CW01021777

The New Land - is a magical tale
Pacific Book Review – A 4 star silver

Bourne does an admirable job in building this into a believable new world and populating it with an assortment of interesting characters. - *US Book Review*

The Land of Twydell & the Dragon Egg - continues the sweeping saga of the *Tales of Avalon*. Daisy Bourne has written a novel that will leave readers ready to continue the series and escape to Twydell for adventure. - *Pacific Book Review* – A 4 star silver review

The Exchange of Rings - Bourne has created a fantasy world especially geared toward the young adult market, where danger or romance must be true-to-life but suitably contained. Once again she welcomes youthful readers back to this enchanted place of kings, queens, flying brooms, mines, pit ponies, and the Forbidden Forest. - A 'RECOMMENDED READ' by the *US Review of Books*

THE TALES OF AVALON SERIES

Books one, two, & three

BY DAISY BOURNE

For my family

First published 2018 in Great Britain by

Text Copyright © Daisy Bourne 2018

British Cataloguing Publication data:
A catalogue record of this book is available from
the British Library

This book is also available as an e-book

Illustrations© Daisy Bourne

CONTENTS

MAP 1

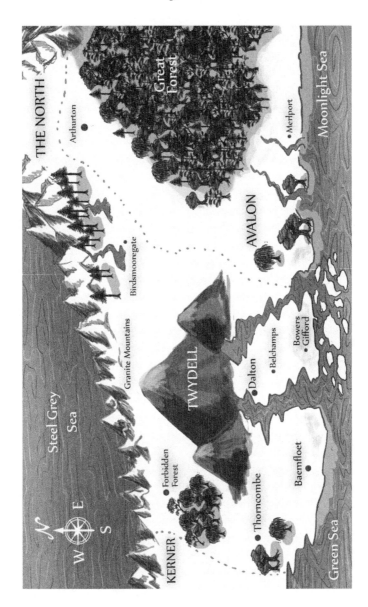

MAP 2

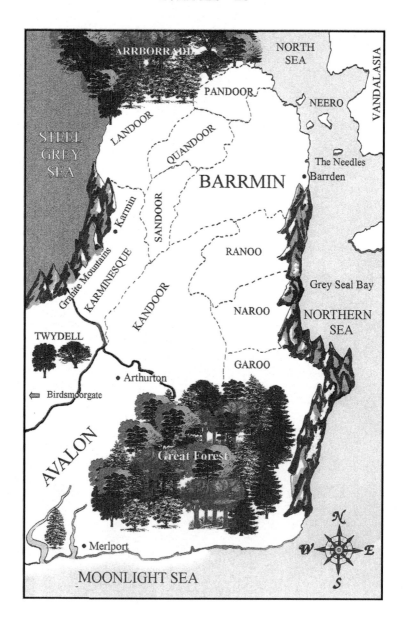

BOOK ONE:
The New Land

1

Prologue

Mankind had been foolish and destructive for far too long. It was with deep sadness that many fairies, elves, and witches made the decision to leave Briton and travel to a new home. Full of hope, they sought a land where nature flourished and all beings could live in harmony. Indeed, the witches were very much afraid that, if they did not leave Briton, their kind would be exterminated by man, who feared their magic and healing powers.

Men were content to war with one another over the slightest quarrel. They were concerned more with wealth than well-being. They had gradually destroyed many of the creatures of the forest so that only one lonely unicorn survived the wicked onslaught. Even mighty animals like the auroch and the mammoth had been hunted to extinction.

Merlin, the wizard, had sought and found a land rich in flora and fauna where he believed magical beings could live in peace. Since finding this new land, the magical beings had built a fleet of sturdy ships. They had been helped by a small group of men and women with kind hearts, who had been persecuted in Briton and who also wanted to find a new and happy home.

For many years, at each full moon, a party of the travellers had sailed to their new world. This coming night would see the last party to leave Briton.

That morning, Maud, Queen of the Fairies, and Elvira, Queen of the Witches, had searched for a four-leafed clover in the meadow. Lennox, the last of the unicorns, trotted along beside them. A four-leafed clover is always a token of good luck. However, a four-leafed clover picked in the morning dew after a unicorn has run through the meadow in which it grew, enables the creation of an even more powerful good-luck charm. The birds of the air had helped the two women find the clover leaf and now hovered above them, keeping watch, ready to raise the alarm in case of danger. The two women hurried away with Lennox. Later, in the safety of Elvira's hut, which was well hidden in the forest, they set the four-leafed clover in a clear wax. Lennox had further obliged by shedding a tear, which, once dropped into the setting wax, would provide even greater enhancement to the spells cast by the two queens. This powerful charm would be carried on the leader ship to bring good luck when it sailed from Briton that night.

While mortal men slept in their beds, three ships slid into a secluded cove on the British coast. Their waiting passengers quickly embarked, and the ships sailed away just as they had appeared: silently, like ghost ships skimming across the sea. Each craft had a hull of intricately carved mahogany and three masts on which fifteen white sailcloths waved proudly in the night breeze. The ships followed the moonlit path which sparkled on the rippling waters of the mighty ocean. They sailed as far as the eye could see from the shore, and then, at the point where the ocean disappeared into the sky, the ships lifted from the sea into the air. A light was shining from a far-away star, and the ships sailed towards its brightness. Their sails flapped in the wind, just as if the crafts were sailing on water.

The faces of the passengers looked up, towards their destination, full of hope and rapture. None felt fear because their journey had been meticulously planned and they carried with them the powerful good-luck charm. However, they still felt a certain sorrow to think that they were leaving the place where they had lived all their lives. The humans, in particular, felt sad that they were leaving friends and family behind, but they knew that if they were to stay in Briton, their lives would be in danger.

Day after day, the ships sailed through the air. Each dawn, as the starlight faded, the cool of the night was replaced by a warming sun. One morning, as the sun rose, the travellers could see a luscious green land with veins of blue water in the distance. A ripple of excitement spread throughout the ships as their passengers leaned over the deck or climbed the masts to get a better view. As they drew nearer, the outline of the land, with

its meandering rivers, grew more distinct. At last, they could see a sandy beach in front of vast grasslands dotted with small copses. In the distance stood a dense forest.

Lennox pawed the deck of the ship with his hoof. He could smell the scent of other unicorns, drifting on the breeze, out from the forest. His wife and children had been slain by men seeking to sell their silvery horns and white skins for profit. Lennox had been lonely for a long time; he yearned for the companionship of others like himself.

The enchanted vessels descended gradually in the direction of the ocean below. Smiles widened on the faces of the travellers as the new land grew closer and closer. In happy accord, many of the witches took to their broomsticks and fairies to their wings. They flew alongside the ships, eager and excited to reach their new home. The witches laughed and sang, as time and again, they soared up in the air and then dipped down towards the sea. Some carried the tiny elves, who could not fly, as passengers on their brooms.

Fairy wings fluttered as they rose towards the sails; some sat or stood on the masts, while others just flew alongside. Sunlight caught the many colours in their translucent wings and reflected on the ripples of the shimmering ocean below. It was as if all the painted glass in a shattered kaleidoscope floated on the sea.

As the flying vessels landed on the water, the sails were lowered. Elves and humans jumped down from the ships and into small boats awaiting their arrival, whence they were taken ashore by oarsmen. The magical beings with wings and broomsticks flew ahead of them.

The gangplank was lowered, and Lennox stepped down into a slightly larger boat waiting especially for him. The boat creaked under the unicorn's weight. Lennox was so excited that he found it hard to stand still, making it difficult for the human oarsmen to keep the boat from overturning. However, when Lennox sensed that the sea was sufficiently shallow, he jumped down into the water and cantered towards the beach. White surf splashed over his silky body as he made his way towards dry land.

The travellers chattered and laughed as they made their way ashore. Many of those who had made the journey before them were waiting to greet the new arrivals. A cacophony of voices filled the air until, as if in unison, all attention was drawn to a tall, imposing figure on the beach. The waiting figure had stood for many hours, watching the ships as they sailed towards their destination.

"Welcome to Avalon, my friends." As Merlin's loud voice was heard, the new arrivals stood in silence and awe of the mighty wizard. The sorcerer stood tall and proud. His satin cloak, flapping in the morning breeze, glistened with all the colours of the rainbow. He held a long staff in his right hand, which he lifted high, in greeting to the newcomers. The end of the staff was encrusted with a round crystal from which emanated a purple glow that embraced all around.

Maud, Queen of the Fairies; Elvira, Queen of the Witches; and Allarond, King of the Elves, took their places beside Merlin.

A middle-aged man, who had been sitting on a rock a little way behind Merlin, forced himself to stand. His face grimaced with pain as he used both hands to push himself up. He steadied himself for a while before limping forward to take up his place alongside the other leaders.

Surprised looks appeared on the faces of the older men and women who had just arrived in Avalon. They could hardly believe their eyes to see the crippled man who stood beside the magical leaders. They pointed and smiled, and then the men bowed and the women curtseyed. Although he was more advanced in years and scarred by war, they recognised the man as Arthur, once King of the Britons. He had been a good king, and they had believed he was killed in battle. They had even mourned Arthur's death. However, Merlin had placed the near-dead king into a small boat and set it to sail for Avalon. The injured man had been nursed back to life by fairies and witches.

Now, the people from Briton were overjoyed to see that their king still lived.

"This is our new home," Merlin said. "Never more shall we return to Briton. Avalon is a good and beautiful place. All the creatures which once roamed Briton are plentiful here, as are the plants we have used in our remedies and spells for millennia. Those who arrived before you have started to build new homes, and the men have started to plough the fields and plant crops. Our little settlement has become a village; one day, it will be a town. As our population grows, there will be more settlements, more villages, and more towns.

"We will endeavour to make our home a happy one, where our descendants will live in peace and harmony with each other. Nevertheless, we should remember that no matter how much goodwill we have come here with, there will always be an element of mischief and evil embedded in some hearts. Therefore, we must have a system of law, punishment, and reward. Each of our leaders – Maud, Elvira, Allarond, Arthur, and I – will be responsible for the behaviour of each of our kind. But enough now! It is time to reunite with your kinfolk and friends. You need to rest after such a long journey. Tonight, we will celebrate."

The magical beings followed those who had come to greet them, whilst the men and women let King Arthur take their lead.

Lennox trotted up to Merlin and nuzzled the old man's wizened face. Wizard and beast exchanged a few words in Unicornian. The beautiful white animal then briefly rose up on his hind legs, whinnied his goodbye, and galloped across the grassland towards the distant forest.

The people of Avalon watched the splendid creature race to find the unicorns of the unknown forest which stood in the distance. They waved their fond goodbyes. Some shouted, "Good luck", but few thought he would need it, for they all felt how fortunate they were to be in this new land – the country now known as Avalon.

Chapter 1 – Avalon

The new arrivals gazed in awe at their new surroundings.
The spot that Merlin and Arthur had chosen to build their new village was on a long stretch of grassland. Colourful flowers had sprung up among the vast meadows – wild pansies, cowslips, daisies, scarlet pimpernel, to name but a few. The flowers mankind struggled to grow in the gardens in Briton grew in wild abundance in Avalon. As the bluebells and daffodils withered and fell, they were replaced by lupins, blue geraniums, and lavender, which contrasted boldly with the green meadow.

Woodbine and honeysuckle intertwined in the wild fuchsia, which formed hedgerows and provided shade for the blackberries and raspberries to flourish. Pheasants, partridges, and all sorts of birds of the air feasted on the ripened berries.

It was not hard to spot deer, hares, or rabbits as they chomped sweet meadow grass and clover. A herd of wild horses also grazed in the meadows. When the sun was too hot to bear, the herd sheltered beneath the cherry trees which grew along the river's edge.

Several woods and small copses dotted the vast meadows. These were bordered by the sea on one side, a river on another; a deep forest lay in the distance behind.

The new village was to be called Merlport, in honour of Merlin, who had found the land of Avalon. Whilst the humans were more than happy to settle in Merlport, it was not unusual for a witch or a wizard to prefer privacy. Many decided to build homes further afield or in the woodland undergrowth. Large, strong leaves and carefully placed broken branches provided comfortable homes. What's more, a home in the remote countryside meant that there were no complaints from neighbours when they brewed smelly potions in steaming cooking pots on open fires.

Fairies and elves had no need of a village or a house made of stone. They were small and fragile, and thus always a little concerned about the clumsiness of larger beings. The footstep of a human could easily squash a fairy or elf, so they preferred to dwell in the meadows and the shrubs. Some found large toadstools, which they hollowed out and made into homes for themselves. Others made little houses out of leaves and twigs, carefully hiding them from view by cunning and magic. Water fairies found shelter near ponds, where water lilies spread like stepping stones from one bank to another.

Those of the earlier arrivals who preferred village life had set to work building houses. Near the site Arthur and Merlin had chosen were heaps of stones that looked as if they had been used for houses before. However, Merlin and other wizards and witches had flown over the land for more than a hundred miles, time and time again. They had seen no sign of humans. There were plenty of bison, mammoths, horses, and other types of animals, but no human beings.

The new village of Merlport started to take form. Houses were built of the stone left by former inhabitants. Timber was taken from the nearby copses, to build the skeleton roofs to which small bundles of hay or clumps of mud were attached. Some of the new dwellings surrounded what was now the village square. This was a busy little place because a well had been constructed in the centre of the square.

Some people had planted flowers round their houses and in window boxes to make their new homes pleasing to the eye. Travellers on the ships had brought seeds. These had been sown either in small gardens, next to the houses, or in enclosures. One enclosure held a sea of sweet corn; potatoes and carrots grew in another, whilst small gardens boasted plants like asparagus and lettuce.

Roads were just dust tracks, but the children gathered shells from the beach and crushed them to make shingle. The shingle was then sprinkled on the roads to prevent them from being so muddy when it rained.

12

Today had been dry and sunny, so the village square was just right for this evening's celebrations to welcome the newcomers.

❋ ✦ ❋ ✦ ❋ ✦ ❋ ✦ ❋ ✦ ❋

A young man stood beneath the cliff with his two friends, watching the new arrivals. He was a good-looking lad who stood at least six inches taller than either of his friends. His name was Edward-Arthur, and he was the illegitimate son of King Arthur.

It had never been planned for Edward to come to Avalon. He was to have remained with his mother in Briton. They had lived in the small village where his mother grew up and where she thought she had many friends. Few knew the identity of the boy's father, and it was thought that the lad was out of harm's way there. Merlin had arranged for the local wizards and witches to keep an eye on the boy and his mother in order to ensure their safety. However, one day, Edward's mother was drowned in a stream whilst the boy was playing. It was thought that the boy and his mother had been betrayed by so-called friends seeking Saxon gold.

Fearing for the boy's life, Esmerelda, the daughter of Queen Elvira, took action. She and her young warlock friend, Tannus, rescued Edward and took him to Avalon. He had been living here with his father and stepmother for six years now.

Arthur had married a witch named Gilda, who'd nursed him back to life after Merlin brought him to Avalon. They had a daughter, Rosalie, who was two years younger than Edward. Edward was very happy with his life in Avalon. When he first arrived in Avalon, his father was almost a stranger to Edward, for he had not seen Arthur in many years. Nevertheless, blood is thicker than water, and father and son built a strong bond over the ensuing years. Edward also grew close to his stepmother and half-sister. However, the young man had a burning desire to return to Briton one day. He was sure that his mother had been murdered, and he was determined to find out the truth and seek revenge.

Edward never spoke to anyone about his wish to return to Briton; it was a secret buried deep within his heart. Today, he was content to watch the newcomers.

Edward watched his father push himself up from the rock on which he sat. He could see the pain in his father's face whenever the prematurely aged Arthur stood up. The crippled man always waddled for a few paces before getting into his lame stride.

Edward had come with his friends to see the last of the flying ships arrive. Many had arrived over the years, but he always felt the same excitement when he watched them descend into the ocean. On this occasion, however, he felt a certain sadness to think these were the last people to arrive in Avalon.

He listened patiently to Merlin's speech. At last, the great wizard finished speaking. Edward had heard the speech so many times over the years that he could almost repeat it word for word.

Before leading his people away from the beach, Arthur spoke to them. He was brief because some already had friends and relatives in Avalon. Many Avalonians had come to greet their friends and kinfolk, and they were eager to catch up on lost time. "We will meet tomorrow and talk together," their king promised. "But please remember that we are all equal here. No one bends a knee to me anymore, and I do not wish anyone to do so. I wish only for a land of peace and harmony. Now I will take you to your new homes, and I look forward to seeing you at this evening's celebrations."

As the new arrivals followed his father, Edward spotted two girls about the same age as he was. "They look nice," he mumbled to his two friends, Alexander and Andrew.

"I like the taller one of the two, with the springy red hair," remarked Alexander.

"Well, that's all right then, Alex," Andrew said with a smile. "I prefer the plump little blonde. Hard luck, Edward. There's only two, so you'll have to fight Tannus for Esmerelda."

"What? Esmerelda?" Edward pretended to choke with laughter. He was often teased about his friendship with Esmerelda, who could be quite a formidable young witch.

"Esmie's more like a bossy big sister to me. Tannus is welcome to her. I feel sorry for him sometimes."

Of course, that wasn't really how Edward felt about Esmerelda. It was true: the young witch was like an older sister to him, and she was bossy, to say the least. Her presence made most humans nervous. However, Edward had travelled to Avalon with her, and he knew that there was a softer side to her character that most people did not see. He loved her almost as much as he loved his younger half-sister, Rosalie.

"There'll be a good party tonight," Andrew commented. "I wonder whether the new girls can dance."

"All girls can dance," replied Alex. "It just depends whether they are too tired. I hear men complaining a lot that women are too tired to have any fun."

"Well, I'll be dancing with Connie, the baker's daughter." Edward smiled confidently. "I won't fight you for the two newcomers."

Edward noticed the two newly arrived girls nudging each other and pointing towards him. Rather than upset his friends, he pretended not to notice the girls' interest in him. Instead, he headed towards Connie, who was standing on the beach and welcoming the new arrivals.

"Are you coming to the celebrations tonight, Con?" he asked.

"Wouldn't miss it for a new world," replied Connie. As she smiled, her nose crinkled, and Edward admired the golden freckles on her nose and the twinkle in her hazel eyes. She reminded him of his mother. "I love to see the spellfolk dancing – especially the wizzwits. The wizzwits look so funny."

"Be careful they don't hear you calling them spellfolk or wizzwits." Edward smiled back at her. "They might be offended and turn you into a frog."

"Oh, I'm sure they know what we call them," Connie replied. "In fact, I've heard them refer to us as the plainfolk."

"Really?" Edward raised his eyebrows, feigning surprise. "I must ask Esmerelda whether she refers to me as a plainfolk. Perhaps she calls me a plainman."

"Plainboy, more like!" Connie retorted. "Although, perhaps you're not so plain." The girl's cheeks turned pink as she paid Edward the compliment.

"Plain or not, I can do a fine jig when the music starts. Will you dance with me tonight, Con?"

Connie blushed an even deeper shade of red but nodded her head enthusiastically before hurrying off.

That night, a feast was prepared in the village square, in honour of the newcomers. A vegetable stew laced with herbs boiled in a huge cauldron. Fresh bread, puddings, and pies had been baked. Away from the vegetable stew, because many of the Avalonians did not eat meat, a wild boar roasted on a spit. The delicious aroma of fresh food cooking filled the air.

Witches and wizards joined the party. A few fairies and elves sat on the rooftops to watch the celebrations, but most disappeared into the surrounding meadows and woodland.

Hops grew in abundance in Avalon, and there were plenty of honeybees, so a sweet mead had been prepared. However, the men generally preferred their beer neat and undiluted by honey. For those who did not wish to wake up with an aching head, there was plenty of fresh spring water and apple juice.

Pipers piped, fiddlers fiddled, and a rather fat man squeezed an accordion. The fat man had a loud but melodious voice, and it didn't take long for other less-harmonious voices to join in.

Soon few were able to stop their feet from tapping in time to the music. One of the men grasped his wife's arm and led her into a space where they started to dance. It only takes one couple to get up and dance for others to follow. The couples danced around the stone well which stood in the middle of the square. Some used steps they had been taught, and others just jigged about in ways that they thought looked good.

It didn't take long for the wizzwits to join the humans – or *plainfolk*, as they called them – in the square. The wizzwits wore their long cloaks and pointed hats. Their dancing seemed to consist of bobbing up and down as they skipped round in a circle, in time to the music. In the firelight, their tall hats cast long shadows across the square. The eerie shadows danced up and down against the surrounding buildings. Smoke from the fires drifted upwards, towards the sky, taking with it bright sparks from the smouldering logs.

Edward grabbed Connie by the hand and led her into a space in the square. They linked arms as they joined other merrymakers in a reel. The couple turned and twirled until they were dizzy. They recovered from their bouts of dizziness by gulping down mugs of sweet mead before re-joining the dancers.

Alex and Andrew had already led the two girls they'd seen earlier into the dancing. However, Andrew was quite a clumsy fellow and kept treading on the plump little blonde girl's toes. She eventually got fed up with him and went off to find her parents, leaving the poor boy standing alone and looking miserable.

Apart from Andrew, everyone else seemed happy. Laughter and singing filled the air.

Edward and Connie danced till the early hours of the morning. Connie had turned to the fresh water for sustenance, but Edward continued to enjoy the sweet taste of mead whenever they took a break. As the evening progressed, Edward's head swirled with a strange sensation he had never experienced before.

Edward couldn't remember finding his way home, but he must have done so because he could hear his stepmother calling him from downstairs.

"Get up, Edward!" shouted Gilda. "You are supposed to be helping to cut trees in the Great Forest today."

"Alright. I'm up," he called back although he was, in fact, still in bed.

17

Edward made an effort to get up, only to lie straight back down again because the room was spinning. His tousled mop of dark hair spread back over the pillow. His head throbbed. Last night, the sweet mead had tasted good, and the more he drank, the more he seemed to enjoy himself. He tried to open his eyes, but they stung, and so he closed them again. At the time, it seemed like a good idea to keep them closed for a bit longer. If he lay in bed for a just a few minutes more, he thought he might awake refreshed.

Edward wanted to get up. For many years, he had looked forward to visiting the Great Forest. When he was younger, he and his friends had attempted to visit the forest several times, yearning to explore its hidden depths. They wanted to climb trees and build a secret den. If they had a den, they would have a place to call their own. They could laugh and tell jokes, without any adults telling them what they should be doing. However, on each occasion, the boys had been seen by the wizards, who had ordered them to head back to the village.

"You boys must learn to wait," the wizards had said firmly. "We need to investigate that forest properly. There's something not quite right about it."

"When are you going to investigate it?" the boys would ask, almost pleading.

"When there are enough of us here to form an investigative party!" the wizards had always retorted as they shooed the boys home.

Edward was just like any other boy: when told not to do something, it always made the yearning to actually do it even worse. Now, the day he had longed for since his first attempted visit had actually arrived. He had planned to get up early. Perhaps it was the headache, or the thought of exploring the mysteries of the forest, which made Edward fall into a slumber. Whatever it was, he dreamed of a forest with a unicorn and other strange beings.

Edward was snapped out of his reverie by cold water dripping on his face. He woke up with a start, opening his eyes to see Gilda standing above him. His stepmother was attempting to rouse him by wringing out a wet cloth over his face.

"Wake up, sleepyhead! It was half an hour ago I called you. You said you were getting up, but, instead, I find you're back in bed! Your father and the other men are almost ready to leave. You'll hold everyone up if you don't hurry!"

Edward pulled on his clothes and made his way downstairs.

"There's scrambled egg and mushrooms in the pan," his stepmother said.

Normally, Edward would have devoured his favourite breakfast with relish, but this morning the smell made him feel sick. He gulped down a mug of water and hurried outside, where his father and a group of other people were gathering.

"Good morning, young man," Merlin greeted him with a wry smile. "Good night, was it?"

"Very good," replied Edward.

He was busy tucking in his shirt when he saw Connie across the road. She waved to him and gave him a wide smile.

Edward crossed the road to speak to her.

The men in the working party busied about, checking that they had all the equipment they needed and that axes had been adequately sharpened. Satisfied that all was as it should be, they began to make their way up the hill towards the Great Forest.

"Come on, Edward," his father's voice boomed.

The tone of his father's voice made the words' meaning clear to Edward. Mumbling his goodbye to Connie, he ran after the working party making its way to the Great Forest.

Chapter 2 – The Giants of the Great Forest

At first, the Avalonians only took the timber they needed from the nearby woods. The trees they cut were carefully selected by Willy the Wood Wizard. Both the humans and the wizzwits were keen not to destroy the trees of Avalon without good reason. They knew that trees were needed to help create the rain which filled the rivers and watered the crops. They were also aware that they would need to share the trees with wildlife as well as future generations of their own kind.

As the building of the village grew nearer to what they now called the Great Forest, they decided it was time to start taking its trees.

Today was the day that a party of men and wizards, including Willy the Wood Wizard, Merlin, and Arthur, went to explore the forest and take its first trees.

Edward, Alex, and Andrew had been brought along to help, as they had done previously when trees were felled in the small copses around Merlport. Tree felling was hard work, and all the boys were expected to assist. To be fair, the trio had never shied away from work, and today they were every bit as eager as before to visit the Great Forest.

Edward always considered Willy to be a strange little fellow. He spent a lot of time muttering to himself. Often, when the boys tried to speak to him, he appeared not to hear. None of the humans seemed to understand how he selected the trees to be cut, but Edward had noticed that before they were allowed to put an axe to a tree, the wood wizard appeared to say a little prayer.

As they trekked up the hill, the boys heard an old, white-haired wizard, Wormald the Wise, chastising Merlin. "We should have sent in an exploratory party before going to the forest. We don't know what dangers may belie us."

Andrew rolled his eyes, and Edward grinned at him.

"We have flown over the forest several times, and not a person to be seen," Merlin replied to Wormald's concerns. "We are only going to the edge of the wood; we are not entering its depths."

"Nevertheless, we should have a standard procedure before entering new territory and putting our working party at risk. These plainfolk have no magic with which to protect themselves."

Alex silently imitated Wormald's concerns.

Although Edward was amused by his friend's mimicry, he shook his head. His father had always made it clear that the wizzwits should be treated with respect; after all, Gilda, Edward's own stepmother, was a witch.

Andrew giggled at Alex's impression of Wormald.

Although Edward was trying to keep a straight face, he was finding it very hard to do so. If Edward laughed at Wormald and his father saw, he would not be amused. The clear air had eased Edward's aching head, and now he ran ahead, needing to avoid his father's gaze.

The mysterious forest had always been like a magnet to the three boys, so Alex and Andrew did not hesitate in following their friend.

The rest of the party shouted for the boys to return.

Better to be told off for running ahead than to be scolded by my father for laughing at a wizard, Edward told himself.

The youths started climbing trees and swinging on branches, like big children at play. Suddenly, Edward felt uneasy, as if he were being watched. The laughter in his face dissolved, replaced by a look of apprehension. Casting his eyes round the dense undergrowth, he saw nothing untoward. In spite of the fact that everything seemed as he might have expected, he slid down from the branch on which he was perched. His two companions must have shared his unspoken concerns because, after exchanging glances, the three friends re-joined the others.

The party had just reached the edge of the wood and had already selected a tree which seemed suitable for roofing timbers.

Willy was just talking to the tree to see if it was ready to be cut when a loud, bellowing voice asked the party, "What do you think you are doing?"

The voice was accompanied by a huge giant who appeared from behind a cluster of trees.

As Merlin and the others looked into the depths of the forest, their eyes grew accustomed to the darkness within, and other large shadowy figures also became apparent. The figures moved forward to reveal large men clad in the same manner of dress as humans. The leader was a red-headed man who wore a green woollen vest tucked into brown dungarees. He had a round face with rosy cheeks. Bushy eyebrows knitted together above enquiring eyes. He stood with his feet placed firmly on the ground, one hand on his hip, and the other holding what looked like a large club over his shoulder.

Edward heard his father speak. His voice was perfectly calm. "Good day to you, sir. My name is Arthur. Our people started to travel to this beautiful land some years ago now. My friend, the wizard Merlin, searched the land to see if anyone else lived here, for we had no wish to steal."

"I saw no one on my visits, and neither did any of my companions," said Merlin. "I am somewhat confused because if my old eyes deceive me, my other senses generally don't. I had no sense of any other race of people – although they have clearly lived here in the past."

Merlin lifted his hands in a gesture of explanation. However, Edward noticed that Wormald and the other wizards, except Willy, were surreptitiously moving their own hands towards their sleeves, where they kept their wands.

"Why did we not sense these giants before?" Merlin whispered to Willy, who stood a little way behind him.

Willy stepped forward, making no attempt to retrieve his wand. He spoke loudly so all could hear. "Ah, you did not sense the mighty Zog and his clan of giants because they are at one with the forest. They have lived in the forest for so long that they belong to it, and so their presence was hidden." Willy bowed his head slowly as a sign of respect to the leader of the giants.

"So, if you didn't know we lived here, how d'you know me name, you weird little man?"

"I am a wood wizard." Willy smiled, and as he did so, his wizened face, which much resembled the gnarled bark of a tree, crinkled. His hair was a greenish grey, and he wore a brown pointed hat and cloak. When he stood next to a tree, he became almost invisible.

Willy continued. "I talk to the trees. They tell me when they are sick and need help. They tell me when they are ready to be cut down to make room for others. This old oak tree here, which has spread its branches wide, has told me that he has shed many acorns, but for more than a century, none have grown because his saplings cannot see the light from the sun. His roots are failing now, and the time has come for him to make room for new growth.

"Sometimes, when I talk to trees, they tell me that their bodies are to be used for a special purpose. This old oak has told me that he wishes his body to be used to make a likeness of the brave warrior whose name is Zog, who stopped the cutting of many trees before their time. Forgive me, Lord Zog, but I believe you already know that your days on this land are limited. This tree wishes to mark its respect for you by using its body to create an image in your likeness."

"Yes, I am Zog." The giant frowned. He seemed unsure whether to believe the wood wizard; nor did he admit that he too knew that his life would not be for much longer.

"That beech tree over there is telling me that his time has come to retire too. He would like his trunk to be used to create the image of another brave warrior, Greatog, who died in battle, but I do not understand some of the words he uses."

Zog looked suspicious but nodded. "My father was Greatog. He died from the injuries he suffered whilst fighting the Trajaens who raided this coast. It was the Trajaens who slaughtered the small people, like you, who used to live here."

"Ah, I know how it is to suffer from the injuries of war," Arthur said now. Looking into the giant's face, he recognised the pain of a kindred spirit enduring the agonies left by battle. "We knew that someone had lived here before because we found the stone which must have once been their houses. Please tell us what happened to the people who once occupied this land, for we have seen no one else except for your good selves."

Arthur was concerned. He had fought enough battles in Briton. He was not sure that he had the strength to wield a sword again. Nevertheless, he knew that few could match his planning and strategy in the battlefield. Even fewer could match his negotiation skills at the end of the fight. Arthur was still a valuable asset to the Avalonians. He was anxious to live peacefully beside the giants. He wanted to find out more about the people who once lived in the place where Merlport was now situated, and also about the people known as Trajaens, who had raided the coast.

Arthur told Edward to listen carefully to what the giants told them and to learn from what he heard.

Edward nodded dutifully.

Avalonians and giants sat down in a circle in the grass meadow. The men had brought jugged hare, elfin bread, and spring water for their lunch. The giants had brought bread, cheese, venison, and red apples. They had also brought some cider, which they shared, somewhat sparingly, with the Avalonians.

Edward sat with Alex and Andrew, and the three lads listened intently. They were still wary of the giants, but the huge men seemed agreeable enough, at least for the time being. All the boys were keen to learn about the possible enemy which the giants were telling them about. The old king had given Edward and his two friends brief lessons on how to use a sword. They had always wanted more lessons, but the priority in Merlport had

25

always been to grow food and build houses. How would they defend themselves if the Trajaens attacked again?

The giants told the party from the village, "People similar to you newcomers lived here before. We've also seen those tiny people with wings, who resembled butterflies, but we've not seen 'em for many years now." The giants went on to say they thought this was a pity because they liked to watch the tiny people flying in and out of the forest. They also said the pretty little things never did any harm. However, although they had heard of them, they had never seen any of the strange people with tall hats, who rode on brooms, in these parts before.

"I wouldn't mind one of them contraptions. It'd save a lot of walking," Zog said, looking directly at Willy's broom.

Merlin explained that it was not the broom that could fly but the special skill of the person riding it. Regrettably, those skills could not be taught to those born without magic.

Zog looked disappointed but continued with his tale.

The giants had lived peacefully next to the people who used to dwell in the stone houses and had called themselves Brewins. The bears of the forest, which also walked on two legs, had been named bruins after them.

"They didn't bother us, and we didn't bother them!" one of the giants stated firmly. "They never came into our forest, and we rarely leave it. We don't like getting wet, so we stay as far away from the sea as possible."

The giants went on to tell them that people lived in the land known as Twydell, to the west of this place now called Avalon. Twydell was ruled by King Frederrick and Queen Elise, who seemed friendly enough. It was a land made up of three tall mountains and two large valleys running in between. The valleys turned into meadow as they spread down towards the sea. However, much of the land along the south coast was marshy and was occupied by a small race of human beings known as the Marsh People.

A few giants lived on the far side of Twydell, near a small country called Kerner. Kerner was ruled by King Jeffrey and

Queen Shirley-Poppy. The Kernans were not as friendly as the Twydellers, according to Zog, but his people hadn't been in contact with the Kernans for many a year. "Not in my lifetime, anyways," as Zog phrased it.

Twydell had two coastlines but its northern coastline consisted of a chain of Granite Mountains which had never been crossed. Kerner was shaped like a triangle and had two vulnerable coast lines. Both Twydell and Kerner were plagued by raids from the Trajaens. Trajaens came in longboats from another land across the sea. They wore silvery covered helmets with what looked like cow horns poking out on either side. Heavy golden and silver bands adorned their muscular arms and necks. They had brown skin and hair the colour of ebony, as were their long moustaches and beards.

"Which they never comb!" said one of the giants, proudly stroking his own silky ginger chin growth.

The Trajaens were strong "for their kind", the giants explained, and they carried many weapons. Not just swords, but axes, bows and arrows, and long spears.

"Them fools, Frederrick and Jeffrey, they only paid 'em to go away!" Zog spoke with anger.

The other giants nodded.

Zog continued. "The Trajaens just used the money to go and buy more weapons to attack Twydell and Kerner all over again. They stole their corn, they stole their jewellery, and they even stole their young people and made 'em into slaves!

"But it wasn't just the Twydeller or Kernan fools they attacked. Oh no! They came back 'ere and attacked the Brewins. The Brewins didn't have no fine armies like Twydell or Kerner. They stood no chance against those Trajaens with their shiny new weapons. It was like lambs going to the slaughter.

"We didn't interfere at first. Thought it was none of our business, like. What arguments go on between the small peoples, nothin' to do with us. We don't get involved.

"We let the Trajaens live in the village for a while, with their Brewin prisoners. But then they started to cut down trees from our forest to make more boats, well, that was a different matter. Those are our trees! We weren't 'aving none of that! They didn't have no tree talkers like you lot. It was just cut, cut, cut!"

Zog described how the giants came out of the forest to confront the Trajaens. The Trajaens tried to drive the giants back into the forest by unleashing arrows at them. He clenched his fist as he spoke. "They went and tied rags to their arrows and set fire to them. The fools set the undergrowth alight. We thought our forest was gonna go up in flames! We could have lost everything – our families, our homes, our livestock, as well as the trees. As luck would have it, the heavens opened up, and the rain fell in torrents."

The giants went on to tell the Avalonians that instead of being driven back into the forest, they were fuelled by anger. They didn't often leave the forest, but, on this occasion, they advanced towards the Trajaens. Many giants were killed or injured in the onslaught, including Greatog, but they chased the Trajaens back into the sea.

Zog continued the story. "It was all too late for the Brewins. Those who hadn't already been slaughtered by the Trajaens, were taken as slaves. When we came out of the forest, the few Brewins left were forced on board the longboats and taken away. There was only one boat left by the time we got to the shore because when they realised what they were up against, they ran for their lives, so they did! We don't like the sea. We don't like getting wet, but we went in after 'em and got hold of the last boat. We lifted it up and tipped it into the water."

The giants laughed at the memory.

"Them there Trajaens, they just sank into the sea and got swept away. There was no way they could swim with all them golden bands round their arms and necks.

"Next, we smashed up the houses to make sure that nobody lived in 'em again. Nobody until you came along, that is. We thought we'd watch and wait."

"I see," said Merlin thoughtfully. "But, why did you do nothing to stop us from rebuilding?"

28

Zog smiled. "Well, if the Trajaens come back, you'll be here to see 'em off, won't you?"

"They'll be back," one giant added, nodding his head sagely. "They took a beating, but they'll be back!"

The others giants agreed.

"No doubt about it." Zog was serious now. "That's why we don't mind you settling here. If you can keep the Trajaens off this land, you can stay here. That is, you can stay here, as long as you don't cut trees from our forest without our say-so. You will also not hunt the animals in our forest because we are big people, with big appetites, and there is only so much food to go round."

Merlin felt a sudden pang of fear. "Do you hunt unicorns too?"

"No," replied Zog scornfully. "What fool would hunt unicorns? Don't you know that it's bad luck to kill a magical beast like that?"

"Indeed." Merlin breathed a sigh of relief. "We brought a friend here with us. A unicorn named Lennox. Lennox is a splendid creature. He was the last of his kind in Briton, the place where we used to live. He hoped that he would find more of his kind here."

The giants laughed.

A ginger-bearded giant with a loud rumbling guffaw told him that a new white unicorn stallion had arrived in the forest. Tyzon, the leader of the forest herd, had not been happy about the appearance of a rival. Tyzon and the newcomer were exact opposites. Tyzon was a sturdy black unicorn, much bulkier than the new white arrival. Nevertheless, the new stallion was a powerful force to be reckoned with, and both were capable of seriously injuring the other. There had been a clash of horns and then a stand-off. Neither was injured, but some of the mares had left the herd and galloped off with the newcomer.

"Not a bad thing to happen!" Zog laughed. "The unicorns could do with some new blood, and Tyzon is a bit full of himself. He needed to be brought down a peg or two."

29

"Please tell us about the other creatures which live here," said Merlin. "Are there any dragons or phoenix?"

The giants told him that there were dragons in the Twydell mountains, which sometimes stole sheep and goats, but were rarely seen in this area. The Trajaens had stolen nearly all of the Brewins' stock. What was left of the Brewins' herds had wandered off into the wild.

The giants were not sure what a phoenix was. However, when the wizards told them it was a large colourful bird, they nodded. They described how a bird with blue, green, and red feathers had risen out of the ashes of the Brewins' settlement.

The wizards exchanged knowing looks. A phoenix rising from the ashes foretold that the Brewins' town would be rebuilt.

"It flew off in that direction." One of the giants pointed towards the west. "My cousin said he had seen it on the plains on the other side of Twydell."

"We do see the thunderbirds sometimes," said one of the giants. "That's one of the reasons our ancestors liked to live in the forest. Thunderbirds are big enough to carry off one of your children. They're even strong enough to carry off one of ours!"

"Amazing." Merlin was interested. "I've never heard of a thunderbird before. What do they look like?"

The giants described a large bluish-grey bird of prey, which some people called the rain bird. They said that when the thunderbird flapped its wings overhead, it often sounded like thunder, and its appearance always seemed to bring heavy rain.

"When yer see the thunderbird, yer head for home and make sure all yer family 's inside," the ginger-bearded giant advised. "Yer hear the flapping wings like thunder, and then yer feel the rain."

"And make sure yer cattle and sheep are in the barns, to keep 'em dry," Zog added knowingly.

Merlin asked how far it was to Twydell.

The giants told him that they could walk there in two days, so it would probably take his shorter legs four or five.

The giants made it known that they wanted to end the parley and make their way home, but Arthur still had some questions.

"Did none of the Brewins survive?"

Zog said, "Far as I know, only one girl is left here. Each time they attacked, the Trajaens took a lot of them off, across the sea, to sell as slaves – if ye can call that survival, they survived. The girl who was left was kept here as a child slave by one of the Trajaens who tried to make a home here.

"When the Trajaens knew we had the better of 'em, they either killed the slaves who were left before they ran, or put 'em on long boats to take with 'em. S'pose they thought we might make use of 'em, but we don't believe in slavery. It's a wicked trade. Anyways, the little maid managed to hide in the woods over there." Zog pointed to a small copse near the village. "She lives in a cave in the hills now. Pretty little thing but very strange. We think the animals must have taken pity on her and brought her up. She talks to wild beasts, like Willy here talks to trees!"

"She's got a pet wolf. A huge grey thing. It'll attack yer if yer go near her," Ginger-beard put in.

"She caught a wild pony and tamed it herself," added another giant.

"And she's got a pet goat," added another.

"The birds come down and feed out of the palm of her hands." An elderly giant smiled at the recollection of the young girl with birds perched on her arms and hands.

"Doesn't the wolf attack the goat or the pony?" asked Merlin.

Zog said, "No. She seems to have trained it not to hurt her pets – but it won't think twice about biting the throat of anyone or anything which tries to harm her!

"She can use a bow and arrow too. We call her Amazon, we don't know what her real name is. She refuses to talk to us. Her aim is deadly accurate. If you get too close, she'll let off an arrow, which will land at yer feet as a warning, but she could just as easily hit you in the eye with it!"

31

Arthur asked the giants if they would show them where the girl lived.

The giants seemed to find Arthur's request amusing.

"We'll tell ye, but we won't show yer." One of the giants chuckled. "We don't want to start a fight with the grey wolf or get hit in the eye by an arrow." He then went on to describe where the girl lived.

"Now. One final piece of business." Zog spoke seriously. "You, Willy the Wood Wizard, you reckon the trees talk to you, and that there beech tree has asked you to create an image in the likeness of my father, Greatog. Now, you've never seen Greatog. I give you my permission to cut down that beech tree, whose foliage I admit looks past its best, and so it probably does need to make way for younger saplings. But, before we allow you to enter our forest and cut down any more, I want to see this image of my father. If you are telling us the truth, and not spinning a yarn, then you'll have our permission to cut other trees, but only those that we permit you to cut."

"That sounds very reasonable to me." Merlin nodded. "Willy, how long will you need to make the image of Greatog?"

"As long as it takes," replied Willy blandly. "I have no knowledge of time when I'm carving. I simply keep going until I know it will reach the old tree's satisfaction."

"Then how will our giant friends know when it's finished?" asked Arthur. "We don't have their permission to enter the forest to look for them."

"That's easy." Willy smiled. "I'll leave a note in the hollow of that oak tree over there. See the hole at the bottom of its trunk? I'll leave it in there."

"What do you mean a note? A note like in moosic?" Zog looked puzzled.

"No. I mean a note, as in a piece of parchment with words written on it."

"Oh, I knows what you mean. We saw them funny squiggles that the Brewins used to draw, and those Trajaens they do the same. We don't bother with all that. Just leave a sock in the tree.

32

Leave a pink one, to make sure we spot it and it just don't get hidden inside."

"But, what if a fairy or elf or animal carries it off?" asked one of the wizards.

"Well, put some stones inside. No small creature will be able to move it then."

"Right," said Willy. "I will put a pink sock, filled with stones, in the hollow base of that oak tree as soon as the image is ready."

The giants watched and helped as the men felled the selected beech tree. When the deed was done, they said their goodbyes and left the men to roll the great tree trunk back to Merlport.

As they rolled the tree trunk down the hill, the Avalonians pondered over the day's events.

Edward was mesmerised. As a child he had been brought to this land by witches, wizards, fairies, and elves. Today, he met giants. Would the charmed life he seemed to be leading come to an abrupt end by a Trajaen axe?

"Father, we need more sword training," Edward said. As the words left his mouth, he realised that they sounded more like a command than a request.

"Yes," agreed Arthur. "Now that we have no trees to cut for a while, we will start training again. Tonight, when you get back, you can speak to all the able-bodied men and ask them to bring what weapons they have to the village square first thing tomorrow morning."

"Mmm, good idea," Wormald the Wise said authoritatively. "I think I will call our brethren together and start practising defensive spells."

For once, the boys did not make fun of the old wizard behind his back.

Chapter 3 – Merlin Plans a Trip

The men of Merlport practised with wooden swords while Arthur watched, barking instructions from his seat.

It was clear that Edward and the other youths relished the activity. They made it known, at every opportunity, that they thought it would be better to practise with real swords. However, even if they had all been sufficiently skilled to practise with blades which cut, rather than sticks that bruised, there would not have been enough swords for everyone. To this end, Arthur commissioned the blacksmith to make enough swords, axes, and maces to arm all the men in Merlport.

Meanwhile, Wormald the Wise sat with a group of wizards, huddled in a nearby copse, away from the sound of clattering wood. An invisible circle surrounded them, which no man would be able to penetrate.

Merlin attended the meeting for a while before excusing himself. He had expected to find Willy at the meeting. However, the wood wizard had given his apologies, advising that he wanted to start creating the image of Greatog without delay.

After leaving the circle, Merlin hurried off to see Willy, but first stopped to speak to Arthur.

The king knew that the sorcerer was present, and listened to him, but kept his eyes on the duelling men as they trained.

"Well, it looks as if Willy will be busy for a few days. I think I will take a trip to Twydell. I would like to meet King Frederrick and Queen Elise. I would certainly like to know more about the dragons and thunderbirds which live there."

"Aren't you going to practise spells with Wormald?" asked Arthur.

"Do you think I need to practise spells? I'm disappointed in you, Arthur." Merlin pretended to sound surprised and hurt.

Arthur smiled.

"No. Wormald is more than capable of teaching our young warlocks a trick or two. My time would be better spent acting as an envoy to our neighbours."

Strengthening his case for the visit, the sorcerer continued. "Our neighbours may be able to give us more insight into these Trajaens. Our people have been here for some thirteen years now, but we have not been bothered by them. That would be because the first arrivals were almost all fairies and elves who might not have been noticeable to the Trajaens as they sailed along the coast. However, even from a distance, our continued building must already be visible. Of course, the Trajaens may be afraid of coming back here because they fear another defeat by the giants."

"I have never seen any boats, other than ours, out at sea," replied Arthur. "We are in a bit of an inlet here, and I suppose not too noticeable because of the surrounding hills and trees. Nonetheless, you are right. We need to find out more and build new allies."

Tongue in cheek, as he kept his eyes on the duellers, the king added, "Of course, you are obviously the best choice to act as envoy. That way, I can keep the able-bodied men here."

Merlin laughed. He liked it when his friend joked. The smile on Arthur's face made him look younger and brought back memories of the handsome knight he once was.

With a sigh, Arthur took his eyes off the men battling each other with wooden swords. He looked his most faithful advisor in the eye. "I sincerely hope that we will not have to go to war again, my friend."

"I sincerely hope not!" Merlin responded. "I will only be gone a few days. The giants said that it would take them two days to walk to the capital town of Twydell and that it would take our shorter legs four or five. It should take me less by broom."

"Then we will see you again in about a week's time." Arthur nodded and turned his head back to watch his men.

"While you are off to Twydell, and Willy is busy making his carving of Greatog, I will send a party to search for that girl. After all, it sounds as if she is a human being just like my people. Despite what the giants say about her ability to look after herself, she must be very frightened and lonely living on that mountain all alone."

"Good idea," Merlin said, nodding. "Poor young lass out there all on her own. I'll look forward to talking to her when I get back. We would all gain by knowing more about the Brewins."

Merlin said goodbye to Arthur and waved to the men practising their sword skills.

Only Andrew saw him, and he raised his sword arm to acknowledge the wizard's departure.

Edward, who was duelling with Andrew, mistook his friend's gesture as a preparation for a vertical head chop. The prince immediately thrust his wooden weapon at his friend's unguarded ribs, expecting him to step back.

Instead, Andrew fell to the ground, crying out in pain.

Arthur barked an angry rebuke at the youth. "Never take your eyes off your opponent, you fool! If that were a real sword, you would be dead by now!"

Andrew was not only bruised, but his pride was wounded too. His face turned a bright scarlet shade of embarrassment.

Edward discarded his wooden sword and fell to his knees to comfort his friend.

Merlin lowered his head in guilt, and then scurried off in the opposite direction to find Willy. He was anxious to see the wood wizard before he became too engrossed in his task. He had seen Willy at work before, and knew how difficult it would be to communicate with him once he started his project.

He found the little man arranging his tools on a bench. The felled beech tree lay in front of him.

Just in time, Merlin thought.

Merlin put his arm round Willy's shoulders and spoke to him in his most endearing terms. "My dear friend, you will be very busy for a few days. While you are engrossed in your work, may I borrow your broom, please?"

"Why can't you use your own broom?"

"I've gotten rid of mine."

"Why?"

"Oh, it was falling apart." Merlin waved his free arm, as if to provide some sort of explanation, but kept his other around Willy's shoulder. "I don't like flying now. I get stiff in the cold wind, and my eyes keep watering. I no longer enjoy it."

"So, if you don't like flying any more, why do you want to fly now?" Willy's question seemed quite reasonable.

"I need to go to Twydell," explained Merlin. He then put forward the best case for borrowing Willy's broom that he could think of. "I will act as an envoy from Avalon to Twydell. It is imperative that we find out more about our neighbours and make them our allies. There may even be more wizards who live there. Wouldn't you like to make more friends, Willy?"

"You could take one of the horses the men have captured and trained, and ride to Twydell," retorted the wood wizard, who remained unconvinced by Merlin's argument.

"Flying is much quicker and safer. I can soon fly out of the reach of hostile men, but I could not easily outride them. Besides, do you think my old bones would stand up to several days' ride on horseback? Come, Willy, my friend, lend me your broom. You won't need it before I return, and I promise I will bring it back safely."

"It's a pity we don't have any wood; we could then make you a boat, and you could cruise round the coast to Twydell."

"It's a pity we don't have wood to make me a carriage, or velvet for cushions, for then I could drive myself to Twydell in a little bit of comfort!" retorted Merlin.

"Alright," Willy agreed. "But if you damage my broom, you repair it!"

"Thank you. I knew you were a good-natured chap." Merlin smiled as he withdrew his arm from round Willy's shoulders.

Chapter 4 – Daisy; The Last of the Brewins

"This will be your first command," the king told his son. "I will listen carefully to how the men who go with you speak about your leadership when you return."

Arthur had been unsure whether to put his son in charge of the party going to look for the Brewin girl. However, after giving the matter some consideration, the king decided that it would not be a difficult task to find the girl and bring her back to civilisation. No one had travelled far from Merlport since arriving in Avalon. Most of the humans had been in the last ships to arrive. They now needed more scouting parties to investigate the outlying areas.

Edward's pride showed in his face. It wasn't because his father had chosen him to lead the group. It wasn't even the fact that he was riding the fine bay stallion his father had selected for him, when still a foal, from the wild horses which roamed the grasslands. It was the steel sword, hanging at his hip, which made him feel that he had truly become a man at last.

The prince had grown into a good-looking lad. He was tall and broad, as his father had once been. He was also thoughtful and beginning to show wisdom beyond his youth. He worked hard no matter what task he was given. His courteous manner made him well liked and respected by all.

Nevertheless, Arthur had chosen the five other men carefully. They were all experienced soldiers. They may have been past their prime, but three knew how to fire an arrow, one was a huntsman skilled in tracking, and the fifth had once been a swordsman. If Edward did not act wisely then they would advise him accordingly, without seeming to argue.

It only took a few hours to reach the hills where the giants had said the girl lived. Edward was enjoying himself. It was the first chance he'd had to ride more than a few miles on Challenger, his bay stallion. He would have loved to have urged Challenger into a gallop, but that would not have been right. The other men's mounts were more like the horses seen working in the fields; a far cry from Challenger and the fast, sleek, horses ridden by soldiers.

There were several winding paths round the hills. At each path they found, Edward looked hopefully at the tracker, who inspected the path carefully to see what kind of animal was using it.

The man would jump down off his palfrey, examine the tracks, but then look at the prince and shake his head. "Goats and sheep," he stated several times.

On one occasion, he spent more time looking at the tracks. Edward started to feel excited, but when the tracker turned and saw him looking at him anxiously he said, "Sorry, m' lord, it's the track of a large stag with a herd of a dozen does. A fine place for hunting, though."

At last, Edward heard the news he wanted. After carefully examining the prints in a fairly well-hidden path, the tracker announced, "It's a pony. The tracks are deep, as if it's carrying a rider."

"It must be the girl," declared Edward. "There are no other humans in this area, and the giants said she had a pony."

The men nodded their agreement.

The path was very narrow, and twisted round the hill. The men did not need Edward to tell them that they should leave their tired horses behind. However, they waited for their leader to give the orders. The prince jumped down from Challenger, looked carefully at the prints the tracker showed him, and gave the order to dismount.

Edward looked at the horses and told one of the archers to stay behind and look after them whilst the others continued on foot. As Edward looked back at the track, he didn't notice the smiling and approving nods of his men. He asked the tracker to take the lead.

The path wound its way up a steep incline. Their ascent was slow because it was hard work walking uphill, and the pathway kept crumbling beneath their feet.

"Ah," said the tracker after a short distance. "Look, m' lord, here is where she dismounted."

Edward examined the track he was shown, and could indeed see the change in the depth of the hoof prints when they were pointed out to him.

At this point, Edward took the lead. He might have been a little bit vain, but he felt that the girl might not be so frightened if she set her eyes on him first. She would see him as the knight coming to her rescue, whereas the scarred and battle-hardened men who followed him might frighten her.

Just as he was rounding a bend, near the top of the hill, an arrow thudded into the ground in front of him. He gasped because the arrow was only an inch or so away from his toe. It had come from farther up the path in front of them.

He looked up but saw no one, and so he called out, "I am Edward-Arthur, son of King Arthur. The giants have told us about the terrible slaughter of the Brewins. We have come to tell you that we have built a new village on the site where you once lived. We wish you no harm, and invite you to join us. You need not hide away in a cave any more. You can return to a proper home in our village of Merlport."

Edward truly expected the girl to come out from where she was hiding and rush down the hill towards them, arms open in gratitude. He was very wrong. To his surprise, another arrow thudded into the ground in front of his feet, and he took a step back.

"We wish you no harm. We come as friends," he shouted as loud as he could, in case she had not heard him the first time.

"Go away!" the girl shouted. "Come another step nearer, and I'll kill you, no matter whose son you are!" With that, another arrow thudded into the ground alongside the others.

Edward remembered what the giants had told them about the accuracy of the girl's aim. The path had wound round the hill, and he ordered his men to step back a few paces, behind the safety of its slope.

Edward stuck his head out from behind the bend in the hill and again shouted at the top of his voice, "We have only come to rescue you! We mean you no harm!"

"I don't want to be rescued!" the girl shouted back.

She shot another arrow, which thumped into the hill just beside Edward's head. He knew that the next arrow would be aimed to kill.

The last arrow had been a surprise, but not nearly so much of a shock as the appearance of a grey wolf bounding down the side of the hill towards him. There was no time to string bows, so Edward and the other swordsman swiftly drew their weapons. The wolf came to a sudden halt halfway down the hill. It looked directly at the group of men before throwing back its head and letting forth a chilling howl. The wolf's cry would have made even the bravest of men shiver with fear, and Edward was no different. Not a man among them failed to feel his hackles rise or his skin turn to goose prickles.

However, instead of attacking, the wolf took a giant leap, taking cover behind a large boulder.

Bows were carefully strung, and arrows poised, ready to shoot the wolf if it reappeared.

"Harm my wolf, and I'll harm you!" This time, the voice came from above the place where the men were standing.

They looked up and saw a pile of small rocks start to move and tumble down the hill towards them. For a few fleeting moments, they caught sight of a young woman before she darted behind the boulder with the wolf. She was dressed in pieces of animal fur and had long, straggly, fair hair.

The men ran for their lives. They stopped after a few hundred yards and looked behind them. There was no sign of girl or wolf.

"She was warning us." Edward tried to stay calm and take back control. "The giants told us that she was deadly accurate with a bow and arrow. If she had wanted to kill me, or indeed any of us, she could have done so."

"Aye," agreed one of the older men. "If she hadn't shouted before she pushed the rocks down the hill, we wouldn't have had a chance."

"And then she hid behind the boulder with that wolf," another man added. "I've seen a few wolves in my time, but never one that wouldn't attack a girl if it had half a chance!" He shook his head in disbelief.

"Best leave her be," said one of the men, who was still trembling with fright.

"Yes," agreed Edward. "We will leave her for the time being, go back to the village, and report what has happened. Then we will decide what to do."

The men walked back a lot quicker than they had come, describing what each had seen and discussing their thoughts.

But Edward was quiet. He was thinking about the girl. He had caught a brief glimpse of her long blonde hair and pretty face. He remembered slender legs and arms, stretching out from the animal skins that hung from her body, as she leapt for cover behind the boulder.

When the party arrived back at the village, Edward told his father what had happened. Arthur looked questioningly at the other men who had been in Edward's party. They confirmed that the strange tale the boy had told was true.

"I think," said Edward, "we may have startled her because we were all men. Perhaps, if we had taken a few women or girls with us, she would not have been so alarmed."

"Hmm." Arthur considered his sons words. "You may well be right, but we cannot risk any more lives trying to speak to this girl. Anyway, it does not sound as if she needs to be rescued."

"I would like to try one more time," said Edward. "I have a plan, which I hope Gilda will help me with."

Edward gave his stepmother one of his winning smiles.

The witch furrowed her brow, wondering what favour he was going to ask of her.

Edward continued to tell his father his plan. "If Gilda would fly on her broomstick, up above the girl's cave and out of the range of her arrows, perhaps we could talk to her together. If Gilda would be kind enough to ask one of her fairy friends to come too," he added, giving his stepmother another charming smile, "the girl could see how beautiful the fairies are, and she would surely be enticed to speak with us."

Gilda, who was used to being persuaded by her stepson's charms, took his side. "Well, I would be willing to give it a try. It would be interesting to see this girl who talks to animals. She might even be a witch or part-witch."

Arthur was worried that his wife was putting herself in danger but agreed to let her go, providing she kept out of the range of arrows. Even if he hadn't agreed, Gilda would probably have gone anyway.

Despite a lengthy argument with his father, Edward was forbidden to go. His father spoke sternly. "I cannot put any of our men at risk, and there is much work to be done here. If that wolf attacked you, there is no way you could fight it off on your own. If you ran away, it would soon catch you. A wolf can run much faster than any man."

Gilda sought the help of Elna, a young witch, and two fairy friends, Cherry Blossom and Franzipan.

However, Edward made sure he was close at hand when the four ladies met to plan their adventure. He still hoped that his father would relent and let him go too. The four friends decided to take the girl a bag of gifts. They planned to drop the gifts on the ground as they hovered above the cave; that way, they could quickly fly to safety if the girl fired an arrow at them.

"It will have to be things that won't break as the bag hits the ground," Elna said thoughtfully. "No good sending eggs or berries. Perhaps she would like some soap. I have some nice soap which I made last week, scented with roses."

"I have some violet essence she can have. I have preserved it in a very sturdy bottle which will not break. I have cast a spell of unbreakability upon it, and I can guarantee that it will not shatter when it is dropped." Cherry Blossom beamed with the pride of her achievement.

"I can make a spray of dried lavender which she can pin to her clothing," Franzipan offered.

"A brush and comb would be a nice gift," said Edward, who had been listening to the plans. "She has long hair which is a lovely shade of blonde, but it is badly tangled."

The women looked at him and passed knowing looks to each other.

"I am sure I can find a brush and comb somewhere." Gilda smiled.

Chapter 5 – Another Visit to Daisy

Edward's father and stepmother had told him most sternly that he was not to attempt to follow the four friends. He was trying to be adult about the situation, doing his best not to sulk. Nonetheless, he made sure he was there to see them off.

I'll put on my best face and not show my disappointment. I would far rather go with them and see that strange girl again instead of building dry stone walls, he thought.

Fairies cannot fly very far in one journey, because their wings are delicate, so Cherry Blossom rode with Gilda on her broom. Franzipan rode with the young witch Elna. The bag of gifts was tied to Gilda's broom.

They waved goodbye to Edward as they set off on their mission. Despite Edward's effort to put on his best face, the envy was apparent to the four friends. They all felt a little sorry for him.

It was fine day, if not a little cloudy, and a pleasant flight. Fairies never flew very high, and so they enjoyed the view below.

When they neared the top of the hill where the girl lived, they could see the opening to the cave. For anyone travelling up the hill, the entrance was concealed by shrubs, but the witches and fairies could see it as they looked down from above. The young girl came out and looked up, her wolf on one side and her goat on the other. A piebald pony grazed at the top of the hill where the land was flat.

"Greetings, young lady," called Gilda. "We bring you greetings and gifts from all who live in Merlport, the new village standing on the one where you once lived."

"What are you?" asked the girl. "I have never seen anyone riding in the air on a brush before!"

49

"I am Gilda. Elna and I are witches. We live with the people who dwell in the village now known as Merlport. Our little friends here are fairies who live nearby in the meadows round our village."

The fairies flew down and sat on some wild orchids a few yards away from the girl. They were afraid to go too close in case the wolf attacked them.

"Edward-Arthur, the boy you spoke to a few days ago, is my stepson. He and his companions meant you no harm. They are sorry that they alarmed you."

"They did not alarm me," the girl replied sharply. "I am happy as I am. I don't need other people. It was other people, called Trajaens, who murdered my family. How do I know that they will not try to harm me? How do I know that you are not trying to lure me back to the village so that you can make me into one of your slaves?"

"We do not have slaves in Merlport," Elna replied. "The very thought is abhorrent to us. No living being should be another man's slave."

The girl looked doubtful, but the fairies, in their tiny musical voices, confirmed what the witches were telling her.

"What is your name?" asked Gilda kindly.

"The giants call me Amazon, but my birth name was Daisy."

"Which name do you prefer?" Gilda dipped her broom nearer the girl, who made no attempt to string her bow.

"I was Daisy born and would like to be again."

"Well, Daisy Born, let us tell you about the people who live in the village."

Daisy listened while the witches and fairies told her about their journey to Avalon. She frowned when they told her that they had come in ships.

"The Trajaens came in boats," she said warily.

Gilda tried to assure her that the people who now lived in the village were not Trajaens, but settlers who would defend their land.

"You do not have to make up your mind now but please think about coming to live in the village. It must be a lonely life for you up here."

"I am not lonely! I have Billy, my goat; and Ruff, my wolf. I am happy here."

"Well, here are some gifts from our people," said Gilda, dropping the bag a few yards away from the girl so that she did not feel threatened. "I hope you like them."

"Thank you." Daisy gave a smile which lit up her pretty face. "You are very kind. I have listened to what you have said, and I will give it some thought." However, she was still wary as she watched the fairies fly back up to the broomsticks. "You really are beautiful creatures," she admitted as she watched the sunlight enhance the rainbow colours of their opaque wings.

Daisy waved goodbye. She watched the broomsticks and their passengers fly into the distance before picking up the bag and taking it inside her cave to examine the contents.

A few days later, the four friends flew back up to the cave to see the girl again. They were sure that this time Daisy would welcome the offer to join the people in the village. They even allowed Edward to follow them because, on their last visit, they had parted from the girl on such friendly terms that they did not feel the young man would be in any danger.

"Don't worry," Gilda had said to her husband before she left. "She has that wolf firmly under control, so it won't try to attack him; if it does, I will issue a stunning spell which will leave it unable to move for at least an hour."

Arthur had experienced Gilda's stunning spell once himself. He knew that her "speciality" spell, as she often referred to it, was very powerful.

It was a fine morning, with a light breeze blowing. Edward took the opportunity to push Challenger into a full gallop across the grasslands. He watched the two broomsticks soaring above him. The flyers preferred a gentler pace, especially since they had passengers on board.

The flyers breezed through a cloud above the cave at the same time as Edward neared the top of the hill.

One arrow after another shot up in the air as the broomsticks approached the cave. The witches were forced to steer themselves and their passengers up higher into the sky. An arrow whistled through the air, missing Elna's ear by just an inch.

"Go away!" shouted Daisy angrily. "Keep away from me, you evil people! Didn't you think that I would notice that lump of lard you gave me frothed like sea foam when I put it in my frying pan? Didn't you think that I would notice the funny smell of that cooking oil you gave me? You tried to poison me! Why can't you just leave me alone? I've done nothing to you!"

She shot more arrows in the air, even though she knew that the deadly points could not reach the witches, who were now too high to hear what she was saying.

"It wasn't lard; it was soap!" shouted Edward from the pathway, as he stuck his head out from behind the curve in the hill. "And the oil was violet oil, not cooking oil. You were supposed to wear it on your skin to make it feel soft and smell nice."

Daisy looked round, and when she saw Edward, she ordered her wolf to attack. Edward turned and ran.

Gilda swiftly dipped her broom, making poor Cherry Blossom hold on for dear life. The witch pulled her wand out from beneath her cloak and pointed it at the wolf bounding towards her stepson. As she uttered strange words, the wolf froze. It stood like a statue of an animal about to leap on its prey. Its lips were drawn back in a snarl, yellow teeth bared.

The young girl ran to the wolf and threw her arms round its neck. "What have you done to Ruff? You wicked people!"

Edward stopped and looked round.

Daisy stood, picked up a stone and threw it at him, but then turned back to the wolf, tears streaming down her face.

Edward ducked to miss the stone, and then stood tall again, watching the distressed young woman. He saw her drop her bow to the ground and throw her arms round the grey wolf again. "Ruff will be alright again soon," he called. "He will come back to life in a few hours."

Gilda was angry now. "Go. Go. Go. You foolish boy. Get away as fast as you can. It won't take her long to string that bow again, and when she does, her aim will kill you."

The two witches flew above Edward keeping watch over him until he safely reached the bottom of the hill. However, even as he reached his horse, Edward seemed reluctant to leave. He turned and looked back up the path, in two minds as to whether or not to turn back.

That poor girl. She doesn't realise that her wolf will soon come back to life. She looked heartbroken. I wish I could make her understand, he thought. However, the memory of the wolf's chilling howl and its bared fangs made the young man shiver.

Gilda shouted at him again. "Move, Edward! Move! Don't just stand there!"

Edward swung himself back into the saddle and urged Challenger into a trot. As he made his way back to the village, his mind was planning his next attempt to speak to Daisy. He just could not get out of his mind the picture of her looking so pitiful, holding the wolf and weeping into its fur. He just did not feel he could leave her. He wanted to make her understand that he was not the bad person she thought he was.

As the villagers saw the party returning, they gathered to hear the news. Everyone wanted to know whether young Daisy, the last of the Brewins, would be coming to live with them. They shook their heads with disbelief when Elna recounted what had happened.

Cherry Blossom's and Franzipan's faces were still white with terror.

"A fairy's wings could never have carried us as fast as an angry witch's broomstick," Franzipan stated.

Both fairies swore they would never travel on a broom again.

Gilda gave them some of Arthur's wine to revive them, and slowly the colour started to come back to their peachy cheeks.

"I don't want anyone else going up there again," said Arthur. "It is too dangerous, and I will not risk any more lives for the sake of one wild girl who seems perfectly able to look after herself."

All nodded their agreement, except Edward, who remained silent and thoughtful. Now was not the time to argue with his father, but he was determined to see Daisy again.

Edward remembered how soft her suntanned skin looked. Her hair was not so tangled, so he assumed she must have used the brush they had given her to comb her long, fair hair. He felt touched by the memory of the tears running down her face as she threw her arms round the ugly grey wolf. He remembered the tears he had shed for his mother when he found her lying in the river. He likened himself sitting beside his lifeless mother to Daisy hugging her immobile wolf, and shared her pain.

Just for a moment, Edward envied the wolf. How nice it must be to have someone throw her arms round you, and love you no matter how ugly you might be.

Chapter 6 – The Image of Greatog

During all the fuss about Daisy, Willy the Wood Wizard was hard at work. From the moment he started work on the trunk of the great beech tree, he seemed to have gone into a trance.

The old wizard had a small, triangular yard attached to his cottage, and it was here that he had gone to work. He had a wooden bench, and all his carpentry tools lay upon it.

Willy had removed his cloak and hat, and now wore only a thin cotton vest and boxer shorts. He looked very thin and old, but he set to work with the strength of a much younger man.

He worked feverishly, stopping only to drink water and swallow the occasional mouthful of soup, which his kindly neighbour had made for him. He hardly stopped, sleeping for just a few hours each night before resuming his task.

As he whittled away at the wood, beads of sweat ran down his wrinkled body and stained his vest. Villagers stopped to watch him, but if anyone spoke, he seemed not to hear them. As the days went by, Willy became noticeably thinner, and his craggy face turned a paler shade of grey.

In marked contrast to the hyperactive Willy, a very old wizard sat – or, rather, slept – in the corner of the triangular yard. He kept his arms folded and tucked inside his voluminous sleeves, and he had his hat pulled over his face. When he did wake up, he revealed a particularly kind face with a beaming smile.

For days and days, Willy maintained the incredible pace of work which no human could have managed.

King Arthur was worried, but the other wizards advised him to leave Willy to his work. They had seen him like this before and knew that he would not stop till he had finished.

While Willy worked, the men of Merlport continued to rehearse their battle skills. Arthur had ordered them down to the grasslands to practise archery. They had tried to practise in the village square, but the arrows which missed their targets proved to be too dangerous for those villagers going about their everyday business.

On their way to the grassland, they passed Willy, who was standing on a ladder, whittling away at the large tree trunk. They all stopped to stare. A few made humorous remarks.

Edward glared at those who joked about the little wizard. His stern face soon stopped the japes.

Edward strode over the rickety little fence which surrounded Willy's yard. He felt the need to ask the little wizard whether he was all right, but before he could reach Willy, Edward heard a voice.

"May I help you, young man?"

Edward turned to see the elderly wizard, who had been sleeping in the corner of the yard, standing at his elbow. He had no idea how the man had moved so quickly, especially when he had appeared to be very soundly asleep.

"I ...," Edward said hesitantly. "I am worried about Willy. He's been working frantically for days now. It is not humanly possible to keep working at that pace for such a long period of time."

"Ah," replied the other wizard, with a gentle smile that made his blue eyes twinkle. "But we are not human, are we?"

Edward shook his head. "No, I don't suppose you are. But," he added as he looked back at Willy, "he just looks so old and frail."

"In some ways, the older you are, the more resilient you are." The wizard beamed. "Willy is fine. He is always happiest when he is working. The harder he works, the happier he is. Thank you for your concern, but please do not trouble yourself." The old wizard bowed his head as if to end the conversation.

Edward mumbled his goodbye, left the yard by striding over the fence again, and set off for archery practice. He looked round, to see that Willy's friend was back in his chair, hat pulled over his face, with all the appearance of being asleep.

The afternoon sun was hot. One of the witches brought some pale-coloured cream for the men to put on their faces to protect them from burning.

"What about Willy?" Edward asked the witch as he took some of the cream and smeared a thick dollop over his nose. "He will need some protection from the sun. His skin is so pale."

The witch smiled a toothless grin. "If Willy needs anything, his friend Tannitus will make sure it is provided."

"Who is Tannitus?" asked Edward.

"Why, his friend who watches over him. The gentleman who sits in the corner of his yard."

"But that gentleman spends his time sleeping!" exclaimed Edward. He then shook his head, remembering the unnatural speed with which the elderly wizard had appeared at his elbow earlier. Smiling at the witch, he conceded, "I am sure you are right."

The witch grinned and continued to offer her tray of soothing potions to the would-be archers.

Edward was still concerned about Willy. On his way back from the village, he stood to watch the little wizard labouring over the image of Greatog. A face and shoulders had been crafted, and the wood wizard was now working on the fingers of the folded arms.

"It's unbelievable, isn't it?" asked a familiar voice at Edward's side.

Edward looked down to see Connie. He had noticed her watching him several times as he practised his sword drill, even seeing her clap her hands each time his arrows hit the centre of the target.

"Yes, it is unbelievable," he said.

She smiled up at him. The same crinkly smile of which he had become so fond. Edward walked away.

"Bye, Con. Can't stop to talk. I need to get home and bathe. It was very hot out in the open today."

"I saw you. You hit the bullseye more often than anyone else," Connie called as she hurried after him.

However, Edward took his longest strides and quickened his pace. He really liked Connie, and it was because he liked her that he did not want to lead her on. His thoughts were now on another young woman, and he did not want to hurt Connie any more than he knew he was already about to do.

Connie realised that the young man who had become her heart's desire was now deliberately trying to avoid her. She felt deeply hurt. Tears stung her eyes and gradually trickled down her cheeks.

Day after day, Edward passed the wood wizard and stopped to watch. The speed and skill with which Willy used his various knives to carve the wooden image was incredible. But, as the days passed, the little wizard's body and vest looked dirtier and dirtier. His friend still continued to sleep in the corner of the yard, seemingly oblivious to Willy's worsening demeanour.

At last, the wood wizard ceased whittling away at the wooden statue, but still he did not stop working. He fetched the paints he had made, from flowers and plants, and set about painting the likeness he had created. Every now and again, Willy would step back and gaze at the likeness before carefully dabbing it with more paint.

Finally, he sat on the ground, exhausted, and just sat staring at the statue.

Almost simultaneously, Tannitus woke up and pushed the hat back from his face. The wizard asked one of the people watching to tell Arthur that Willy had finished his creation.

As soon as the king heard the news, he headed towards the triangular yard, limping as fast as his crippled legs would allow, to see the end result of the wood wizard's labours.

"It's amazing," said Arthur as he stared at the round face which Willy had carved. The face revealed a strong jawline with a mouth shut firmly, and a protruding nose. The head stood upon broad shoulders and folded muscular arms. The detailed carving stood upon a wooden, ornately decorated plinth. All had been carved in one solid piece from the trunk of the beech tree.

"But are you sure that this is what Greatog looked like? After all, you've never seen him. What's that funny little black lump underneath his eye?"

"The image you see is the image the tree gave to me. Nothing more, nothing less. You can leave the message for Zog, and you can see what he thinks when he gets here." Willy was not willing to discuss his work of art. "By the way, is Merlin back yet? I will need my broomstick again once I am rested."

The king told Willy that Merlin had not yet returned, but it was not unusual for the mighty sorcerer to be gone longer than he planned. He told Willy not to worry. He was sure that Merlin would return the broom soon, and in good condition.

One of Willy's wizard companions took a pink sock to the forest. He filled it with small stones and, as agreed with the giants, put it inside the hollow of the oak tree. The sock was carefully positioned, with a little bit sticking out of the hollow, to make sure that the giants saw it.

The next day, Zog and a band of giants marched down to the village. The villagers knew the giants were on their way before they saw them. The ground had already started to tremble with the weight of their heavy footsteps. Luckily, Willy lived on the edge of the village, so the giants did not have to venture too far into Merlport. The very stone walls of the newly built houses shook as giants passed.

When Zog saw the statue, he was delighted. "It's exactly like my father! You even put the black mole under his left eye! He hated that mole, but it was there, and it's a true likeness alright."

Arthur breathed a sigh of relief. He had not been convinced that Willy could carve a likeness of Greatog without ever having seen him.

The giants were invited to sit, take refreshment, and parley. Plate after plate of sandwiches, pies, and cakes were brought out to them. They ate and drank so heartily that the villagers were worried that they would run out of food and ale.

"So when will you make that old oak tree into a statue of me?" Zog asked.

"Let me rest for a while," said Willy. He looked strained and could hardly keep his eyes open.

"While we wait for Willy to rest, do you think we could select some trees to cut?" asked Arthur. "We really do need to strengthen our roofs with timber before winter sets in."

Zog nodded his agreement, and then he laughed. "I see you've been trying to talk to the girl we call Amazon. That young lad of yours is persistent, isn't he? We were watching the goings-on from the edge of our forest. She didn't make you very welcome."

"Well, a lot of it was a misunderstanding," admitted Gilda as she collected the empty plates. The giants had devoured a large quantity of home-made cakes and scones smeared with cream and strawberry jam.

Gilda continued. "I flew up there this morning to make sure her pet wolf was alright after the effect of my spell had worn off. After all, the wolf will protect her, and I wouldn't like to see her come to any harm. I see she's got a pet mountain lion now."

"Pet mountain lion?" asked one of the giants. "Are you sure?"

"Well, there was a mountain lion in the grass above the cave. I think it had injured its back because there was a long scratch which looked as if it had been bleeding. I couldn't see Daisy anywhere. The pony wasn't there either, so I assumed she had gone out for a ride," replied Gilda.

"That sounds like the lioness with the cubs." The giant looked concerned. "My brother had to kill the male on his way back from Twydell a few days ago. He'd been there to visit relatives, and the lion attacked him on the way back. He didn't like killing a lion, as there are only a few around. The lioness tried to have a go at him too, but he cut her with his sword. She ran away, with two hefty cubs at her side. Good job the cubs didn't join in; otherwise, it would have been my cousin lying dead instead of the lion."

"The lion wont attack when the wolf is there," said Zog. "But if it wanders away from the girl, she will have little chance against a hungry lioness with cubs to feed."

Young Edward was alarmed. He had sat in the parley with the giants but had kept quiet, listening intently while they discussed Daisy. Now he stood and faced his father. "We must go and warn her!" he shouted. "It wasn't her fault. She didn't know that the soap wasn't lard or that the violet scent wasn't cooking oil! We have to save her!"

"No," the king snapped. "I'll not put any of my people at risk for that girl again."

Father and son glared at each other and started to argue.

The giants looked at one another. Zog looked at his companions and winked. They had no wish to listen to the small people row with each other, so they politely said their goodbyes.

"Anyways, we will wish you good afternoon," said Zog loudly.

Arthur and Edward ceased their quarrelling – at least until the giants had taken their leave.

Zog continued, as if nothing had happened. "We'll take this magnificent statue of Greatog. Now, if Willy comes to the edge of the forest tomorrow to meet our forest master, I'm sure they'll come to some agreement about which trees can be cut."

Two of the giants lifted the heavy statue, and they all made their way back up the hill to the Great Forest, waving to the small folk and humming a merry tune as they went.

Chapter 7 – Lions

When the giants were out of earshot, Arthur and Edward turned on each other again. It was a rare sight for father and son to argue, and the ferocity of the argument was unprecedented. Wizzwits and humans alike stood back and watched, until Gilda intervened and put a halt to the argument.

"Edward is right, my love," she said gently to her husband. It was not often they disagreed, but her maternal instinct had come to the fore. "The boy is right. Daisy did not understand what the gifts were for. I've been thinking that we should go back and try to speak to her again. Now I know we must."

"Let me ride with you, Mother," Edward said.

"Two on a broomstick will slow me down." Gilda rushed off. "I must go."

Arthur sighed noisily. He knew that if his wife intended doing something, he could not stop her. However, he was determined that Edward would not risk his life again.

"Edward-Arthur, you come back here!" Arthur shouted as his son ran off after his stepmother. The king always used his son's full name when he was angry with him.

However, Edward was not going to be stopped by anyone – even his father. He mounted Challenger and urged the stallion into a gallop. He could see his stepmother soaring above him. When he got to the base of the hill, he dismounted and left his horse behind. He hurried up the path, panting heavily, but not stopping once to catch his breath. All he could think of was that Daisy might already have been mauled by the lion. She might be lying dead and lifeless, and he was too late to help – just as he had been too late to help his mother.

He could hear the agonising yelps of the wolf before he was anywhere near the cave. As he turned the bend, he could see the lioness on top of the wolf, her teeth sinking into its throat. Daisy lay pale and motionless, a few yards behind the wolf. The blood-drenched body of the dead goat lay beside her.

Edward's heart beat fast. *Am I too late?* He wondered as he reached for his bow.

Gilda dipped down on her broomstick, with her wand drawn. She issued the stunning curse just a second before her stepson released an arrow from his bow. The arrow hit the lioness in the chest and sank deep into her heart. The lioness was dead, but the stunning curse had left the ferocious beast lying rigid on top of the wolf.

Edward rushed to Daisy, who was now stirring and trying to sit upright. "Are you alright?" He put his arms round her, and for few moments, she sat rubbing her head and trying to focus her eyes. "I'm so glad you are still alive! I thought I was too late – again."

Daisy continued to just sit, leaning against Edward, waiting for her head to stop spinning. She tried to focus, and when she did, she saw her wolf still lying beneath the lioness. She pushed Edward away and forced herself to stand. She staggered towards the wolf, which was bleeding heavily and struggling to breathe underneath the weight of its foe. The wolf had suffered deep claw marks to his body, and the lioness's sharp teeth were still entrenched in its neck.

"Ruff! Ruff!" Daisy sobbed.

Gilda, who had been circling above to make sure that the lion cubs were not nearby and likely to attack, landed her broom. She and Edward helped Daisy lift the lioness from the wolf's body, but it was clear that the poor creature was dying.

Edward felt helpless.

The distraught Daisy tried to comfort Ruff, tenderly stroking his head as he breathed his last. "He was trying to save me. The lioness attacked Billy, my goat. I ran to help Billy, but the lioness turned on me. It was about to pounce when Ruff came between me and certain death. I fell back and hit my head."

Tears streamed from Daisy's eyes until they were puffed and swollen. The young girl sobbed so much so that her breath caught and her shoulders heaved. It was a long time before she stopped crying.

Gilda and Edward sat with her, trying to offer comfort.

"I must bury my pets," Daisy said. "I must get rid of this lion carcass before any scavengers see it. I don't want any thunderbirds smelling the blood."

"I'll help you," Edward volunteered.

"I will get help from the village," Gilda said. "You will need spades." Without any further hesitation, the witch flew off towards Merlport.

Daisy covered the dead animals with blankets. She and Edward walked to the top of the hill, where the ground was soft, and selected a place to bury the dead pets. Daisy was not sure what to do with the lioness. Edward thought she might want to make use of the animal's skin, but Daisy said that she would not want to wear anything that reminded her of the creature which had killed her pets.

"How did you know that the lioness was nearby?" she asked.

Edward told her about the giants' visit and that the male lion had been killed a few days before. He explained that the lioness had two growing cubs, and she'd probably been looking for enough food to feed all three of them.

"What?" Daisy said with a gasp. "You mean there are hungry lion cubs out there? We must find them, or they will starve!"

Edward was astonished.

Daisy forgot her grief and started following the tracks that the lioness had left. She followed the tracks back until she found the two hungry cubs hidden in the undergrowth. At first, they growled and bared their teeth, but Daisy spoke to them. She had a calming way with animals, and the cubs eventually allowed her to stroke them.

"I have some preserved meat in my cave," said Daisy. "I'll go back and fetch it. I'll set up a camp, here beside the cubs, until they trust me enough to come back to my cave."

Edward protested. "They are big cubs, Daisy, and will soon be able to fend for themselves. What if they attack you? They look pretty strong to me!"

Daisy laughed at him. It was the first time he had seen her laugh, and it brought a warm feeling to his heart.

"You must come back with us to the village." Edward tried to be firm with her. He was genuinely worried for her safety.

"No. I can't. I must stay here and look after the lion cubs. They will be my pets just like Ruff and Billy were. Ruff was just a pup when I found him. I trained him, and he eventually became my protector. These two cubs will take the place of Ruff and Billy, and then I will have two new protectors." The smile slipped away, and the sadness appeared in her face once more. "Although I am not sure that anything can actually replace my cuddly wolf or loving goat."

By the time Gilda returned from the village, a makeshift camp had been set up alongside the den in which the cubs were nestled. Gilda had flown above some volunteers from the village and guided them to the spot where the three dead animals lay. The men had brought spades, and they dug graves for Daisy's pets and the lioness. The bodies were carried up to the top of the hill and buried in the spot chosen by Daisy. She asked that the lioness be buried next to her pets. She had forgiven the lioness. She understood that the beast which had killed her pets was just a mother trying to feed her cubs in the only way she knew how.

The men grumbled that it was a waste of a good lion skin, let alone a wolf pelt. Edward hushed them and bid them not to speak of such things in front of Daisy. The men stayed no longer than was necessary. They lit oil lamps to guide their way down the spiralling path towards their horses. They hurried down the path and did not look forward to riding through the night to get back to their homes.

Edward insisted on staying with Daisy. The night had drawn in, and he was worried about her staying alone with the lion cubs without Ruff to protect her. Daisy did not want him to stay. She said that she had lived alone for a long time before she had Ruff, and he was just a little orphaned cub when she found him.

Edward was hurt by her rejection. However, Daisy was oblivious to the hurt she had caused him and adamant that she wanted to be alone to grieve for her pets.

"Well, if you insist on being alone, then so be it," he stated firmly, his face full of displeasure. He then added in a gentler tone, "I'm not going home, though. I'll sleep in your cave. If you get frightened, or just feel you need a bit of company, then all you have to do is call."

"Thank you, Edward." Daisy came towards him, stood on tiptoe, and surprised him with a kiss on the cheek.

The young man wanted to take her in his arms, but Daisy would have none of it.

Daisy didn't linger. She went straight back the cubs, kneeling beside them and stroking their fur. One of the cubs nuzzled up against her arm, just like a house cat.

Edward made his way back to the cave, using an oil lamp that Gilda had left for him. All the blankets had been taken, either to cover the dead animals or to use in Daisy's makeshift camp. There was straw on floor, and he pushed it together to make a soft place to lie, but he slept little. On a few occasions, he walked back up the hill to make sure that the girl who had stolen his heart was all right. Each time he checked, she looked snug, wrapped in the blankets, with the lion cubs curled up against her.

As he lay on the floor of the cave, the morning light eventually penetrated the entrance. Yesterday, he hadn't taken too much notice of the inside of the cave. Now he could see the herbs she had dried hanging from the ceiling and the smoked meat suspended above the fireplace she had made. On the floor were home-made baskets in which he could see dried fruit and nuts. Daisy was a remarkable young woman to manage alone here for so many years on her own. He had longed to hear her voice calling for him in the night, but Daisy had not found the need to rouse him. The young woman was self-sufficient and needed no one.

He found her where he had left her. Her eyes were still red from copious tears, and circled with dark rings. She obviously hadn't slept as well as he had thought. She must have heard his footsteps during the night and pretended to be asleep. But her bond with the lion cubs had grown stronger: one sat at her side, and the other on her lap.

She gave Edward a weak smile when she saw him. "Thank you for staying, but there was no need."

"Well, I'd better be on my way then." Edward was reluctant to leave, but it was clear that Daisy wanted to be on her own. He had come here without his father's permission, and he knew that the longer he stayed away, the angrier his father would be with him.

"You'll find some berries in the cave, and some nuts. Help yourself to anything you want to break your fast," Daisy called as he walked away.

Edward hoped that she still might follow him, but, sadly, the girl made no effort to do so.

Chapter 8 – Prearations for Winter

King Arthur forbade his son to visit the "wild girl", as he called Daisy, again. He was livid with his son for disobeying his order not to go with his stepmother. The way Arthur saw it, the boy had put his life at risk for one individual.

"One day you will be king of the people who live in Avalon. Look at me! I am no longer a healthy man. Soon our people will need a strong leader who is also wise. You may be physically strong, Edward-Arthur, but you are not wise. You cannot risk your life for the sake of one wild girl when you are responsible for so many others. There is no wisdom in helping one person when there are a hundred others here that need you. There are houses and barns to build before winter sets in. This is where you are needed, and this is where you must be!"

Edward knew his father was right. Reluctantly, he obeyed the order to remain in Merlport. However, Gilda found the time to visit Daisy on several occasions. She told Daisy that Edward had angered the king and been forbidden to visit her. The witch explained that the king was worried about his son's safety. As Prince of Avalon, Edward was expected to work alongside the villagers. He had a duty to make sure that there was sufficient food and shelter to see his people through the winter.

Daisy said she understood. She asked Gilda to give him a message thanking him for all he had done, and to tell him she was sorry for the trouble she had caused. She asked Gilda to tell him that the lion cubs were growing fast. They were living in the cave with her now but had just started hunting for themselves.

Gilda passed Daisy's messages to Edward. She added that Daisy was just like a young mother, running after the cubs when they went out in search of prey.

Edward longed to see Daisy but did not want to make his father angry again. Besides, he did not want people to think that he was shirking his responsibilities in Merlport. There were still a lot of preparations which had to be done before winter.

Willy had taken time to rest after finishing the statue of Greatog. A few days later, he had started work on the statue of Zog, going through the same process of working feverishly, in a trance-like state, while his sleeping friend kept watch. Zog had been as pleased with the likeness of his own image as he had been with that of his father. The giants had carried the statues back to their own village, and, under the supervision of Willy and their own forest master, allowed the Merlporters to cut more trees.

Merlin was still not back, so Arthur had a cart made for Willy to travel back and forth to the forest to select the trees for cutting.

When he was not travelling back and forth to the forest, Willy was resting. His hard work had taken its toll, and he needed time to recuperate. This was just as well because, otherwise, he might have wanted to use his broom.

"Have you heard from Merlin?" Willy asked Arthur as they sat watching Edward and the other boys sawing the tree trunks into timber roofing structures. "He promised he would be back with my broom in a week's time. It must be nearly three weeks now, and we still haven't heard from him. What's worse, he's still got my broom!"

"No, I haven't heard from him," replied the king. "But you know how unpredictable Merlin is. I'm sure he will show up soon, with enough stories about his adventures to fill a book."

The king tried to sound confident, but Merlin's failure to return was beginning to worry everyone.

Chapter 9 – The Battle of Merlport

Since learning about the marauding Trajaens, one of the Merlporters was posted at the top of the cliff, day and night, to act as a lookout. The lookout kept a loud horn beside him, which he would blow if he saw any approaching danger.

For weeks, the men took turns sitting on the cliff, but no peril was seen. Late summer turned into early autumn. One day, just as the new houses in Merlport were getting close to completion, longboats appeared on the horizon.

The bellow of the horn made one and all stop in the midst of what they were doing, turn, and look out to sea. Goose prickles rose on the skin of everyone.

The Merlporters had not come to this new land prepared for war. They thought that Avalon would be a land of peace. They prepared for battle as best they could. Those who had swords, or bows and arrows, picked up their weapons. Others, who might have been considered too old to fight, took up pitchforks and axes; they were joined by some of the women. Other women and children gathered baskets of stones to throw.

The makeshift army made its way to the beach.

The old women found rags and tore their petticoats into strips to make bandages, knowing that battle brought with it much bloodshed.

King Arthur donned his old armour, but it was now heavy on his aching shoulders. He took it off and told his son to wear it instead. He and Edward then mounted their horses and identified the positions that their men would try to hold. Eleven archers stood on the cliff-top; another sixty men stood on the beach, armed with swords, pitchforks, axes, and anything else they could use to fight with.

The women and children with stones knelt above the path leading up to the cliff. From that vantage point, they could throw stones when the Trajaens crossed the beach, as they surely would.

The witches, who were present in the village, sent messages on the wind to gather as many of their brethren and sisterhood as possible.

As the boats sailed closer into view, the villagers could see their foe. The boats were full of angry-looking, black-bearded men with brown skin, wielding swords and other spiteful weapons. They wore metal helmets with what looked like cow horns poking out on either side. The men on the boats were just as the giants had described the bloodthirsty Trajaens.

At last, the boats came close to the Merlport beach. As the Trajaens started to disembark, the witches and wizards dipped down on their broomsticks. With wands drawn, they each uttered their own special spells. Gilda issued a stunning spell which left one would-be marauder standing motionless half in and half out of a boat. Another cast a spell which melted the sword of a burly Trajaen.

A clever old witch called Azgoose created a cloud which rained pink goo over one of the boats. The Trajaens inside it found that their feet were stuck to the deck and their arms glued to their bodies, so that they could not use their weapons. Azgoose used her spell on another boat and shook her fist with glee as she saw the men inside struggling to move in the sticky substance which rained over them.

Arthur looked up and saw Bizzbuzz, a large, plump wizard flying overhead. He was so large, he needed a very sturdy broomstick which resembled a small tree trunk. Unfortunately, the weight of the broom meant that he could not fly very high or very fast. "Bizzbuzz is going to get shot down by an arrow if he gets too close," he told his son.

However, Bizzbuzz stopped short of the enemy boats, and hovered. He drew a bag out of his coat. Holding up the bag to his lips, he appeared to speak into it. Out flew a swarm of insects.

"He's releasing his honeybees on the Trajaens!" Arthur realised. "I hope the insects don't get near our people. The last thing we want is to be stung by bees."

"No," replied Edward. "They're heading straight for the Trajaens. I don't think they are honeybees, though. Bizzbuzz wouldn't risk his precious bees. It's his wasps. Esmie said he was trying to develop a type of wasp that could make honey, but he's not been successful."

Bizzbuzz took another bag from his pocket, spoke to the contents, and then released even larger insects, which buzzed towards the Trajaens.

"He's been trying to breed honey-producing hornets as well." Edward laughed. "Unsuccessful at making honey, maybe, but his little pets seem to be doing a good job at assaulting the Trajaens, alright!"

The Trajaens tried to swat at the attacking wasps and hornets, and some of the raider suffered stings. Unfortunately, the insects seemed to be attracted to the pink goo. Many got stuck in the sticky substance, where they died.

Meanwhile, Azgoose was so pleased at the sight of a third raider boat inundated by the rain from her cloud of pink goo that she hopped aboard her broom and stood on it. She was an ugly old witch, so thin that she looked like skin over bone. Her nose was hooked, and her chin poked out and curved upward. The old hag made a bizarre spectacle of herself: she not only stood on her broom but actually started to dance. The Avalonians cheered the old woman on, but, alas, the triumphant witch was overconfident. Her foot slipped, and she tumbled head first into the sea. The Avalonians groaned to see their newly found heroine fall. Azgoose was last seen swimming out to sea, in an attempt to avoid Trajaen arrows. Meanwhile, her broom continued to fly along without her until it crashed into a cliff.

As the pink goo began to dry, the raiders were able to pick the goo, as well as the wasps and hornets stuck in it, off their bodies. Gradually, they were able to lift their feet from the decks of their boats. The pink goo had only caused a delay.

Willy the Wood Wizard was still without a broomstick. He took up a standing position halfway up the cliff. From this point, he threw disarming spells as far as his wand would allow. Many Trajaen swords fell to the ground before they could harm anyone.

Few magical people are able to cast a spell without a wand, and even fewer are strong enough to issue a killing spell. Now Willy's friend Tannitus, the very elderly wizard with the kind, smiling face and twinkling blue eyes, boarded his broom. No one had ever seen him fly before because he seemed to spend most of his time asleep. The old wizard did not need a wand. He dipped his broom till he could look into the eyes of his chosen victim, pointed a crooked finger at the victim's heart, and issued his spell. Five enemy warriors fell lifeless to the ground before Tannitus himself was brought down by a Trajaen axe. He, too, then lay dead in the shallow water, beside his victims.

As the enemy made their way out of the shallow water and onto the beach, Arthur gave the order for the archers to fire. Eleven archers poured their arrows down from the cliff-top, bringing several Trajaens to the ground.

About twenty witches and wizards had joined the battle, with others joining the fray when they heard the call on the wind. Queen Elvira hovered above her witches, shouting commands to her people and sending her own hexes at the enemy. It seemed as if an array of spells had been cast, almost in unison, sending one Trajaen after another into the sea.

However, the people of Merlport were still heavily outnumbered. There were at least ten longboats, each containing thirty murderous Trajaens. The odds stacked against the people of Avalon were high.

The men of Merlport rushed towards the Trajaens as they stepped out of the sea and onto the beach. Some of the

Merlporters were on horseback, and others were on foot. Insults were thrown as metal clashed against metal.

Esmerelda was fearless. She uttered incantations and cast spells which issued green sparks from her wand. Each spell struck one of the would-be invaders dead.

Queen Elvira saw an arrow aimed at Esmerelda. The old witch pursed her lips to blow the arrow off course. The arrow shuddered and landed harmlessly against a rock. However, the old woman momentarily lost concentration as she watched her daughter veer her broom to safety, and was struck by an enemy spear. Elvira fell from her broom and plummeted to the ground.

King Arthur and his son sat on their horses, on the edge of the cliff, watching the fight. Edward was angry because he wanted to join the battle, but his father would not allow him.

"If you go to the battle and are slain, our people will give up hope," said Arthur.

"And if I do not join the battle, our people will call me a coward! Look! Our men are falling, and even Elvira, Queen of the Witches, has been brought down."

Edward felt helpless sitting above the battleground, watching people die, and he told his father so.

As the two argued, they did not see Trajaens climbing the cliff beneath them. The Trajaens had avoided the pathway, and the overhang of the cliff hid them from view. Three crept stealthily up on one side, and four more on the other. They knew that if the leaders fell, the Merlporters would give up hope and surrender to slavery.

A Trajaen with a large sword suddenly seemed to appear from nowhere, and he ran towards Edward. Another grabbed the reins of Arthur's horse and tried to pull him to the ground.

Edward raised his sword to deal with the Trajaen heading towards him. As he did so, he caught a glimpse of another emerging over the edge of the cliff, just a few feet behind the first. He knew he could not fight two burly warriors, and his heart sank as he saw a third rising up from the cliff.

As the prince's sword clashed with that of the first Trajaen, he heard a strange deep growl. He glanced sideways and saw a golden, partly grown lioness leaping at the second Trajaen and bringing him to the ground. Seeing a third Trajaen fall as he clambered up from the cliff, with an arrow in his chest, Edward knew that Daisy was close.

Edward could feel himself shaking, but he managed to bring his sword down on the first Trajaen. The man had also caught a glimpse of the lion, out of the corner of his eye, and quickly turned to see where it was. It was enough time to allow Edward to gain the advantage. A second blow rendered the attacker senseless, and he toppled off the precipice.

Just as the fourth Trajaen was pulling himself onto the top of the cliff, yet another arrow found its mark. At first, the man tried to pull the arrow from his neck, but it was stuck firm. His lifeless body slid back down the cliff.

The prince turned to see what had happened to his father. King Arthur, old and frail as he was, had managed to turn his horse, which had reared up and knocked his first attacker to the ground, unconscious. His second attacker lay struggling under the teeth and claws of the other partly grown lion, and the third lay dead, with an arrow in his back.

Edward was still shaking. He thought at first that it was fear because his heart was beating fast, but then he realised that it was not he who was trembling, but the ground beneath him. The giants were running through the village, waving menacing clubs and axes as they came. Down the hill they ran, towards the cliffs. They had always had the appearance of being big, clumsy men, but they descended the cliffs with an abundance of energy and agility.

The men of Merlport, and the magical beings, were heartened when they saw the giants coming to their aid. Just one swipe of a giant's club could render two or more Trajaens senseless.

The giants hated the Trajaens and were eager to get into the midst of the battle, sending enemy after enemy to the ground.

They laughed heartily each time a Trajaen fell beneath their blows.

"I'm going into the fight!" Edward cried, ignoring his father's orders to stay where he was.

He looked to his left and saw Daisy taking her place alongside the Merlport archers. He felt proud of her.

Another witch, who could issue fire spells, had joined the battle. The Trajaens watched with dismay as they saw two of their boats burst into flames.

A horn sounded to the prince's right. It was a deep mellow sound which he did not recognise. The young warrior looked round, just before descending the cliff towards his first battle. He saw Merlin on a white horse, galloping across the meadow towards the beach. Merlin was followed by six soldiers, one of whom was blowing the horn. Another was carrying a standard, but Edward was too far away to see what the standard depicted.

The Trajaens looked startled when they heard the horn because they recognised its sound. They had not expected the vicious onslaught from the giants, who had never come out of the forest to protect the Brewins. Nor could they have expected the strange spells that left them disarmed, motionless, or covered in sticky pink goo. Now it seemed yet another threat was heading towards them.

Many Merlporters lay dead, more were dying or injured on the beach. However, as Edward entered the battle, his armour shining bright and his war cry loud and clear, all rallied round him.

Edward could see his friend Andrew lying on the ground, and hoped that the lad was only injured. The sight made the prince rage even more. Edward found a strength and fury he did not know he possessed. His sword felled Trajaens to his left and right, and he kept his blade at work.

Merlin was the first of his group to reach the cliff-top. The crystal hilt of his staff was glowing red. He pointed the hilt of his staff towards a party of well-armed Trajaens who were edging towards a group of Merlport farmers equipped only with pitchforks and scythes. Lightning streaked forth from the glowing staff, striking Trajaens in its fiery course, knocking them to the ground, lifeless.

As the soldiers who followed Merlin reached the cliff-top, the Trajaens saw the familiar standard of Twydell: three mountains above two green valleys. The Trajaens did not know that there were only six soldiers, because they could not see beyond the top of the cliff. They thought that that a whole regiment of trained Twydell soldiers had come to the aid of the Avalonians.

The Trajaens turned and ran back to their ships, leaving their dead and dying behind.

The giants ran after them. Although they did not like the feel of the salt water on their flesh, they ran into the sea. They chased the marauders as far as their height would allow in the depth of the water. Two giants caught a longboat by its tail, tipping it upwards so that the Trajaens within fell into the water. The Trajaens were unable to swim because their armour and metal adornments were too heavy, so they drowned.

The witch who issued the burning spells followed the boats out into the sea and managed to set one more alight, so that the boat, along with its passengers, sank into the deep ocean.

Edward looked towards his father. The look of triumph which had filled his face swiftly disappeared. The king had fallen from his horse. The prince turned and urged Challenger up the path towards the cliff-top; as he did so, he saw Daisy run towards his father.

"One of the Trajaens must have cut him with a sword before Leo reached him," she said. The young lion, whose shaggy main was now beginning to grow, sat proudly on top of the Trajaen he had felled.

"Don't worry about me," the king managed to say, though he spoke with difficulty. "I will live, but Gilda has fallen. You must find your stepmother, but even if she is dead, you must be strong. Act like a leader. Tell the men of Merlport that they have done well, and honour their dead. Thank the giants and the people of magic. Thank those strange soldiers who arrived with Merlin. Your people need you, Edward."

A woman with bandages rushed towards the king. Daisy was kneeling at the king's side, trying to stem the flow of blood from his leg with her hands. The older woman fell to her knees and tore the king's trousers, revealing a long, deep gash. Arthur winced with pain as she tightly wrapped the ugly gash with pieces of linen, but he pushed himself up on his elbow to speak.

Edward just stood and watched. He knew he should return to the beach with his people who had fought there, but he found it difficult to tear himself away from his father.

"Go, my son. Go, Edward-Arthur. Be the leader you will shortly be," the king commanded.

This time, Edward did as his father bid.

Edward found his stepmother lying on the beach, another witch and Cherry Blossom tending her. The fairies and elves had not joined the fight but had stayed close, ready to use their own special kind of magic to try to heal the wounded.

"She is alive, but badly injured," the witch said of Gilda. "She hit her head when she fell, and she is unconscious. We will take her back to the village, along with the other wounded."

"I will stay with her," Cherry Blossom told Edward. "You must go and do what you must do. I will find you if Gilda awakes." The fairy seemed to understand that the young prince had duties to attend to.

Edward thanked her and then set off to speak to each of the Merlporters who had taken part in the battle. He sympathised with those who had lost loved ones; he shed tears when he heard that Alex and Andrew, the two brothers who had been his friends, had died side by side. He praised those who had fought bravely and listened while they recounted their actions; he thanked the giants and the people of magic. Finally, he introduced himself to the small band of soldiers who had entered the battle last of all, alongside Merlin.

As evening approached, Edward felt exhausted. All the dead and wounded had been taken to the village, except the Trajaens.

Elvira, Queen of the Witches, had been slain. Esmerelda, her daughter, wanted to execute the wounded Trajaens. Many of the other magical beings and humans agreed with her.

Edward tried to think what his father would do, and so took a different point of view. He argued that the prisoners should be put on their longboats, with enough drinking water to get them home, taking a message from Avalon. He said that the surviving Trajaens should tell their people that the Avalonians had been merciful on this occasion. They should make it clear to their people that the Avalonians were people of peace. However, if the Trajaens ever attacked Avalon again, they would be shown no more mercy.

Tannus, the son of the Tannitus, the elderly wizard who was able to perform the killing curse, challenged Edward. Tannus's father was dead, and the angry warlock wanted revenge.

"We should slay all the Trajaens and pile their bodies high in their boats," he argued. "We wizards and our sister witches can use our combined powers to blow their boats back from whence they came. Let their people know what will happen if they dare to come here again!"

Merlin supported Edward's plea for mercy. "I understand your anger," he told those who had lost loved ones. "Many of those who died were my friends. But if we slay the prisoners, we will then be as bloodthirsty as our attackers. Let them go home with a very clear message that we are a peaceful people, but strong, well organised, and able to defend ourselves."

"I agree," said the blacksmith's wife, whose two sons, Alex and Andrew, had been killed in the attack. Her face was full of pain, and tears ran down her face as she spoke. "Killing more of these savages will not bring my sons back. Send the marauders home in disgrace, with a message not to come back. If they do return, I'll take a sword and slay them myself!"

The Avalonians who wanted to execute the Trajaen prisoners knew it would be difficult to challenge Merlin and Edward. Now that the blacksmith's wife had stated her wish for leniency, those with opposing views reluctantly ceased to argue.

Although Tannus had begrudgingly stopped arguing to have the prisoners slain, he wanted to identify them in case any returned. "We should mark each of them so that, if any do return, we will recognise them and know that they have not learnt their lesson. They must understand that if they come back, they will pay with their lives."

All agreed to this proposal.

Tannus ran three fingers across each Trajaen's left cheek, leaving stripes like tattoos.

Merlin and Edward spoke to the prisoners before putting them on their boats, to find out more about them. The Trajaens told them that they were people of the ocean and had no fixed home. They thanked the Avalonians for their mercy and asked if they could take their dead so that they could be buried at sea. The Avalonians agreed; after all, they did not want the murderous Trajaens buried on their land.

The prisoners and the dead Trajaens were stripped of their weapons, their armour, and the gold and silver ornaments they wore. The survivors were carefully guarded, by armed Avalonians and Twydell soldiers, as they piled the bodies of their dead on to one of the longboats. The Trajaens pushed the boat containing the bodies of their dead warriors out to sea on the receding tide. They then clambered aboard the other remaining boats for their journey home. A group of witches stood on the beach and, puckering their lips, blew a wind which pushed the boats far out to sea. They watched the boats grow smaller as they sailed into the distance, until they gradually disappeared.

Chapter 10 – After the Battle

When Edward returned to the village, he found his father lying on a bed of straw in the village hall. His wife lay next to him. Daisy knelt beside Gilda, mopping the sweat from the witch's brow. The two lion cubs had curled up together nearby.

An exhausted Cherry Blossom had draped herself along the top of Gilda's pillow, and fallen asleep. Gilda had regained consciousness, waking from time to time but soon drifting back into a feverish sleep.

"They are doing all they can for her." The king looked sadly at his wife. "I thought my battle days were over." The cut at the top of his thigh was bandaged, but blood had seeped through, staining the cloth a deep shade of red. "I certainly never thought I would see my beloved Gilda in battle. She was magnificent, wasn't she?"

"She was indeed," agreed Edward.

"And you too, my dear!" The king spoke to Daisy this time. "I owe you and your pets my life."

"As do I." Edward looked tenderly at Daisy, who lifted her head to look at him. "I thank you with all my heart."

"I am so sorry I accused Gilda of trying to poison me." Daisy let her guilt pour out. "I was so foolish. I remember that my mother spoke of something called soap, which she thought to be a luxury. I should have realised that it was not lard because it smelt of flowers when I tried to cook with it."

"It was an easy mistake to make, Daisy. I'm sure Elna will make you some more."

"I still have some of the violet oil, though. I tried to smash the bottle. I threw it hard against the rocks many times, but it wouldn't break."

"Cherry Blossom put an unbreakability spell on it," explained Edward as he gazed at Daisy.

Cherry Blossom stirred when she heard her name mentioned, but simply smiled and fell back into her slumber.

"I rubbed some on my skin after I washed. Here, smell," said Daisy, offering Edward the crook of her arm.

Edward looked rather taken aback but did as he was bid. He took her hand and gently breathed in the scent of her skin. He noticed how soft and warm she felt.

"It's lovely," he said and then noticed his father watching them.

Embarrassed, he changed the subject. "Your lion cubs have grown. They are much bigger than last time I saw them. Obviously, you managed to train them, and train them well."

"I have named them after my parents, Leo and Sybil."

Daisy spent the rest of the evening amusing the king and the prince by telling them about the antics of the two lion cubs she had taken in. As night fell, she laid a blanket beside Gilda and lay down to sleep at the witch's side.

Edward offered to find her a bed, but she declined, saying that she wanted to stay close to her witch friend, in case she woke and needed help.

With a tinge of jealousy, the prince watched as the lion cubs curled up close to Daisy. He had no wish to leave his parents or Daisy, but he knew that he needed rest, as there was much to do in the morning. He decided not to go home to his bed, but, instead, fell asleep on a nearby pallet of straw.

Merlin had left Arthur to his family on the evening of the battle but was on his way to see him the follow morning when he spotted Willy. Willy was sitting on a stool outside his house. The elderly wood wizard had fallen against the cliff during the battle, and his arm was in a sling.

"Where is my broom?" Willy demanded.

"I'm sorry, old friend. It is broken and beyond repair. I will buy you another."

Merlin expected Willy to be cross and give him 'a piece of his mind'. However, the old wood wizard was still thinking of the events of the previous day, and he was melancholy.

"Never mind," he said. "I'm getting old now and don't really want to travel by broom any longer. The king has had a cart made for me to get backwards and forwards to the forest, did you know?"

"No," replied Merlin.

"Yesterday, it was used to bring back the dead and injured from the beach," he said sadly. "We thought that when we travelled to Avalon, we were coming to a new world full of peace."

"Yes," Merlin said with a sigh. "We lost old friends yesterday, but we have also made new ones." He tried to lift his friend's gloomy spirits. "I hear your images of Greatog and Zog were outstanding, and the giants came to our aid yesterday."

Willy pulled his lips, attempting a smile, but try as he did, his face remained cheerless. He simply looked more like a grizzled piece of bark than usual.

Merlin reminisced with his friend for a short while, but his errand remained, and he hurried away to the king.

"Where have you been for so long?" Arthur asked irritably as Merlin approached.

"It's a very long story, which I am eager to tell, but first I must give your response to an offer from King Frederrick of Twydell. The captain of the Twydell soldiers who escorted me home is to take your answer back to his king. He and his men are anxious to leave, as soon as their horses are ready. They all have families of their own and need to warn the Twydellers that the Trajaens have returned to our seas."

"Speak, then." Arthur was in pain but intrigued to hear the offer that the neighbouring king had made.

"Frederrick has a daughter called Jeanette and a son called Derrick. Both are of marriageable age. A marriage between Avalon and Twydell would form a powerful alliance."

Arthur understood. "It would indeed," he said thoughtfully, but he nodded towards where Edward and Daisy sat. They had spent much of the night watching over Gilda. Leo and Sybil curled up beside them, purring contentedly.

"I think Edward has already set his store with that girl. She saved both our lives. If he has fallen in love and wishes to marry her, I will give them my blessing. A loveless marriage to Princess Jeanette would not be fair to either of them and might also end up with a falling out with King Frederrick.

"Rosalie is still too young to be married. But if Derrick is willing to wait awhile, and they like each other when they meet, perhaps that would be a possibility."

"Very well." Merlin was disappointed, but he did not argue. He, too, could see the close bond that had developed between the young prince and Daisy. However, he added, "Derrick is a very affable young man. I think Rosalie will be impressed."

Merlin then hurried away to give Arthur's response to the captain of the Twydell soldiers.

The people of Avalon had fought a hard battle, and many had lost their lives in the process. Humans, wizards, and witches had fallen in the Battle of Merlport. However, the Avalonians had learnt much. They knew that they had neighbouring allies in the giants and the Twydellers. Most of all, they realised that the humans and the people of magic, together, were one people. Avalon was a peaceful nation, but the Avalonians would work together to protect their land from whatever dangers might come their way in the future.

BOOK TWO: The Land of Twydell and the Dragon Egg

Chapter 1 – The Demise of Twydell

The leaders discussed the terrible happenings of the previous day. Tears were shed for those who had been lost. A plan of action was put together to help protect Merlport if the Trajaens broke their promise not to return. The leaders had taken a break from the meeting to partake in refreshment, but they were now seated again, anxious to hear about Merlin's adventures in neighbouring Twydell.

King Arthur; Esmerelda, now Queen of the Witches; Maud, Queen of the Fairies; and Allarond, King of the Elves all sat at Arthur's round table.

Prince Edward was also invited to the meeting. Edward's invitation was significant. Arthur had suffered many battle injuries during his lifetime. Yesterday's fight with the Trajaens had been no different: he had suffered a deep sword slash to his leg. The ageing king was pale, and all noticed how he winced with pain at even the slightest movement. Edward's presence identified him as the next leader of the humans in Avalon.

Merlin took a long swig of apple juice before beginning his tale.

The wizard started by telling them that he had borrowed Willy the Wood Wizard's broom and flown in the direction of the country which neighboured Avalon. He then gave a brief overview of the land known as Twydell. The country's name meant "two valleys" in an ancient language – twy meaning "two", and dell meaning "valley". Merlin had flown further inland than he had ever ventured since coming to Avalon. He had also flown very high, and in the distance, could see three sprawling mountains with two valleys between them. It was obvious as to how the land had got its name. However, the kingdom was much larger than just the mountains and the two valleys. There were meadows which swept down to the sea. But the land near the sea bordering Avalon was very marshy, and small islands dotted the water round the coast. To the west of Twydell, near the border with the land of Kerner, stood a small forest.

The capital of Twydell was called Dalton, but there were also several towns and large villages in the country. Beamfloet was a small town which stood on the coast, guarding the country against the Trajaens. Bowers Gifford was a large village which stood near the marshes. Thorncombe was another small town; it had a busy farming community near the small forest, and traded much of its produce with Kerner. Birdsmoorgate, another farming community near the border with the north, used to do a lot of trade with the northerners but now did very little business with them. The northerners had worked hard to develop arable land and now grew sufficient crops for themselves, so Birdsmoorgate was left with little trade.

Merlin had learnt there was a lot of infighting between the people of the north in years gone by. The north had once been made up of several different kingdoms. Now they had all come under one leader. The ancestors of some of the northern kingdoms had been friendly with the Twydellers, but the new regime did not like people from the south crossing its borders. There had also been some trouble between the northerners and the Brewins, but the people of Twydell didn't know much about what had happened.

The Twydellers had little to do with the Brewins, who liked to keep to themselves. The Twydellers regarded this to be a pity. If the two countries had joined forces, they might have been able to defend themselves better against the Trajaens.

Having described the land neighbouring Avalon to his fellow leaders, Merlin took another swig of apple juice before telling them about the rest of his eventful journey to Twydell.

"It's been a long time since I travelled by broom. It makes my old bones ache, sitting for hours on that thin handle and bending forward to hold on to its end. I must admit, though, I had forgotten how good it is to see the sunrise from above and feel a light breeze blowing in my face.

"I was enjoying my bird's-eye view, watching the herds of animals make their way along the plains, when I spotted a long trail of people. I steered the broom a little closer, and could see that some were carrying bags or trundling wheelbarrows with what appeared to be their possessions inside. Some rode on horses, and others rode in carts drawn by oxen or ponies, but most were on foot. Naturally, I was curious to find out what was going on.

"I flew down to speak to the people, but they were startled to see me. I suppose the sight of a man riding a broomstick must be a queer sight to any human other than an Avalonian. I tried to call out a greeting, but they were frightened and picked up stones and threw them at me. I knew the stones couldn't reach me, but when I saw one preparing to fire an arrow, well, that was another matter. I flew up high, out of reach, and travelled on towards Dalton.

"I needed to talk to someone to find out what was going on. Eventually, I spotted a small family travelling together. The man was pushing a cart, and there were two small children with the woman. I guessed that the children had not been able to keep pace with the other travellers, so they had fallen behind. They didn't appear to be armed, so I swooped down, landing on the road in front of them."

Merlin smiled as he related their reactions to him dropping out of the sky and onto the road: the man's jaw dropped, and the woman screamed; however, the children only laughed.

"Good day, young sir and young lady." The wizard bowed his head in greeting to the young family. "I am on my way to Dalton, the capital of Twydell, and want to make sure that I am travelling in the right direction."

The man and woman continued to stare in disbelief.

"Would you like to share my lunch with me?" Merlin opened the bundle he was carrying on his back, to reveal a loaf of bread, a wedge of cheese, and a red apple.

It was obvious that the children had been crying. Tears had left clean trails down their dirty, travel-stained faces. They looked eagerly at the food the strange old man offered, and ran to take it.

"Don't touch it!" shouted the mother as she moved between her children and the wizard. "It might be poisoned."

The children looked bewildered. The food looked so tempting, but their mother was usually right.

Merlin smiled. "My food has not been poisoned." He took the cloth in which the food had been bundled, spreading the fabric on the ground and laying the food on top. He drew a small knife from his pocket, pulled a bite-sized piece of bread from the loaf, and cut a small piece of cheese from the wedge. He squeezed the cheese between the bread and popped it into his mouth.

"What do you want from us?" asked the man nervously as his eyes looked longingly at the food.

"I only want to know why so many people appear to be travelling away from Dalton, taking all their belongings with them." Merlin cast his eye over the contents of the cart. There were some cooking pots; what seemed to be muddy, folded blankets; and a heap of clothes, which appeared to be wet because they left water stains on the edge of the cart.

"We are leaving Dalton because it has become a dangerous place to live. We have lost everything we owned. Now we are travelling to Birdsmoorgate, as far away from Dalton as we can get without entering the north. We pray that we will find safety there."

Merlin noticed that the young man's hair was matted with mud. All the family wore mud-splattered clothing. "Please tell me what has happened in Dalton. You can rest awhile and share my lunch. You can then resume your journey feeling a little refreshed."

Although the father and mother were still wary of the oddly clad man who had flown down from the sky on a broomstick, they accepted his offer. They were amazed when Merlin pulled a short stick from his pocket and, waving it over the food, doubled the size of the bread and wedge of cheese. Another apple appeared from nowhere. Another wave of his wand, and the quantity doubled again.

"There! That should be enough to go round. Please help yourselves."

"How did you do that?" asked the woman, her mouth gaping.

"I am a wizard," explained Merlin. "I can do all sorts of magic tricks. Doubling food is one of them."

As they tucked into lunch, Merlin told the young family about Avalon and his mission to speak to King Frederrick. He asked them again about why so many people appeared to be travelling east, with all their possessions in tow. "What is it that has frightened you so much that you feel the need to leave your homes?" he asked.

The young couple looked downhearted. Tears started to run freely down their despondent faces. They said that a pair of dragons lived in the central mountain just above Dalton. Dragons had lived there for as long as anyone could remember, and they had never bothered the Daltonians.

"Now and then, when we went fishing, we used to see them skimming across the mountain lakes, taking fish for themselves," the young father remembered sadly. "We would hide in one of the caves or in the trees, and watch. Afterwards, we would rush to swim in the lake because the flames from the dragons' breath heated the water. They never harmed us, and we used to look forward to seeing them. Sometimes we thought they warmed the water just to amuse us."

The young father went on to tell Merlin that suddenly, and for no apparent reason, the dragons started attacking the Twydell towns and villages. Tears filled the man's eyes as he remembered the terrible night not that long ago, when the thatch on his family's cottage roof caught fire, and he and his wife and children had to run for their lives. Many other families suffered the same fate. The townsfolk worked together to put out the fires, forming a human chain to carry buckets of water back and forth from the river.

No sooner had they put the fires out than a thunderbird appeared in the sky, bringing with it a strong wind and an assembly of dark clouds. Very few people had ever seen such a huge bird before, and no one knew where it had come from. As the dark clouds blew across Dalton, a heavy storm erupted. Thunder clapped, and lightning zigzagged its sharp, bright needles above the town. A lamb ran from a burning barn, and the thunderbird picked the creature up in its talons, carrying it off and flying back in the direction from which it had come.

Although the thunderbird disappeared into the distance, the storm continued. The palace was struck by a fierce streak of lightning, which brought down part of the wall surrounding the courtyard. The river filled with rain and burst its banks. Many of the young family's possessions which had not been devastated by fire were destroyed by the flood.

The king organised some temporary shelter for the homeless families, but even that was destroyed.

The two-pronged attack – the dragon's fire, followed by the thunderbird's storm – happened time and again. Reluctantly, people began leaving their homes to find new settlements where there were no dragons or thunderbirds.

Merlin thanked the young couple for the information and conjured up another helping of food, for the family, before parting. He would like to have provided more but explained that performing magic spells was tiring and he needed to preserve his energy for the rest of his trip. He suggested that the young couple might find safety in Avalon.

Wishing the young family well and bidding them goodbye, Merlin continued on his journey to Dalton.

As the wizard neared the capital of Twydell, he was shocked to see the devastation below. Smoke billowed in grey ribbons into the sky, forming a smoky haze that smelt most unpleasant. Some houses quenched of flames still smouldered. The remains of other houses, which had been burnt to the ground, were now covered in thick mud. Old people, too frail to travel, were sitting or standing in what was left of the palace courtyard. They sat there, hoping that the king would provide them with food and shelter. Soldiers were trying to set up makeshift tents. The palace itself, and other more ornate marquees, appeared to have been put to use as a hospital for the sick and injured.

Merlin walked to the palace door, but armed guards stopped him. He asked to speak to the king, but the guards just laughed. The old wizard was dressed in his travelling attire of a long grey woollen cloak and a tall grey hat; his waist-length grey hair and long grey beard were tangled from his long days of travelling on the broom. He carried the broom in one hand and his wooden staff in the other. The soldiers made fun of the new arrival's bedraggled appearance, telling him that the king would have no time for such a strange-looking person.

The sorcerer ignored the guards' mockery. "Tell the king that I am Merlin, a wizard well respected by Arthur, king of your neighbouring land. The land once known as Brewin but now re-named Avalon. Tell King Frederrick that I can talk to dragons and will try to speak to the angry beast before it attacks again."

The soldiers laughed heartily. It would have been hard for any human to believe the unkempt traveller in front of them. They thought the strangely dressed man, with long tangled hair, was some kind of fool. Still laughing, the armed men pushed him down the steps of the outer hall. The wizard ended up sitting on his backside in the courtyard below.

"If you can really speak to dragons," one of the soldiers yelled, "you'd better go and find them, and tell them to keep away from Dalton! If you come back here, we'll throw you into one of our dungeons."

With a sigh, Merlin simply picked himself up, brushed himself off and walked back into the town. He did his best to mingle with the people milling about in the streets. At the outset, people were cautious and reluctant to speak to the peculiar stranger, but when he showed how his magic could help them, they started to befriend him. He cast a spell which created a light wind that dried clothing soaked by the rain. He found a child who had been parted from his parents. One of his spells helped lift a cart which had turned on its side and got stuck in the mud.

The stories told by the townsfolk were the same as that told by the young family he had met. No one knew why the dragons had started to attack the Twydellers. Nobody knew where the thunderbird had come from, as its like had not been seen for many years.

Merlin learnt that people of magic had been shunned and driven from the town many years ago. The Twydellers believed that there were still some people of magic living in the Forbidden Forest, which lay on the border with Kerner. The forest was forbidden because those who tried to enter were trapped in a binding plant which wrapped itself round their bodies. Several townsfolk knew people who had tried to enter the forest and escaped only by hacking themselves free of the weed. They had heard stories that the creeping bindweed could grow two or three feet in a matter of minutes. There were stories that people determined to enter the forest had been suffocated in the coils of the deadly binding weed. The forest had indeed forbidden anyone to enter its depths.

Merlin was resting with other folk on the town's walls when a warning blast of a guardsman's horn echoed across the town. Terrified people ran for cover, and children screamed. Merlin turned to see a large green dragon in the distance, heading towards Dalton. He placed his staff in the long hidden pocket inside his travelling gown, and then mounted Willy's broomstick. The old wizard soared high in the air, flying his borrowed broom in the direction of the oncoming dragon.

People hesitated from pursuing their search for shelter. They pointed at the strange man flying through the air, on a broomstick, towards their deadly enemy. The guards who had ridiculed Merlin stood at their posts, with jaws dropped and mouths wide open.

As Merlin drew close to the dragon, he raised his arms to show that he carried no weapons. However, the gesture seemed meaningless to the dragon, which blew forth a trail of fiery red flames. Merlin lowered his arms and expertly steered the broom above the dragon, missing the deadly flames aimed at him. The dragon turned, ready to blow forth its lethal flames again, but before it could exhale its fire, Merlin shouted to it in a language it would understand.

"I am no enemy of the dragon. I seek only to speak to you."

The dragon hesitated for a moment, hovering in the air. "Well, I have never seen a man flying through the air on a brush before. Nor have I ever heard a man who spoke our language. Therefore, I will allow you to speak. But, I warn you, I am angry, and in a hurry to hurt those who have hurt us. I have no time for idle chit-chat!"

"I am Merlin. I came from an unhappy land far away to live in a world where mankind could live in peace and harmony with nature. I am told that the dragons have lived near the people of Twydell for many years, and neither has bothered the other. Please tell me, my friend, what has happened to make you so angry that you wish to harm the people of Dalton? What have they done to you?"

"They stole our egg." Merlin saw anger glitter in the dragon's eyes. "My wife and I have waited years for a child. She laid an egg and guarded it well. But then, one day, while I was out looking for food, she left the nest. She was not away for long, but when she got back, our precious egg was gone. The people stole it, and now they must either give it back, unharmed, or suffer the consequences."

"But, my dear dragon, the people to whom I have spoken know nothing of your egg. Why do you think that it is they who stole it?"

"Who else could have stolen it? A cow could not carry an egg, nor could a goat or a horse or a sheep!"

Merlin nodded. "If someone stole your egg, then whoever it is does indeed deserve to be punished. However, surely not every single person who lives in Twydell?"

"All who stay will be punished, including you!" The dragon took a deep breath, ready to breathe out fire again.

Merlin rose swiftly into the air. "Allow me to speak a little longer!" he cried. "I may be able to help you."

The dragon continued to hover. "Speak."

"Let me go back to Dalton. I will speak to King Frederrick, asking him to search every home, shed, and barn in his country to try to find your precious egg. If the egg is hidden in Twydell, and you keep burning the houses and barns, surely your egg will be destroyed too."

The dragon looked thoughtful for a moment, continuing to hover.

Merlin persisted. "Let me try to find your egg. I cannot promise that I will find it, but I swear that I will do my best. I need time, though, and so will King Frederrick. Sending his soldiers to search every nook and cranny will take weeks."

"You speak sense, strange man called Merlin," replied the dragon. "I cannot wait weeks, though. The next full moon is fifteen days hence; if our egg is not returned to me and my wife by then, we will destroy the town known as Dalton, and every other town in Twydell and Kerner."

"Thank you for listening to me." Merlin bowed his head in gratitude. "However, I beg you to consider that the egg may not have been taken by the Twydellers or the Kernans. I would like to speak to your wife so that I can try to put together the pieces of this puzzle for myself."

"Very well," replied the dragon. "She is in poor spirits, and the sight of a man flying on a brush, without wings, and who can speak our language, may amuse her. On the other hand, she is so angry that she may cook you alive in her fury."

"I will take that risk. I shall go now to King Frederrick and tell him of the truce we have agreed upon. I will then look forward to visiting you and your charming wife."

The two parted company. The dragon turned and flew back in the direction from whence it had come. Merlin steered his broomstick back to Dalton Palace as quickly as it could carry him. When he arrived, he did not need to look for the king, because the king was waiting for him in the courtyard, coming forward to meet him when he landed.

Frederrick was an old man whose face was pale and lined with worry. He wore no crown. He had spent much time in the town, comforting his people and organising shelter. His fine velvet gown was spattered with mud.

"So you are the man who said he could talk to dragons, but my guards did not believe you," said the king. "I would never have believed such a thing myself if I had not seen it with my very own eyes. I apologise for the way you were treated."

"Sire," said Merlin. He nodded his head to the king but did not bow. "The dragon believes that one of the people of Twydell or Kerner has stolen his egg. The dragon has waited many years for his wife to bear the egg. The egg is precious to them, for dragon eggs are rare, and she will probably never lay another. He is furious. He has given us till the new moon to find his egg. If it is not found, I fear that your towns and the people who remain within them are doomed. I have told him that you would search every house and building in your land to find the egg."

"I will order every inch of Twydell to be searched," said the king. "Furthermore, I will offer a reward to anyone who can give us information as to where the egg might be. My people and I will do all we possibly can to find it."

"You must also send a message to King Jeffrey of Kerner, telling him to do the same."

"I shall do so straight away. Now tell me, strange man, will you help us search for the missing egg? Will you speak to the dragon again on our behalf?"

"My name is Merlin," the wizard said, correcting the king.

The king's pale cheeks reddened, but he smiled warmly.

"Ah, yes. My guards told me that you and a new king, Arthur, had settled in the land to the east of us. I look forward to meeting our new neighbours."

"King Arthur will look forward to meeting you, if you survive the revenge of the dragons. But now I would be grateful for some food and drink, and then I must go to meet the mother of the egg. I hope that she will agree to speak to me. It may not be one of your people, or indeed anyone from Kerner, who stole the egg, and I need to understand what happened."

King Frederrick invited Merlin into the castle. This time, the guards bowed respectfully as Merlin swept past them. Queen Elise ordered food and wine to be brought to the table in the king's parlour. The royal couple shared a hasty meal with Merlin before his departure, which gave them a little time to parley.

"Tell me, sire," said Merlin. "Is there a soothsayer in Dalton from whom I might seek advice?"

"A soothsayer! We do not encourage such nonsense here." The king stopped. "I apologise. Your kind has not been welcome here, but you have proved that you are a good man. I realise that you are trying to do all you can to help us, and did not mean to offend you. There has been no soothsayer here for many years. I believe there was a woman once, but my grandfather banished her. It is said that she went to live in the Forbidden Forest. She will be dead and gone by now, but she had a husband. It is possible, I suppose, that they had children who still live there, but I doubt it."

"Yes, the Forbidden Forest. Who will search that?" Merlin wanted to know.

"That cannot be searched," replied the king, "for no one who enters ever returns."

"Then that will be my task!" responded Merlin. "If I have my bearings right, I will need to travel north-west to the mountain to visit the home of the dragons, and from there, I will travel west to the Forbidden Forest."

"Your directions are correct, but I fear that I shall see you no more," the king said with regret. "For those who try to enter the Forbidden Forest suffocate in the creeping weeds that surround it."

"I hope that is not the case, and I hope that I will return to Dalton with good news. Now I must make haste. We both have much to do and little time in which to do it."

Thus, Merlin left Dalton. The king and his people wished him good luck as they waved goodbye. However, few believed that they would ever see the brave old wizard again.

Chapter 2 – Ajax and Blitzen's Grief

Merlin flew to the mountain where the dragons lived. It did not take him long to find their cave. He simply looked for the red glow of fire.

First, he flew round the cave, to see how easy it would be to climb up to the entrance. The mountain was steep, and there was no pathway. It would have been very difficult for any man to climb up to the dragons' home, let alone leave carrying an egg.

Merlin flew to the entrance of the cave, feeling the heat exuding from within. He drew his staff and issued a cooling spell before calling out to say that he had arrived.

The deep voice of the male dragon bade him enter.

A fire shielded the cave from the cold outside. On the other side of the fire, the cave opened out into a large room. In the middle of the room was a round nest made of straw and leaves. The dragons sat opposite each other on either side of the nest, looking sadly at the centre, where the straw had become depressed into an oval shape. Merlin guessed that this was where their precious egg had rested.

Whereas the male dragon was green, with lizard-like yellow eyes, the female dragon was dark blue, with eyes just a shade lighter. The blue dragon was some five feet shorter than her husband, who was thirty feet long. She was not as muscular as her husband, either; even so, she was a powerful force to be reckoned with.

"So you think you can find my egg?" she asked, without any hope in her voice. "We have unleashed our fury on the people of Twydell and Kerner, but it has not helped. We do not know what else to do. We never harmed any human beings. We used to like watching them swim in the lake after we had heated it for them with our fiery breath. Why would they want to hurt us so?"

"They believe that by stealing our egg, they will kill us off, as we will then have no children to replace us when we die!" the male dragon said angrily. As he spoke, he raised his tail and cracked it back down hard against the rock floor.

"I understand your anger," said Merlin. "But I have looked round, and can see no way that a man can easily climb up here. There is no path and, presumably, no other entrance."

"You got here," replied the female sharply as she fixed her cold blue eyes on the wizard.

"Yes, that is true," conceded Merlin. "But as I understand, it King Frederrick's ancestors banned people of magic from Twydell many years ago. Your husband has told me that he has seen no other people flying on broomsticks."

The blue dragon nodded slowly.

Merlin continued. "The king has ordered every building in his kingdom to be investigated, and he sent a message to King Jeffrey of Kerner, urging him to do the same. I will do my best to search the Forbidden Forest, where other men will not tread. Please, now, tell me what happened. I need to understand it all before I make my way to the forest."

Merlin learnt that the green male dragon was called Ajax, and his wife, the blue dragon, was called Blitzen. Dragons rarely lay eggs more than once in a lifetime, and the couple were delighted when Blitzen yielded her heart's desire. She made a comfy nest and rested the precious egg inside it. The egg would take nine months to hatch.

She sat on the egg, keeping it safe and warm, rarely leaving the nest for nearly seven months. Ajax brought her food – a task he found increasingly difficult, as Blitzen's tastes had changed since her pregnancy, even though she had laid the egg.

One day, she asked him for oysters, which could only be found on an island a longer distance away than he usually travelled. Ajax always sought to please his wife so he set off on his long journey. However, he was gone a long time, and in the meantime Blitzen was hungry. She fancied some fresh air, and at the same time thought she would catch some fish in the lake. She thought it might be fun to watch the people swim after she had heated the water for them. However, by the time she got to the lake, storm clouds had started to form, and the fishermen had already left the lake to return to their homes. She caught a few fish as she skimmed across the water, but decided to return home. However, she heard a clap of thunder, followed swiftly by a lightning streak, and decided to shelter in a nearby grotto until the storm had passed.

Blitzen told Merlin that by the time she got home, the egg was gone. She described how she flew frantically over the mountain, time and again, to see if the thief was still in view. However, she could see no one.

"So there were no people near the lake," Merlin re-capped her story to make sure that he had not missed anything. "And you could see no one running from the mountain when you returned home."

"No one," Blitzen concurred.

"You say that there was a clap of thunder and then a streak of lightning?" Merlin's tone was gentle as he continued his questions. "Did you see any strange bird in the sky?"

"No." Tears dropped from Blitzen's huge, sad eyes as she shook her head. "I took cover until the rain stopped. It rained in torrents. I doubt whether even a clever man like you could fly in such a storm. Why, oh why, did I leave my nest?"

"I could not have flown in such a storm." The wizard tried to alleviate the poor creature's guilt. "I can only think of one creature which apparently can, although I have never seen one myself."

"The thunderbird!" Ajax jumped to his feet, and his tail rose again, quickly thumping back down on the floor, with a loud smack.

Merlin wondered why this repeated action left the dragon in no pain.

"I have seen the thunderbird flying towards the towns and villages after I have reaped my vengeance on them," Ajax said. "The bird brings with it thunder, lightning, and heavy rain!"

113

DAISY BOURNE

"It is possible the thunderbird is the culprit," said Merlin. "It could easily spot your cave from above because it exudes such a warm glow. We must not jump to conclusions, though. I must find this bird and speak to it. I hope I speak a language it understands."

"I have a language it understands," snarled Ajax as a long, sleek tongue of flame emitted from his mouth.

Even though the flame was not aimed at Merlin, the heat made the old wizard tremble, and he stepped backwards to avoid being burnt.

"I know you wish to question the thunderbird, but I am afraid that you will frighten it so much that it may lie to try to save itself," Merlin said. "Please let me speak to it. If, and I mean *if*, it is guilty, then perhaps I can persuade it to tell the truth."

Ajax and Merlin argued for some time. However, neither knew where the thunderbird lived, and without such knowledge, neither would be able to question it anyway.

Eventually, Merlin said, "I will travel to the Forbidden Forest and see if I can find anything there."

"How will you do that?" asked Blitzen. "Not even we can get near that forest. We have tried to land there, but the weeds entwine our wings and feet."

"Then best leave the Forbidden Forest to me, my dear," said Merlin. "You and Ajax can scan the mountains by flying high in the air. The thunderbird may just as easily nest in the mountains as in the forest. Now I will bid you goodnight. If I find anything in that mysterious piece of woodland, I will return immediately."

The dragons offered to let Merlin stay in their cave overnight, but he was anxious to get to the forest, which was a good night's journey away. He flew under the starry night, the gentle wind ruffling his hair and beard, his cape blowing behind him. He nearly fell asleep more than once, but woke with a start each time he felt himself slipping from the broom.

114

Chapter 3 – The Forbidden Forest

As the sun rose up from behind the mountain, Merlin could see the Forbidden Forest in the distance. Trees nestled against the tall mountains which separated Twydell from Kerner. He brought the broomstick down at the edge of the forest and spent a few moments listening to the dawn chorus. He then drew his staff, which was concealed in the long pocket inside his cloak.

Sure enough, bindweed, as thick as rope, wound an intricate pattern round the forest. Merlin was considering what spell to use to cut away the powerful bindweed, when, suddenly, a patch of the plant unwound its vines to provide an opening.

The wizard hesitated, wondering if it was some kind of trap, and then he heard the sound of hooves approaching. He looked into the depth of the forest and saw a pale horse-like shape drawing close. As the shape drew nearer, he could see that it was not a horse, but his old friend Lennox, the pure white unicorn, who had travelled on one of the ships from Briton.

Merlin threw open his arms and wrapped them round the unicorn's neck. Lennox nuzzled up against the old wizard's face. Both felt the warmth of their genuine friendship.

"Well, my old friend, how glad I am to see you!" Merlin spoke in Unicornian, a language both he and Lennox understood.

"I am happy to see you too, my wise wizard. I am not a beast of burden, but, on this occasion, if you climb on my back, I will take you to the lady you seek."

Lennox lowered his front legs to make it easier for Merlin to climb on his back, but the old wizard hesitated.

"What lady?" Merlin asked.

"The lady who is expecting you. Climb on to my back. I have never offered to carry a human being before. If you do not wish to take up my offer, I will walk ahead, and you can follow."

Merlin climbed onto Lennox's back, thanking his friend for the lift. He was tired because he had travelled all night, and was most grateful to have the opportunity to ride. It was indeed a great privilege to be borne on the back of a unicorn, and much more comfortable than a broomstick handle.

As Lennox trotted into the forest, Merlin heard a rustle, and looked behind to see the entrance into the forest closing over. Lennox wound his way along a slim path with dense forest on either side. The bindweed formed a lace-like canopy over the top of the trees. In effect, the forest was sealed.

Lennox continued along the winding path for several hours, carrying Merlin on his back. The sun shining through the lace-like canopy formed a dappled effect on the narrow track which the wizard found mesmerising – so mesmerising he could hardly keep his eyes open. It was early afternoon when they eventually reached a waterfall. An opening in the forest canopy, just in front of the waterfall, allowed an expanse of grass to grow. A small herd of unicorns grazed in this small pasture.

"These are my wives," said Lennox.

Merlin raised his eyebrows. "Congratulations! A fine herd you have here. I don't believe I have ever seen such an excellent brood of mares!"

A chestnut mare with a silver mane and a white blaze on her face whinnied, as if to acknowledge Merlin's comments.

"And this is where you dismount, my wise wizard. The lady you seek awaits you. She lives in the cave behind the waterfall."

The old wizard slid down from the unicorn's back and, after thanking the unicorn, carefully made his way up the steps in the rocks, which led to a hollow behind the waterfall.

"Merlin! At last we meet! I've been waiting to meet you for a long time." A slim, handsome woman, wearing a cream smock over a floral blouse, stepped out of the entrance behind the waterfall.

The wizard squinted because a rainbow had appeared in the waterfall between him and the person greeting him. Through the rainbow he could see that she wore a colourful scarf round her hair and gold hooped earrings which glinted in the sun. The arm she extended was covered in gold bracelets, which jangled as she held out her hand to shake his. She reminded him of a Gypsy.

"Greetings, my lady." Merlin bowed respectfully as he took her hand. "I am sorry. I do not know your name, nor did I realise that anyone was expecting me."

"Come in, come in. You must be tired. You've been travelling all night and not had much rest for many days. I've been watching you. Here, have a cup of hot mint tea – I find it so refreshing. I have a plate of fresh fruit and vegetables prepared for you too."

Before Merlin could ask who she was, or how she knew he was coming, he was ushered into the cave and told to sit on a patchwork quilt. The mysterious woman served him a cup of hot brew, and provided bowls of delicious fruits and vegetables. Despite being widely travelled, Merlin had never seen the like of some of the fruits he was offered. The bowls contained ripe peaches, grapes of both black and green varieties, oranges, cherries, and plums, plus raw carrots and cucumber.

"This is delicious!" said Merlin, who was very hungry. The first genuine smile in a long time cracked his wrinkled old face, and his blue eyes twinkled. "Where did you get this wonderful fruit? I've never tasted anything like it before."

"I'll show you later," replied the Gypsy-looking woman as she munched on a carrot.

The visitor noticed a table on which stood a round object covered by a purple velvet cloth. Spread next to the object were cards illustrated with colourful pictures. Merlin recognised the shape of a crystal ball and the images of the Tarot cards.

"Ah, I see now. You are a soothsayer!" he exclaimed.

"Very observant of you! I am Helen-Joy."

"What a lovely name," said Merlin, who had taken an instant liking to the woman sitting in front of him, sharing the plate of fruit and vegetables.

"My parents couldn't decide whether to name me Helen, after a mythical queen, or Joy, because I was always happy. They ended up giving me a double name."

"How long have you lived here?"

"I was banished from Dalton by King Frederrick's grandfather almost eighty years ago. I came here with my dearest husband, Bryan, who was a minstrel. He could have stayed in Dalton, you know, but he chose to leave his friends and family and to follow me here. We were so happy, but Bryan is gone. He died more than twenty years ago." A look of sadness spread over her face.

"You must be an expert in the spell of youth! I would not have taken you for a day over 40!" It was not often Merlin looked amazed, but he did so now. He knew that witches could cast such spells, but they never lasted very long.

"Spell of youth!" said Helen-Joy with a laugh. "I wish. I have no magic powers; I am only a soothsayer. I read the Tarot, look into the crystal ball, and sleep on my pillow of dreams. I merely try to interpret what I see! I have no magic."

"Then who charmed the bindweed to seal your forest, and who released it this morning to allow me entrance?" The old wizard raised an eyebrow quizzically.

Helen-Joy giggled. "Oh, you do look funny when you are in an interrogation mode!"

Merlin felt himself blush. He could not remember the last time that he'd felt his cheeks redden with embarrassment.

"It is not my forest. I am just lucky enough to live in this fantastic place! The girls charmed the bindweed to 'seal the forest', as you put it. When I told them you were coming, they charmed the bindweed to open when you arrived and to close again behind you. They can't wait to meet you!

"The girls will be here tonight. They're cooking your dinner. I don't eat meat, but the girls are going to make a barbecue in the garden. They do that every now and again. I supply the wine and the fruit, and we have a good old get-together. Better when Bryan was alive, of course, because he used to play his guitar, and we used to dance and sing. ..."

"Excuse me," Merlin interrupted. "Who are 'the girls'?"

"Local coven. There's only seven of them, though. The Bramble family of witches. Really good fun. You're going to enjoy yourself, but you need to get some rest first."

"Helen-Joy, I am sorry but I cannot stay. It is true that I have sought a soothsayer, but I need to search the forest for a dragon's egg which has been stolen. I cannot stay, because I am anxious to get back to work. If we do not find the egg before the next full moon, the dragon may destroy Dalton and every other town in Twydell and Kerner. I beg you to look into your crystal ball and tell me what you see."

"So that's what it's all about," said Helen-Joy. "I could see dragons and flames and floods, but couldn't make sense of it all. I saw you flying round, talking to old King Freddy and then cosying up with the dragons. Where do those giant birds come into the story? I've seen them flying about in my crystal ball a few times, and in my dreams too. It seems they only fly with the rain."

Merlin told Helen-Joy all he knew about the missing egg, beseeching her to help him.

"Best sleep on it!" she declared. "Now take your choice. You can either sleep on the floor in here, or use the hammock in the garden. I'll have a nap and try to put the pieces of all the bits I've seen together. Then we'll party it up with the girls tonight. They'll be able to throw some light on the subject for you, and they can help you search the forest, if you must – but you would be wasting your time. If the egg were here, one of us would know."

The guest could not argue with his new friend, and he was desperately in need of sleep, so he agreed to Helen-Joy's plan of action.

Helen-Joy led Merlin to the back of her cave.

A bed with satin quilts lay in a cleft at the far end of the cave. Lace curtains separated the bed from the rest of the cave, but Merlin had not realised that the cave turned to the right just in front of the bed. Helen-Joy pulled back heavy red velvet curtains to reveal the beauty of her secret garden.

The garden lay in a hollow inside the mountain, forming its own small valley. Fruit trees grew in abundance, as did vegetables. Flowers of many different varieties and colours flourished. Grapes grew on vines which clung to the side of the tall rocks that surrounded the garden like a wall. A stream ran down the mountainside, into a pool beside which an inviting-looking hammock was strung between two apple trees.

Merlin chose to sleep in the warmth of the afternoon sun. He cast his cloak and hat to one side, and climbed into the hammock. For a while, he listened to the birdsong as he gazed round the secret garden, but his eyelids were heavy, and he soon drifted into the welcome world of slumber.

It was late afternoon when he awoke. It was still warm, and it would have been all too easy to close his eyes again, but he slipped down from the hammock and climbed the stone steps leading back up to the cave.

Helen-Joy had left open the red curtains separating the cave from the garden. He could see her through the lace curtains in front of her bed, lying with a satin sheet across her body. She was fully clothed; she seemed to be in a fitful sleep. Every now and again, she would mutter to herself. It seemed as if she were about to sit up, but then she would simply turn to one side and continue muttering.

Merlin helped himself to a cup of mint tea from the pot which was boiling on the fire. He watched the soothsayer for a while, then made his way back into the garden, ate a ripe peach which he picked from a tree, and then lay back on the hammock and fell asleep again.

The sun was going down, and it was starting to get a bit chilly when Merlin awoke for the second time. He made his way back into the cave. This time, he found Helen-Joy at her table.

Tarot cards were spread out in front of her, and the purple cloth had been removed from her crystal ball. She seemed so deep in contemplation that Merlin thought she must be unaware of his presence. However, she told him to help himself to a cup of mint tea, and to pour one for her as well.

She did not thank him as he placed the cup carefully on the table. She simply looked from cards to ball, and back again, just as if she were reading a book. Lifting her cup and sipping the hot brew, she continued to read the tools of her trade.

Finally, she put down her empty cup and smiled at the wizard.

"Yes, I think you are right: the giant birds have stolen the egg. I can see them in some sort of cave. After all, if they bring rain and thunder, they need somewhere to keep dry."

Merlin nodded. What the soothsayer said seemed to make perfect sense.

"They wish the egg no harm. In fact, they seem to love it; but the egg will harm them. Sounds strange, doesn't it? I'm still trying to understand it all." Helen-Joy paused and then added. "There is a lot of sadness. The egg seems to bring them hope, but I am certain that it will harm them!"

"If Ajax or Blitzen find the thunderbirds with their egg, they will certainly harm them!" Merlin stated the obvious.

"No, I don't think Ajax and Blitzen will be the ones to harm the thunderbirds, although I'm sure there would be one almighty scrap if they met!" Helen-Joy pronounced and then said, "The egg is safe, though, and the baby dragon within it is healthy. That's one thing I'm sure about. Anyway, I'll sleep on it again tonight, and, fingers crossed, we might figure out what is going on tomorrow."

Merlin nodded.

"Now. Let's get ready for tonight," Helen-Joy said. "I suggest you have a good old wash, and spruce up. Take those dirty clothes off, and I'll wash them for you. They'll be dry by tomorrow lunchtime, when you set off again. You can wear some of Bryan's old clothes tonight. You're about the same size, so they should fit all right. Even if they don't, it's better than being dirty."

Giving Merlin no chance to reply, she continued. "Have you got a brush or comb for that mop of yours? It looks like you haven't put a brush through it for weeks. I've got some oil you can put in your hair and beard, and that should make it easier for you to comb it through. If you hurry, I'll have time to give you a trim before the party starts."

Merlin was taken aback. No one else had ever spoken to him in the way that Helen-Joy did. Nevertheless, he did as he was told, and felt much better after he had bathed in the stream and combed his hair.

Helen-Joy washed his clothes while he bathed, and seemed to be totally oblivious to the old wizard's nakedness. He wrapped himself in a towel while she cut his hair and beard, and the birds carried away the trimmings to help strengthen their nests. The clothes she found for him fitted him perfectly, and when he looked in her mirror, he considered himself to look ten years younger.

The girls could be heard before they were seen. Laughter and chatter interrupted the still of the late evening as they wound their way along the forest path. They greeted Merlin with friendly excitement. Their ages ranged from teenager to very old. Merlin found out from talking to the very old cackling witch that they were all related – the Bramble family of witches, just as Helen-Joy had said. The cackling witch was the great-grandmother of the teenage girl. The old witch went on to say that her mother had been banished from Dalton at the same time as Helen-Joy. She and her family had been brought up in the forest, and knew no other life. They felt safe here.

"Tell me, Merlin," she said. "Are there any more fine-looking wizards like you in Avalon? If there are, send them over here. We've run out of men." The old witch cackled.

"I will tell them of your needs," Merlin said in a joking tone, and the old witch cackled even louder.

"You say that your mother left Dalton with Helen-Joy – so how old is she? She looks so young!"

The cackling never stopped. "She must be, let me see, 106, I think. Ask her yourself!"

"I wouldn't dream of asking a lady how old she is. Are you sure? She's nearly as old as I am, if she's 106!"

"Hey, Helen-Joy, Merlin wants to know how old you are!"

Merlin felt himself blush for the second time that day.

"Hmm … .I lose track a bit, but I'm pretty sure I'm coming up to 107 soon." The soothsayer laughed.

"Good. Another excuse for a party!" called out one of the witches.

"We'll make the cake. You supply the wine!"

"Sounds like a good idea to me!" Helen-Joy laughed. She always seemed to be laughing when she wasn't working.

"Shall we invite Merlin too?" One of the witches spoke loudly, into Helen-Joy's ear, but it was the great-grandmother witch who answered.

"Yes, Merlin will come, and he'll bring along the pick of Avalon's wizards with him!" she said with a cackle.

"Oooh …" replied the girls in unison. "We could do with some men."

Merlin smiled. He wanted to be serious and speak to the witches about the thunderbirds and the lost egg, but he felt that he could not interrupt their party without causing offence. So he settled back on a comfy bench to watch them as they laughed and danced and joked.

However, the great-grandmother sensed his anxiety. She sat herself next to him. "Now don't you worry," she said gently. "While we were preparing dinner, Helen-Joy told me about the egg you seek. I can tell you for sure that it is not in this forest; nor are those birds. If they were here, one of us would've seen 'em.

"We'll come back tomorrow, and all of us together will help piece together this mystery. I don't have too much sympathy for King Freddy or the Daltonians, but I don't suppose I'd like to see young kiddies get hurt.

"I'll get my girls home soon, so they don't suffer with too much of a hangover tomorrow. Even if they do, Helen-Joy's got a good remedy already made up. So don't you worry now, Merlin. You just enjoy yourself tonight and then get a good night's sleep. You need to be well rested because I think you will have a lot of work in front of you. Now then, come and try this rabbit pie I've made. By the way, my name is Bertha."

So Merlin enjoyed his night with the girls. Bertha's home-made rabbit pied was delicious. He ate well and enjoyed a fair amount of home-made wine. By the time the girls left his head was spinning.

The wizard and the soothsayer stood at the entrance to the cave to wave goodbye to the girls. As the darkness of the forest enveloped Bertha and her family, they disappeared from view. However, Merlin could still hear their singing and laughter for several minutes after he lost sight of them. He smiled as he thought of the girls, singing and joking as they made their way home, along the forest paths.

Helen-Joy laid a colourful patchwork quilt on the floor of the cave for Merlin to sleep on, and gave him another quilt with which to cover himself. She then bid him goodnight and went to her bed of dreams.

The next morning, Merlin awoke to find Helen-Joy again sitting at her table. The Tarot cards were spread in a different arrangement this time. As he stretched, he watched her looking from cards to crystal ball, and back again. He noticed that there was not a grey streak in her brown hair, and he tried to imagine her brown eyes, serious for a change, staring at the images on her cards and into the depths of the glass ball.

She seemed completely oblivious to his presence, but without looking up, she said, "There's hangover remedy in the jug, if you need it, and mint tea in the kettle. Help yourself to anything you want. The unicorns are out front; you might like to go and talk to them, seeing as you know their language. Good idea, that. Go and talk to Lennox. I'm too busy to chat. Give them some of those apples in the bowl by the door. They prefer green ones."

Merlin raised his eyebrows. He hadn't uttered a word, but he did as he was told, smiling as he did so. He tried the hangover remedy, liked its taste, and filled his cup. Picking out a bowl of green apples for the unicorns and a ripe peach for himself, he went outside.

The unicorns lifted their heads from the small patch of grass, and then came towards him expectantly.

"She's a remarkable lady," stated Lennox, as he trotted across the pasture to where Merlin was offering the apples to the mares.

"Remarkable indeed!" Merlin replied.

"The only trouble with this forest is that the bindweed canopy does not allow much sunlight, so there is little grass. The witches have opened it up in small patches so that we get these grazing areas. Helen-Joy feeds us cabbage, carrots, and apples so we don't go hungry."

"Do you never go outside the forest?"

"Rarely, and if we do, it is always at night. The girls are afraid that we might be seen by men, who would then try to enter the forest to catch us. If they did find a way of breaking in, the girls would not be safe either."

"Are there no other people here?"

"No, and no giant birds either. I heard the girls talking about them on the way home last night. There are no giant birds here, my friend, nor a hidden egg. I am sorry you have wasted your time, but perhaps Helen-Joy can help you. Just don't rush her. Now I want you to meet my wives. I have not yet introduced you properly."

Apart from Lennox, the unicorns had never before met anyone who could speak their language. Merlin was enjoying light conversation with the mares when he heard the girls approaching. The laughter and cackling preceded the appearance of the family of seven. The girls waved when they saw the wizard and hurried towards him.

Chapter 4 – The Bramble Family

"Look how clever he is, talking to the unicorns," one of the witches said.

Merlin heard her clearly; she spoke deliberately loud enough for him to hear.

"Our luck seems to be changing, girls!" said the witch, gesturing towards the unicorns. "First, those lovely creatures find their way here; next, we get a visit from a man!"

Merlin laughed with them, greeting them warmly.

Helen-Joy appeared at the door, with a tray of cups, a jug of the hangover remedy, and pot of mint tea.

Without being asked, Merlin went back into the cave and came back with a bowl of fruit to share.

Helen-Joy smiled.

"Got him trained already," cackled the great-grandmother witch.

They sat on the grass, and Helen-Joy explained what she had seen in her dreams and what the tools of her trade had revealed to her. Most clearly of all, she could see a mountain with a rain cloud hovering over it constantly. She was sure that the egg was safe, but the two giant birds which had stolen it were in danger. She said that Merlin must act swiftly if he was to stop the catastrophe which would occur before the next full moon.

"Unfortunately, girls, Merlin must leave today!" Helen-Joy said.

The girls sighed in unison, and Lennox, who understood the human language but could not speak it, gave a whinny of disappointment.

Merlin asked, "Do any of you know where the mountain with the rain cloud hovering above it lies?"

"None of my family has ever left the forest," replied Great-Grandmother Bramble. "So we wouldn't know."

All the witches, except the youngest, shook their heads.

"I have seen it," said the girl, looking at the ground, as if she were filled with shame.

"How can you, Heather?" exclaimed her mother, who was called Sally. "You have never left the forest!"

"Yes, I have," admitted Heather. "I did not want to be deceitful. I love this forest, but sometimes it feels like a prison. One night, not long ago, when you asked me to open the bindweed for the unicorns and keep guard for them, I borrowed Great-Grandmother's old broomstick. I flew up in the air. I felt like I was free. It was wonderful. I could feel the wind in my face and blowing through my hair."

The older witches gasped, and Sally shook her head in dismay.

"I wasn't gone for long," Heather said in a quiet voice, her head hung low. "I saw a mountain in the moonlight, with a cloud above it. The strange thing is that it was only raining on that one mountain."

"Thank you for being honest," Merlin said gently. "If you had kept your journey a secret, I might not have known that the place I seek is so close."

However, the witches were not so gentle with her.

Sally got up, strode to where her daughter sat, and slapped her hard across the face.

"You foolish girl! Don't you ever do anything so foolish and dangerous again! You know what happened to your father and your uncles! Do you want to disappear too?"

The other witches shouted their agreement, and Heather covered her face and ran inside Helen-Joy's cave.

"She will not do it again without your permission," the soothsayer said. "I saw Heather in my dream that night, although I did not see the mountain of which she speaks. The next day, I told her that she must not go off on her own again."

"She won't go off anywhere again," Heather's grandmother, who was called Nora, said sternly. "Because none of us will ever leave the forest!"

"I can't believe she would do such a thing." Sally shook her head. Her face had turned white. "She knows what happened to her father."

"What did happen to her father?" asked Merlin.

"Well, that's just it – we don't really know!" Great-Grandmother Bramble replied, and then she went on to tell Merlin the history of her family.

The laughing and cackling stopped now, and gloomy expressions replaced smiles. The whole family sat with hunched shoulders as Great-Grandmother Bramble recounted the past.

"My mother and father brought me here as a child. They came with Helen-Joy and her husband, Bryan, when King Freddy's grandfather told all our kind we had to leave Twydell. A wizard and his son already lived here, in the same house where we all live in now. I married Ernie, the son, and we were happy enough. We had two fine daughters: Nora and Maura." She nodded towards each of her daughters. "Maura never married, but Nora found a husband, a good man called Dillbert. He came to the forest from Kerner, seeking refuge, because our kind was being persecuted in Kerner too."

Nora took up the story, with much sorrow in her voice. "Dillbert and I had three beautiful daughters before he died: Dilly, Dally, and Sally."

The three sister witches nodded.

Merlin looked at the three women, all of whom were not just plain, but ugly. *Ah*, he thought. *Beauty is in the eye of the beholder.*

Nora continued. "We thought our daughters would never marry for there were no more men in the forest. But then, one day, a man came to the forest from Dalton. He was the son of a half-witch. He had very little magic in him, but his sons – Jerry, Garod, and Isaiah – had started to do strange things. His wife was horrified, afraid the neighbours would see the boys making their toys fly through the air.

"The father feared for his sons' lives, so he brought them to the forest. Stood outside yelling for a witch, he did. Anyway, he left the boys with us, and Mum and Maura brought them up, just as if they were their own."

The elderly witches nodded, their thoughts lost in the melancholy of remembrance.

"They were good kids. They liked it here in the forest. Their father and mother used to come and visit sometimes. You could see they really loved their sons. If they didn't love them, they wouldn't have brought them here, would they?"

The question didn't require an answer, but everyone, including Merlin, nodded in agreement.

"The boys were happy enough, and they married my girls," said Nora. "But their parents stopped visiting. We didn't know why. One day, the boys decided that they hadn't seen their parents for a long while, and thought they'd walk into Dalton to find them. Heather was already born, and Isaiah wanted to tell his parents that he had a child. The boys promised they would do no magic when they got to Dalton because they didn't want to draw any attention to themselves. The last thing they wanted was to cause trouble. So, off they went, but they never returned. We think the people of Dalton must have recognised them and killed them."

"Or they might have found some other women and stayed with them!" snapped Dilly.

"Speak for yourself," retorted Sally angrily. "My husband would never have left me! He loved me, and he loved our daughter!"

"Stop this!" Helen-Joy broke into the argument. "I can tell you this. Your husbands did not abandon you willingly. They all loved you, and they wanted to return to the forest. The forest was their home! I know this, but I cannot tell you any more."

"Can't, or won't?" Nora Bramble's voice had become angry. "You have said this before, but you never tell us what happened to them. I can only believe that your reluctance to tell us means that they are dead."

Helen-Joy hung her head low but did not reply.

Merlin saw the great sadness that the girls suffered. They had laughed and joked the night before, but now they were filled with anguish.

"I do not know what happened to your husbands," he said. "But if I am successful in my mission, I will not be afraid to ask King Frederrick for the truth. If I finish this mission alive, I promise that I will come back and tell you what, if anything, I have found out."

"Thank you, Merlin." Great-Grandmother Bramble looked into the wizard's face. "You are a good man. I would like to know what happened to our boys before I die. I can't say it will make me die in peace, but not knowing is what makes it so difficult."

Maura wrapped her arms round her mother, holding the old witch close.

Merlin felt helpless. He tried to think of something to do or say to lift the unhappiness which now weighed so heavily in the air.

Helen-Joy tried to lighten the mood. "Girls, Merlin has to be on his way. Sally, will you let Heather go with him to the edge of the forest to point him in the direction of the mountain with the rain cloud hovering above it?"

"To the edge." Sally wiped the tears from her eyes and looked up. "But not an inch farther!"

"Thank you, Sally." Merlin smiled at her. "I would appreciate your daughter's help."

"So, now it is time to pack your things and go, Merlin," Helen stated firmly. She reached into the pocket of her smock and pulled out a sealed piece of parchment. "I know that you want to ask me if your mission will be successful. If I tell you I think it will be successful, you may be overconfident. If I tell you it won't, then you might give up. What I think may not even be right. So, I have written what I predict in this parchment, but you

135

must swear, in front of the girls, not to open it until your work is complete."

"Very wise," stated Great-Grandmother Bramble.

The other witches murmured their agreement.

Merlin raised his right hand and smiled. "I swear most solemnly, in front of the Bramble family of witches who reside in the Forbidden Forest, not to open the parchment till my mission is over, one way or another."

"Well, let's get you packed and ready to go!" said Helen-Joy as she hurried back to the cave, disappearing behind the waterfall.

Lennox trotted up beside Merlin. The unicorn's chestnut mare with the white blaze stood a little way behind.

"We are not beasts of burden, but you may ride on my back one more time, my wise wizard," Lennox said. "Sheba, one of my mares, will take the young witch."

"That is most kind," Merlin said in Unicornian, bowing his head in thanks to the beautiful mare.

The mare lowered her head in acknowledgement.

Merlin told the witches that Sheba would allow Heather to ride on her back.

The witches clapped their hands with glee.

Although Sally's eyes still glistened with tears, she gave a wide smile at the honour bestowed on her daughter.

"What a privilege!" sighed Nora, the proud grandmother of Heather.

Merlin packed his things.

Helen-Joy rolled up some thin strands of leafless bindweed into a ball, like string. She insisted that Merlin take it, although she could give no reason why.

Without bothering to ask questions, the sorcerer dutifully placed the ball of bindweed in his pocket. *A ball of string in one's pocket is always handy. I can always find a use for it*, he reasoned to himself.

The wizard, who was genuinely sorry to leave, said his goodbyes. Helen-Joy waved goodbye from the waterfall, but the

Bramble family ran behind the trotting unicorns for as far as they could keep pace. The misery of earlier had left them. They were now in high spirits as they watched Heather bobbing up and down on Sheba's back, holding tightly to her mane. The young witch's face beamed with delight as she clung to the unicorn.

At the edge of the forest, Heather muttered a spell which sufficiently unravelled the bindweed to form a narrow opening. She pointed towards a mountain above which hovered a rain cloud.

Merlin could just see the strange spectacle, between the passing white clouds.

He boarded Willy's broomstick, but before he set off, he made Heather promise that she would go straight home. Steering his conveyance towards the mountain, he turned only to wave goodbye to the young witch and the two unicorns.

Chapter 5 – Storm and Thor's Folly

It took Merlin little more than an hour to reach the mountain upon which the rain poured. Pulling up his collar and wrapping his travelling cloak round himself in an effort to keep dry, he circled round, trying to locate the entrance to a cave. As he wound his broom round the top of the mountain, he smelt the unpleasant stench of burning. Wiping the rain from his eyes and squinting, he thought he could see smoke coming out of a narrow crevice. He dipped the broom and landed on a slippery ledge just outside the opening.

The smell was far worse as he reached the entrance to the cave, making the old wizard gag; nevertheless, he rushed inside. Two giant birds were flapping their burning wings and tail feathers in terror. They were trying to get outside and into the rain, but a small, fiery dragon, breathing flames, stood in front of them.

The small green dragon was having great fun. It was setting fire to a large nest which stood in the middle of the cave, burning it a bit at a time, blowing out the flames, and then reigniting them. The creature seemed completely unaware of the deadly state of affairs in which it had placed the birds.

With one hand, Merlin used his cloak to cover his mouth. With the other, he raised his staff to quench the flames devouring the nest. Next, he issued a stunning spell on the tiny dragon, which rendered it motionless. Finally, he put out the flames burning the birds' wings.

"Quickly!" he spluttered. The smoke was getting into Merlin's lungs, his eyes were stinging, and he was starting to choke. "Get outside, and let the rain cool your wings!" He managed to shout between coughs, hoping the language he used was one the birds would understand. He was not sure whether they understood him or simply acted on instinct to half fly, half race out into the rain.

He looked at the ashes of the nest and saw the remains of a broken egg. *Well, little fellow – or perhaps it's little lady – you have arrived early. You are still supposed to be in your shell for a few more weeks yet.* He checked the tiny motionless creature, to make sure that it was all right, before picking it up and rushing outside.

In the open air, the thunderbirds were languishing in the rain. Merlin coughed and spluttered, but, after taking a few deep breaths of fresh air, he eventually managed to speak.

"What, in heaven's name, made you steal the dragon's egg?" Merlin asked angrily from the shelter of the cave entrance. He held his staff ready to cast another spell if either of the birds attacked him. However, the large creatures looked petrified as they stood on the ledge, allowing the cool rain to soothe their wings.

"We had no egg of our own," replied the male. "There are so few of us left, and we wanted children so badly. One day, we were sheltering in a cave near the lake. We saw the dragons approaching the same cave. We did not know whether they would attack us, so we hid at the back. We heard them talking about the egg they were expecting, and we thought how lucky they were. We followed them back to their cave. We kept a good distance behind them, and they were so absorbed in each other's company that they did not see us. When we got home, we talked about taking the egg to make it our own. The dragons would have another sooner or later, and then they wouldn't miss the one we took."

"Fools!" bellowed Merlin. "Dragons only usually have one egg in a lifetime! You have caused the deaths of many people, and rendered others homeless. On top of that, when the dragons find out what you have done, they will no longer unleash their vengeance on the people of Twydell and Kerner. They will unleash their vengeance on you!"

The birds squawked in alarm.

"We are sorry," replied the female. "I wanted an egg so badly. I had heard of a bird called the cuckoo, which always lays its eggs in another bird's nest. I always wanted to come home and find that a cuckoo had visited my nest and left its egg behind.

"I have been obsessed with the thought of having an egg of my own. I was envious of the dragons, and I found a little place in the mountains from where I could keep watch on their cave.

"One day, I saw the green dragon fly off, and sometime afterwards I saw the blue one go down to the lake. I knew where the entrance to the cave was, so I decided to pop in to take a look at their nest. I only intended looking, but when I saw the egg, I fell in love with it. It was such a big egg, just like the one I always wished I would be blessed with. I couldn't resist it. I picked it up in my talons and carried it home."

"What could I do?" asked the male. "Of course, I was worried when I saw that she had actually taken the egg. We had talked about stealing it, but I never thought that we would really do such a thing. The idea of stealing someone else's egg was more of a game. Once it was taken, I couldn't risk taking it back, chancing the dragons' anger, could I? It is true we both wanted an egg, and I agreed to keep it. We didn't know that dragons could only have one egg, though.

"We took good care of it, but when it hatched … well, you can see for yourself. We did not expect the fire.

"We never thought that the little thing would breathe fire before we could train it. I am sorry about the people who suffered the dragons' anger, but if people had their way, we would already be dead. Our kind is not wanted here!"

Merlin sighed. "Our kind is not wanted here. How often have I heard that?"

After a moment, he added, "I must return the baby to its parents before the stunning spell wears off; otherwise, the creature will set me alight too. I noticed you have plenty of food stored."

141

"Yes," replied the male. "We stocked up well to prepare for our ... I mean 'the' baby."

"Well, I suggest you stay in the cave, and do not attempt to go outside till your wings and tail feathers are re-grown. The dragons know that it was you who stole their child, and they are looking for you."

The birds looked shocked. For a long while, they stood stock-still, frozen with fear at the thought of being the target of a dragon's fury.

Merlin continued, still very cross himself. "I will tell the dragons that you kept the egg safe, believing it was one you lost. I will tell them that you gave the baby to me willingly when you realised the egg it hatched from was not yours. I will tell them that you flew off towards the ocean, saying that you would not return here again. I suggest that, when your feathers grow back, you do just that – fly far away, where the dragons cannot find you."

"Thank you, strange man," said the male as he closed his singed wings gently round his wife, who nodded her head in quiet acquiescence to Merlin's plan.

"Now I must leave, or this little perisher will roast me alive on our way back to its parents. I don't want to issue another stunning spell on it again, in case I harm it."

The wizard suddenly realised why Helen-Joy had given him the twine. Taking it out of his pocket, he wound it round the tiny dragon's snout and tied it securely. He then picked up the little creature, got on the broomstick, and left the thunderbirds still standing in the rain on the wet ledge.

The wizard travelled as fast as he could. As he sped through the air, he felt the baby dragon start to move. He held it tight and was relieved to find that it fell into a natural slumber. *It must be the motion of the broom, rocking slightly in the evening breeze, that is lulling the baby to sleep*, he thought.

It was the middle of the night when Merlin dipped the broom towards the dragon's cave. A warm glow exuded from the entrance. As he landed, the baby awoke and made a simpering noise. He loosened the twine from round its snout, and as he entered the cave, he set the child free.

There was a fire in the middle of the room within the cave. Ajax was lying at the other side of the room, his wings wrapped round Blitzen, who rested her head against his muscular shoulder.

They both looked up when they heard Merlin approaching, and they gasped with joy when they saw their child trotting along in front of the wizard.

The child headed straight towards the fire, which seemed to attract it like a magnet. In no time at all, the small creature was soon breathing out its own fiery breath, so that flame met flame.

The dragons arose, as if in one movement, and rushed, one either side of the fire, to greet their offspring. They blew warm air from their nostrils over the tiny green creature, and licked it with such powerful strokes that the child kept falling from one of its parent's tongues to the other.

Merlin smiled. "I shall leave you. The thunderbirds who took your egg are sorry." He told the dragons the tale he had concocted with the thunderbirds. He did not think that the dragons altogether believed him, but they were too busy fondling their child to argue.

"Thank you, Merlin." Blitzen's voice was barely a murmur. A large teardrop slid down her leathery blue face and onto the baby's head, extinguishing a small flame emitting from its nostril.

"If I can do anything for you at any time, Merlin," said Ajax, "you know that I am indebted to you. We have kept our side of the agreement and have not unleashed any more of our wrath on the Twydellers or Kernans."

"I am glad to hear it," said Merlin. Not wishing to intrude any further on this, their special time, he turned to leave the dragon family.

The dragons, including the baby, who trotted along in front of its parents, followed Merlin to wave their goodbyes. In its excitement, the baby dragon let forth a flame which caught the brush end of Merlin's – or, rather, Willy's – broom.

Merlin stamped on the broom, swiftly putting out the flames.

"Oh, dear, I hope it will be all right!" exclaimed Ajax.

"Oh, I'm sure it will be," replied Merlin politely, very much doubting his own words.

He launched the broom from the ledge outside the cave, immediately feeling it plummet. He managed to bring it back up, and waved to the family of dragons silhouetted against the firelight of the cave. The broom then plummeted again.

As the broom rose and fell sharply, over and over again, the dragons thought Merlin was just showing off his flying expertise.

"Look at that!" said Ajax. "He really knows how to fly that thing."

Ajax and Blitzen turned, taking their child back into the warmth of its rightful home.

Chapter 6 – The Soothsayer's Predictions

Merlin had a difficult ride back to the capital of Twydell. Throughout the flight, the broom shuddered and lost altitude, regaining its height only to lose it again. However, it managed the journey back to Dalton safely.

The guards had spotted the broom and its passenger in the distance, as dawn was breaking, and summoned the king. By the time Merlin landed somewhat ungracefully in the courtyard, the king was waiting for him.

In between gulps of breakfast, Merlin told King Frederrick about the events of the last few days. Merlin hadn't realised how hungry he was. He finished with gusto the plate of bacon, sausages, and egg, and was just wiping the plate clean with a piece of bread when he remembered the parchment.

While the king was dictating a message to his secretary, to send the good news to all the towns and villages in Twydell, Merlin opened the sealed parchment to read Helen-Joy's prediction:

1. Your mission will be successful, and you will return the baby dragon to its parents. You will earn their gratitude, and one day you will ask them to repay the debt.

2. The three men who left the Forbidden Forest – Jerry, Garod, and Isaiah – are suffering much harm in a prison dungeon. They are so weak that they have lost their magic powers. Please ask the king to release them and let them come home.

3. You will come back to the Forbidden Forest, but first you must waste no time in returning to Avalon.

Merlin was stunned. He felt sickened to think that three wizards might be imprisoned in the dungeon below the very palace in which he was enjoying hospitality. He sat staring at the parchment.

The king turned away from his secretary and started talking to Merlin again. Frederrick expressed his gratitude to Merlin, promising him anything he wanted.

Just then, Merlin raised his head. The stern manner in which Merlin looked directly into the king's face startled the king because, up to this point, their talk had been amicable.

Merlin's voice was loud, and his tone was no longer friendly. "I believe you hold three of my kind – three wizards – in your dungeon cells. I ask you to release them and give them safe passage back to the Forbidden Forest."

"You are wrong, Merlin," stated the king. He looked bewildered but spoke his words firmly. "It is true I have had no love for your kind in the past. My people have never liked those of magic. However, we do not harm anyone unless they do wrong. My ancestors ordered all those with magic powers out of Dalton and all our other towns and villages. But, to my knowledge – and I am willing to take oath and swear – no person of magic has ever been harmed."

Merlin looked into the king's eyes. He felt puzzled because Helen-Joy had been right about everything else, and yet he felt sure that the king was telling the truth.

"The wizards, whose names are Jerry, Garod, and Isaiah, were travelling to Dalton to visit those they knew. They never returned to their wives, who live in the forest. It is those same women, all of whom are witches, who have helped me to find the dragon child."

"I swear I know nothing of these missing magic men," King Frederrick reiterated. "But I make this oath, on my children's lives, that I will try to find out what has happened to them. It would be a small thing to repay such a large debt, but I cannot promise I will find them. Furthermore, I will issue an order stating that people of magic must no longer be shunned from our towns and villages. They must be treated with respect."

"I believe you," said Merlin, and the coldness left his eyes. He did not wish to linger any longer, because Helen-Joy's message had urged him to return to Avalon. He asked the king to lend him a horse, as his broom had been badly burnt by the baby dragon.

"The least I can do, my good fellow." Frederrick beamed, delighted that he could reward the wizard in some way for his services.

Whilst the king's staff busied about, organising a horse and escort for the wizard, the king took the opportunity to tell Merlin about the royal family.

Merlin responded by telling the king more about Arthur and Avalon.

At last, the hurried preparations for Merlin's departure were ready. Merlin was presented with a fine white stallion, which he called Comet. An escort of six soldiers had been arranged to ensure the wizard's safe journey through Twydell and back to Avalon.

As Merlin was about to leave, King Frederrick called him back. "I have been thinking about these missing magic men. Although I am unaware of any Twydeller harming a person of magic, I am aware that King Jeffrey of Kerner offered a reward for any such persons."

"Alive or dead," Frederrick added after a pause, and Merlin saw the shame in the king's eyes.

"Bounty hunters crossed the borders into Twydell. For their reward, they took some people of magic who had been living in the mountains back to Kerner. I am sorry to say I did nothing to stop them."

Merlin sighed, but he appreciated the king's honesty.

The king continued. "I will send a messenger to King Jeffrey forthwith, asking him if the men you seek are there and further asking him to release them into my custody. I shall make it clear that Kerner is as much in your debt as Twydell. If he releases the prisoners, I will tell my men to deliver them safely back to the Forbidden Forest."

"Thank you, sire," said Merlin. "I do not like what I have heard, but I respect your honesty. I hope you will also bid Jeffrey to release any persons of magic or soothsayers he might hold in his cells."

"I will indeed; that I promise," said the king, looking Merlin straight in the eye.

At that, with goodbyes said, Merlin mounted Comet, escorted by six of the king's men, and made his way back to Merlport. The strangely clad man with straggly hair, whom the kings' guards had shunned on his first visit to the palace, was now leaving as an honoured foreign diplomat.

Chapter 7 – Merlin Ends His Tale

Merlin finished telling his tale to the Avalonian leaders. Esmerelda, the new Queen of the Witches, looked severe. "These men must be found and released. I sincerely hope that this Jeffrey has no more of our kind held in his torture dungeons. I should like to meet this evil man."

"I agree," Merlin said with a sigh. "He may not be evil, but he is certainly blind and unknowing. *If* King Jeffrey holds the brothers, as we suspect he does, then let us hope King Frederrick can persuade him to set them free. Of course, we do not know for sure that they are in a Kerner prison – or, indeed, any prison. We only have Helen-Joy's prediction."

"Your soothsayer seems to have been extremely accurate in her predictions so far." King Allarond's tiny elf voice joined the conversation.

"Yes, well, she's certainly right that I will return to the Forbidden Forest," said Merlin. "I owe Helen-Joy my gratitude. She probably already knows what has happened since I left. Nevertheless, I will return and tell the soothsayer and the Bramble family all that I know. They deserve to be kept informed."

"As soon as our brothers and sisters here have recovered from the battle with the Trajaens, we will send visitors to our sisters in the Forbidden Forest." Esmerelda remained very serious.

"Oh, I agree! It is most important that we do so! The people who live in the Forbidden Forest are happy, but I know they would appreciate the opportunity to make new friends." Merlin remembered watching the lonely figure of the young witch, Heather, waving to him as he left the forest.

"Yes, you must return to Twydell," stated King Arthur. "I am interested to hear what Frederrick thinks of my offer of Rosalie's hand to his son Derrick. That is, if they like each other. Such an alliance will truly strengthen both our countries."

The group stared at Arthur, unaware of the potential marriage contract which Merlin had suggested to Arthur the previous night.

In particular, Prince Edward looked bewildered. He could not believe that his young half-sister might soon be betrothed.

King Arthur, aware of his audience's surprise, continued speaking to hold that attention. "Merlin has already shown the Twydellers the power of magic. The Twydell soldiers will tell their countrymen how well the people of magic, and those without magic, fought alongside each other yesterday. Let us hope that our neighbours will learn how strong our combined forces can be. I still believe we can create a land where we can all live in peace beside each other."

The other leaders nodded their agreement, for this was their ultimate aim.

Edward waited for the others to leave before asking his father, "Is there anything you wish to tell me?"

Arthur smiled at his son. He told Edward about King Frederrick's offer of the hand of his daughter, Princess Jeanette. Edward breathed a sigh of relief to learn that his father had turned down the offer and not tried to force him into a marriage he did not want. The fact that his father had recognised his love for Daisy took a huge weight off Edward's shoulders. He had feared that his father would oppose a relationship with the so-called wild girl from the mountains. The other burdens he carried since the losses in the battle with the Trajaens were heavy enough.

Edward was in love. He thought he had hidden the feelings he felt so deeply in his heart. But, if his father had seen through him, other people would as well. He knew he must tell Daisy how he felt.

However, despite his relief that his father had accepted his love for Daisy, Edward had a new concern. He was worried that his little half-sister might soon be encouraged to wed someone she did not like. If Rosalie did not like Derrick, and did not wish to marry him, Edward would defend her decision.

BOOK THREE:
The Exchange
Of Rings

Part 1:
The Alliance

Chapter 1 – Daisy's Story

It was like the calm after a storm. The Avalonians were victorious but no one celebrated. Too many had died, too many were injured.

"How are you today?" Edward asked a shepherd who had been injured by a Trajaen axe. Each day, he walked through the village, talking to his people, trying to motivate them, and answering any concerns they had.

"Healing, m'lord," replied the man, trying to kneel.

"Don't kneel to me, shepherd. If it were not for all those who fought on the beach, my father and I would be dead."

"If it were not for you, m'lord, and the good King Arthur, we would have all been taken for slaves on those Trajaen boats." The shepherd knelt despite Edward's protest. "And that little maid, she saved the both of ye with her arrows, as well as me. I know 'twas her arrow that slew the warrior bearing his axe down on me because I saw the arrow in his throat. 'Twas made of wood, and with a stone point; different to the arrows of our men. The stone point pierced his gullet before he struck me with the axe. The axe only hit me in the shoulder when it fell. I took it, his weapon. It's a fine piece of equipment."

"I hope you only ever have to use it to chop wood, and never need to use it as a weapon," said Edward. "Alas, the time may come when we have to fight again."

"I felt proud to be one of your men, m'lord."

Edward thanked the shepherd and bid him good day. He was making his way to the next villager he intended to speak to when he saw Daisy. She was taking her lions down to the grassland.

Daisy had remained in the village after the battle. She spent her time caring for Gilda and, if she had time to spare, tending other injured folk. The problem was that her lions needed a lot of attention. Leo and Sybil needed to eat, and they could not be trusted to roam free in the village. The Merlporters kept their sheep and goats guarded in pens whilst Daisy and her pets stayed in the village. While Daisy was with the lions, they would not try to attack any creature without her consent. Nevertheless, as they trotted along beside their mistress, Leo and Sybil frightened the chicken which pecked the village streets for insects and snails. When the animals in their pens smelt the predator lions, they became restless and cried out in alarm.

The best way to prevent the lions from attacking the villagers' stock was to keep their bellies full. Each day, Daisy took them down to the plains, as far away from the village as she could comfortably travel. The lions were then free to catch rabbits, deer, or other creatures which roamed wild.

Edward's heart missed a beat when he saw her. "May I join you?"

"If you wish, but I don't know how long we will be. Leo and Sybil are hungry. They like to hunt, eat, sleep, and eat again."

"Then I shall keep you company while they hunt, eat, sleep, and eat again."

It was good to leave the village for a while. The sight of the grasslands with the river running through had a calming effect after visiting the sick, wounded, and bereaved. Edward breathed in the cool air. But as he scanned the scene in front of him, he noticed the wildlife moving. The deer were the first to move, leaping and bounding away. The wild horses whinnied and started to canter, following the deer. The rabbits disappeared below ground. "They have the scent of the lions already. They are moving away."

"Yes, your hunters will not be happy if we stay here much longer," Daisy commented.

Edward noticed a slight sadness in her voice. "Everyone in the village was glad of your arrows which felled the Trajaens. No one wants you to leave." *Least of all me.* Edward spoke from his heart. "Surely it must have been good to come back to the village where you once lived."

Daisy stopped and stared into Edward's face. Her face was a complete blank. "Good! How can you think it is good to return to

162

the place where you saw your brother taken away as a slave? What is good about bringing back memories of your mother being beaten? I have no happy memories of this place!"

She turned and started walking again, at a faster pace than previously.

Edward was stunned. He stood, just watching her for a while, unsure as to what he should do. He decided to follow her and made haste to catch up with the girl and her lion cubs.

"I'm so sorry, Daisy," he faltered. What a fool I am! "I did not think. I had no idea. I don't know what to think. I know nothing about your life except what the giants told us. They said you hid when the giants attacked the Trajaens. I know that those who escaped took your people as slaves and, afterwards, you lived in a cave and fended for yourself."

"I was only a child. I remember little of what happened." Daisy looked away to hide the tears welling in her eyes.

"If you feel up to telling me, I would be interested to hear what you remember," Edward softened the tone of his voice.

Edward wanted to put his arm round Daisy and draw her close. He could smell oil of violets on her skin, and he wanted to hold her and breathe in her scent. It didn't matter that she was dressed in ill-fitting trousers and an old blouse she had borrowed from one of the village women. Daisy was not beautiful, but she was pretty. And she mesmerised him.

The young woman remained silent, lost in her thoughts. Edward decided not to ask her more questions. He simply kept pace with her. At last, they reached a small coppice.

"Off, Sybil! Off, Leo!" she said.

The two lions were eager to be free, and bounded away to seek their prey.

Daisy walked into the coppice and sat on the stump of a tree felled long ago. She faced the opposite direction to which the lions had raced. Looking across the grassland, she could see the village.

Edward sat on the grass beside the tree stump.

Daisy was silent for a long while before speaking. "This is where I was when it happened," she said at last. "Not here exactly; just over there." She pointed to a tree. "I was sent to pick fungi. My mother had taught me which fungi were edible and which were not. She used fungi to flavour stew. If our Trajaen master was not happy with the meal she cooked, he beat her. He probably beat her whether he liked the taste of the stew or not. I knew he liked beating her because I could see the pleasure in his face."

"Did he beat you, too?"

"Yes, but not so hard. He said that my fair hair would bring him a lot of money one day – when the right buyer saw me. He was careful not to break any of my bones. But he broke my mother's nose and then accused her of being ugly.

"I had a brother – an older brother – but he was taken away. I had a father, but I don't remember him. I don't know whether he was taken away and sold to slavers or killed when the Trajaens came here.

"I remember a lot of fighting. And then, one day after one of the battles, a Trajaen moved into our home. He slept with my mother, and she had a baby. The Trajaen was the father of my baby brother. I used to look after him, and I loved him. It was my job to care for him while my mother worked.

"My people used to be fond of bears. We would never harm them because we believed we were related to them. We both walked on two feet. I remember before the Trajaens took over our village, the bears used to come down to the river to catch fish. Mother and the other women used to bring bread for them, and they would take it from us as if they were our pets."

"Weren't you afraid of them? Bears are fearsome creatures," Edward said it half as a question, but it seemed as if nothing Daisy said or did surprised him any more. He was fascinated by her.

"No more afraid of them than I am of Leo or Sybil." Daisy looked him straight in the face. Her expression was impassive.

"There was a big, old bear. She was much bigger than most of the others. We used to call her the grandma bear, and we named her Ursula. She was so old that her brown fur had started to turn grey."

Edward watched a smile flicker across Daisy's face as she remained lost in her thoughts. *She has one pleasant memory at least*, he thought as he stayed silent. She was telling him about her past, and he was afraid that if he spoke, she would end her tale.

The smile soon passed. "The Trajaens slew the bears. They liked bear steak. The Brewins could never eat bear meat. It would be like eating our own flesh, but that horrible man made my mother eat it. She retched, and he beat her. He tried to force me to eat it once, but I spat it out, and he clouted me.

"The bears stopped coming to the river. We didn't know if they'd all been slain, if some had hidden in the forest, or if they'd travelled further away. I remember thinking that Ursula was too old to travel far.

"The day the Trajaens tried to burn the forest, I came here to pick fungi. There was a loud commotion, and I could see that the giants had come out of the woods to fight the Trajaens. It looked as if the Trajaens were setting the forest on fire. But it poured with rain, and the flames were doused. The giants were very angry. We knew they lived in the forest, but they never bothered us Brewins. That day, they chased the Trajaens down the hill. I didn't know what to do. I was going to run and get my mother, but I saw her being taken to a boat. She was carrying my baby brother in her arms. I knew I couldn't reach her.

"I saw the giants chase the Trajaens down the hill. They ran into the water after the boats and turned some of them upside down. I don't know if the boat my mother and baby brother were in got away, or if they drowned. I was frozen with fear, and I just stayed where I was. I cried like a child."

Daisy stopped speaking. She looked ashamed.

"You *were* a child, Daisy."

"I should have tried to save my mother and brother."

165

"You were a child. You could not have helped them. You were lucky to survive."

"Lucky? Yes, I was. Lucky to survive, and lucky not to have been a slave. Guilty? Yes, guilty that I alone was saved; no one else." She gave a long, weary sigh.

"I lay here for what must have been more than a day. Afraid to move, in case any of the Trajaens had come back to look for me. Afraid to move, in case any of the giants came and beat me to death like they had beaten the Trajaens.

"I was hungry, and ate raw fungus and mushrooms. There were berries growing here. Like this one." She picked a cloudberry from a plant growing at her feet and offered the fruit to Edward.

Edward took it, looked at it, but did not eat it.

"I was thirsty, but I waited until nightfall and then went down to the river to drink. Afterwards, I came up here to sleep. When I woke up, Ursula was sitting where I am now, watching me. She held out her arms, and I ran to her and cried and cried. Ursula the Grandma Bear became my mama.

"She carried me up to the forest. On my own, I would have been afraid of the giants, but Mama Ursula was not afraid of them. I felt safe with her. It was nearly winter, and Mama had made a home in a large hollow tree. I helped her gather lots of autumn leaves to keep us warm. We gathered berries and nuts, and Mama collected honey."

Daisy laughed, and Edward was pleased to see the sadness begin to ease from her face. "I tried to help her collect honey once, but Mama must have known that my skin was not as thick as hers because she shooed me away.

"I knew which roots were safe to eat, so I pulled some of those too. I knew how to light a fire, and we pulled the roots called potatoes and cooked them on the fire. Mama had never tried potatoes before, but she loved them. She couldn't speak to me, but I knew she was pleased, so I gathered as many potatoes as I could before the winter set in. We stored them in our tree, with the nuts and dried fruit. It was so warm and comfortable

166

cuddled up against Mama's warm body. I never felt cold all winter! It was the happiest I had ever been. I still cried for my real mother, though. There is not a day that has passed that I still do not think of her."

"I know how you feel!" Edward's stomach lurched. He remembered his own mother lying dead in the river.

"How could you possibly know?" asked Daisy scornfully.

"Because I lost my real mother too," said Edward.

As he admitted the truth to Daisy, for the first time for many years, tears welled in his eyes. He started to cry as he told her about his mother.

Daisy still sat on the tree stump, and Edward remained beside her on the ground. She stroked his head as she recognised his sadness, and put her arm round his shoulders. Edward pulled her down beside him and gave her a long kiss.

Daisy accepted his kiss and returned his embrace. After a while, she pulled herself free.

"Oh, Edward, I am so sorry," said Daisy. "I knew that Gilda was your stepmother, but I did not know what happened to your real mother. I am sorry I never thought to ask."

"And I never thought to ask you about yours." Edward held her face in his hands. "I am sorry I brought you back to this place that holds so many bad memories for you. I can understand now why you did not wish to come here."

He wanted to hold Daisy, but he also wanted to know about what happened to Ursula.

Daisy continued. "Mama Ursula was very old. She knew I would have to fend for myself before long. When the winter came to an end, we went back to the village. The giants had flattened it to the ground, but I found a bow and arrow, an axe, and some other tools. I'd seen the men fire bows and arrows, and Mama watched me as I practised.

"We took the weapons back to the wood, and I practised there. I learnt to throw an axe too. The giants could not have known about me before, because they had never bothered me, but they must have seen Mama and me go to the village. They started leaving food for me, but I was afraid of them. I fired arrows at them; I never hit them, though. I just aimed an inch in front of their feet, to warn them off."

"You did the same to me." Edward laughed, and this time Daisy joined in.

"Yes, I remember," she said with a chuckle. "How bold of you to come and rescue me!"

Edward reddened with embarrassment. "I had no idea, at the time, what an independent woman you were! I thought you were a helpless young girl."

He shook his head, remembering his naivety, "How could I possibly have guessed what an incredible woman you were? I must admit, though, when I saw your bare legs, I felt a stirring inside of me."

"Edward, Prince of Avalon, I'm surprised at you!" Daisy hit him playfully round the head.

Sybil must have heard them, and came to see what they were doing. "*Grrr. Grrr.*" They heard a growl, looked round, and saw the lioness. Her jaws were red with blood, and she was not sure what to make of Daisy hitting Edward. Leo heard his sister's growl, and trotted to her side. Both looked wary, but neither seemed about to attack. Their mistress did not appear to be in danger.

Daisy got up and walked to where they were standing. She tousled their heads, avoiding their bloodied jaws. "There, there; calm down. It's all right. Edward is just playing."

Edward stayed where he was. The lions were still eyeing him. A sudden movement might alarm them.

"What happened to Ursula?" he asked again.

"She died. She was very old. I found a spade in the village and took it back to the tree which we had shared, and I buried her there. I didn't want to stay in the forest, because I was afraid of the giants."

Daisy continued to stroke the lions, who were still watching Edward. Eventually, they turned and went back to the prey they had brought down.

Daisy stood up and turned to Edward. She looked past him, towards the village. "I must have heard sometime in the past that there was a cave in the hills. I can't remember when I heard about it, but it was where the Brewin huntsmen used to take shelter when they were away overnight. I'd found Ruff sometime previously, and Mama and I had cared for him. I think the giants must have killed his mother and the rest of her litter. He was like a kindred spirit."

"I feel like you are a kindred spirit." Edward stood. Stepping towards where Daisy stood, motionless, he put his arms round her. "We both lost our mothers at a very young age. It was a traumatic experience for both of us."

Daisy pushed him away.

Edward wondered what he had done. He thought she had felt as happy to be in his arms as he was to be in hers.

"That's enough," said Daisy firmly. "You are a prince, and I am just a wild girl. Please don't treat me like a plaything. I've seen how the village girls look at you. I'm not to be made a fool of!"

A mixture of bewilderment and shock filled the young man.

"I'm not playing with you, Daisy. I love you. I've loved you from the first moment I set eyes on you. I can't hide my feelings from my father, and I don't think I'm hiding them from anyone else. Can't you see how I feel about you?"

"What do you mean?" asked Daisy suspiciously.

"My father knows how I feel about you. The King of Twydell asked Merlin to arrange a marriage with his daughter, Princess Jeanette, but Father told him that I had already fallen in love with you."

Daisy stared at Edward, her eyes wide. Looking into her eyes was like looking into pools of blue water.

Edward gently took her by her arm and sat her on the tree stump. He then knelt on one knee in front of her.

"Daisy, last of the Brewins, will you marry me?"

169

Daisy fell to her knees in front of him. Edward felt her warm arms wrap round him, and breathed in the scent of the violet oil on her skin.

"You would prefer me to a princess?" she asked, her face full of puzzlement, as she looked directly into his eyes.

"I prefer you to any girl I have ever met."

"Oh, Edward, I feel like I'm in a dream."

He pulled her closer and kissed her.

Leo and Sybil reappeared, but after watching the strange behaviour of their mistress and her friend, they settled down to sleep.

"So, is the answer yes?" Edward managed to stop kissing her.

"Yes, yes, yes," replied Daisy, before pulling his lips back onto hers.

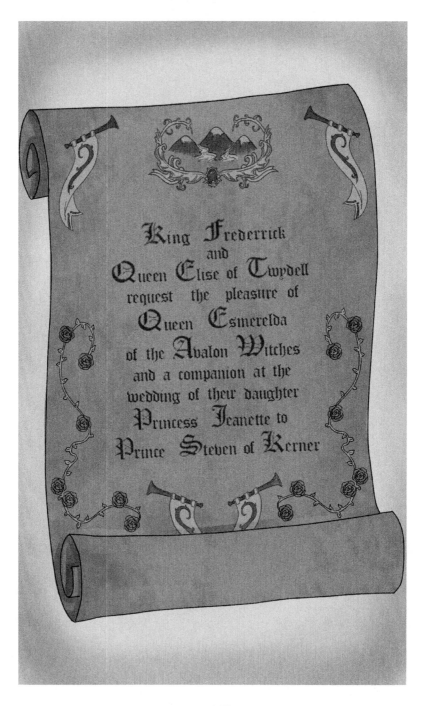

King Frederrick
and
Queen Elise of Twydell
request the pleasure of
Queen Esmerelda
of the Avalon Witches
and a companion at the
wedding of their daughter
Princess Jeanette to
Prince Steven of Kerner

Chapter 2 – Preparations for the Wedding

Rosalie jumped in the air with glee when the parchment arrived.

It was no surprise that King Arthur and his family received a parchment inviting them to the wedding of the lovely Princess Jeanette of Twydell to Prince Steven of Kerner. It was customary to invite dignitaries from neighbouring countries to such events.

It was not even a surprise that Merlin was invited, because he had saved Twydell from the wrath of the dragons. What was a surprise was that Esmerelda, Queen of the Witches; Maud, Queen of the Fairies; and Allarond, King of the Elves, had also received invitations. In fact, the invitations to the people of magic, other than Merlin, came as quite a shock because King Jeffrey of Kerner was once known to despise such beings.

However, what excited Rosalie so much was that this would be her opportunity to meet Prince Derrick, the young man her father hoped she would take a liking to. In fact, King Arthur hoped his daughter would take more than a mere "liking to" the prince. A marriage between Rosalie and Derrick would create a strong alliance between the neighbouring countries of Avalon and Twydell.

A parley of the leaders was hastily organised to discuss the invitations. Edward was looking forward to the meeting. Although he was not a leader, he had started to attend council meetings with King Arthur so that, when the time came, he would have the knowledge necessary to enable him to replace his ailing father as king. Edward rarely spoke at such meetings; rather, his father told him to listen and learn. Sometimes he thought that his father's favourite words were "listen and learn" because he repeated them so often.

Edward did not usually look forward to meetings, but Maud and Allarond were coming this time. Esmerelda, Queen of the Witches was like an older sister to Edward, but he had only met the Queen of the Fairies and the King of the Elves on a few occasions. The fairies and elves did not live in Merlport, preferring to live further afield.

Zog, the leader of the giants, had also been invited to the parley; he, too, had received a parchment inviting him and his family to the wedding. Zog had declined both invitations. However, he said he would send three barrels of cider and some young apple trees to Jeanette and Steven as a wedding present.

The only contact the Avalonians now had with the giants came through Willy the Wood Wizard. The protocol of never cutting a tree without the permission of the giant's forest master was working satisfactorily, and the giants said they had no reason to meet with the small people unless it was urgent. The Avalonians were disappointed that there was so little communication with the giants.

Arthur and Merlin were delighted that all the leaders had been invited to the ceremony to exchange the ring of Twydell with the ring of Kerner. They wanted their friendship with Twydell to be strengthened. Arthur and Merlin were also keen to meet King Jeffrey of Kerner. However, Esmerelda did not want anyone from Avalon to accept the invitations.

Edward grinned as she threw back her head, allowing her tall hat to slip to the floor, letting free her wonderful black hair. The long ebony locks seemed as unruly as the young woman herself. He could guess the tirade which would follow when he saw her eyes flash like bright emeralds.

The prince had known Esmerelda for so long now that he had learnt to judge her mood by her eyes. When Esmerelda was thinking or relaxing, her eyes were the colour of moss. But when she was excited or angry, they flashed like brilliant gemstones.

"The only reason Jeffrey sent us invitations is because he is afraid of Merlin. Jeffrey probably thinks that if he does not pander to keep him happy, Merlin will set the dragons on Kerner.

Does he think that we have forgotten that he has imprisoned the wizards of the Forbidden Forest?" snapped the young witch queen.

Esmerelda looked directly at Merlin. "Surely you are not going to accept the invitation, Merlin!" She glared at the old sorcerer. "Don't tell me that you are going to the wedding of the son of the king who holds our brethren in his prisons."

Edward copied his father's example by staying silent. It was always best to let the leader of the wizards deal with disagreements with the Queen of the Witches.

"Now, now, Esmerelda." Merlin tried to pacify her. "We do not know for sure that our people are held in Kerner. King Frederrick of Twydell has promised that he will speak to King Jeffrey. However much we might wish to interfere, I believe we must be patient. The invitation to the wedding is the first step to acceptance by the Kernans."

Esmerelda's mood did not improve. She made it clear that she would have liked to have flown, with as many witches and wizards as she could muster, and cast devastating spells on Kerner. She talked of burning their land, covering King Jeffrey's palace in pink goo, and rendering his guards immobile while they searched the palace for the missing men. It was only Merlin's continued pleas for patience that had kept Esmerelda, and many other people of magic, from declaring war on Kerner.

Edward was glad that Merlin was still in Avalon and had not left on another journey. He was quite sure that Esmerelda and Tannus would have been off to do battle with the Kernans weeks ago had it not been for the wise old sorcerer. Like any young man, Edward had wanted to be a soldier and fight in a glorious battle. In reality, the Battle of Merlport had been terrible, and he had seen too many of his people dead and injured to celebrate the Avalon victory. A war now, with another enemy on another front, would be devastating.

The fairy queen and elf king were also unsure as to whether to accept the invitation to the wedding. They had heard that many fairies and elves had once lived in Twydell and Kerner.

They wondered what had happened to them – did they leave or were they destroyed?

Arthur decided that it was best to help his old friend. Voicing his agreement with Merlin, the King of Avalon tried to persuade his counterparts to accept the invitation. He argued that the invitation was not only from the royal house of Kerner, but also from the King and Queen of Twydell. He said that the people of Twydell had grown fond of Merlin and that all Avalonians would be as safe in Dalton, just as Merlin had been.

The fairy queen and elf king were eventually pacified. The tiny people thought that as long as Merlin was there to protect them, it would indeed be an opportunity to find out more about the fairies and elves who had once lived in Twydell and Kerner.

After the parley, Edward spoke to Esmerelda, trying to reason with her, "Esmie, I understand your anger with the humans. Your mother was killed by the Trajaens, and the Kernans are probably holding three wizards against their will. But we humans are not all bad."

Esmerelda looked at him with her piercing green eyes, "Of course you aren't. I know that poor old Merlin is right. But that doesn't make it easy to accept an invitation to a jolly when one of the hosts has no love for our kind – 'wizzwits', as you like to call us. Nevertheless, I shall attend the wedding, and Tannus will accompany me. I am intrigued to see King Jeffrey and King Frederrick. Don't expect me to curtsey to any humans, though!"

"You mean you won't curtsey to me when I'm king?"

Esmerelda gave him a playful cuff round the ear. "I'll turn you into a toad if you're not careful, plainboy!"

"I could never imagine you curtseying to anyone," Edward responded in a gentle tone. "I don't think Jeffrey would expect it, anyway. After all, you are a queen." He watched her eyes return to a soft moss green before teasing her again. "I'm so glad you're going to come with us. I always enjoy Tannus's company."

"Well, I hope you're not going to be as much trouble as you were last time we travelled together!" Esmerelda put her hands on her slender hips, feigning a haughty countenance.

"That sounds more like my bossy big sister!" Edward planted a kiss on her cheek.

Esmerelda screwed up her face and pretended to rub the kiss away. "Ugh! That's enough of that messy human stuff. If you keep that up, I'll change my mind and stay at home!"

She turned and walked away, head held high. "Bye-bye, plainboy ... very plain boy, actually."

Edward smiled fondly after her.

Although the witches and wizards were wary of the invitation to the wedding, the people of Merlport thought otherwise. The invitation was an opportunity to lift the sombre mood that had enveloped the village since the battle. The rumour that Princess Rosalie would meet Prince Derrick had spread, and all were anxious to know if the two would like each other.

They also knew that if Derrick and Rosalie married, with Derrick's sister married to the prince of Kerner, a firm alliance of the three countries would ensue. They hoped a strong triple alliance would bring with it the peace they all craved. A three-pronged defence against any future Trajaen attack would be a powerful force to be reckoned with.

Preparations for the wedding began with a lot of enthusiasm. One of the women owned what was once a beautiful blue satin gown, which she was happy to give to Rosalie. The gown was moth eaten, but the water elves searched the river for freshwater seed pearls, which they gave to the fairies. The fairies dried flowers and preserved them. They then sewed the flowers and seed pearls on the satin, so as to disguise the holes in the gown. Their tiny stitches created a delicate gown fit for any princess.

The fishermen found more pearls in the oysters which lived in the sea. The blacksmith melted down a piece of one of the gold rings which had been worn by the Trajaens, and made it into a fine chain. He then threaded the pearls onto the chain to make a gorgeous necklace. While the gold was still warm, he took a small quantity, which he divided in two, and wound each into intricate matching patterns. The fairies helped him hang a large pearl on each one, so as to form a pair of exquisite earrings.

Gilda, Arthur's wife, had survived the battle with the Trajaens but lost much of her sense of movement. The poor witch found difficulty moving her lips to speak and her legs to walk. She either hobbled along on a stick or floated, a few feet above the ground, on her broom. Nevertheless, the people of Avalon wanted her to go to the wedding looking like a queen. They melted more Trajaen gold to make her a crown, as well as a torque and a bracelet. Gilda had an old red velvet gown and cloak, which she spruced up with a few spells. When she put on her outfit, she looked truly regal with her gold adornments. However, after giving the matter some thought, Gilda insisted that she was a witch and proud to be so. She decided she would wear the pointed hat that identified her kind, and gave the crown to Edward, to mark his rank as Prince of Avalon.

Arthur worried that they had no carriage and that he would have to take his wife and daughter to the wedding in Willy's wood cart. Willy would not hear of such a thing, and started to build a carriage. He said that some old trees with withering branches, growing near the sandy beach, had said that they were ready to be cut down to make way for new growth. The trees said they would be honoured to be made into a carriage fit for a king. The trees requested that the carriage be painted gold like the sun, and cared for so that it could be appreciated for generations to come.

Arthur and Gilda visited the trees themselves to thank them and to tell them that their wishes would be honoured. It was strange standing in front the trees and talking to them. The trees made no sound and no movement, other than a rustling of their leaves. However, the wood wizard assured the king and his wife that the trees understood and appreciated the couple coming to see them.

The trees surrendered their lives to the axe. Willy went into one of his trances and set to work on cutting out an ornate carriage. Two boys, who were apprentice carpenters, had come to the village from Twydell when their homes were destroyed by the dragons. They were very happy to help Willy. Although Willy hardly spoke to the boys, they seemed to understand what he wanted. They made sure that he had all the tools ready when he needed them. While Willy worked in a trance, the boys made spare wheels for the carriage, in case any broke during the journey.

More Trajaen rings were melted, and this time the molten gold was used to paint the carriage. The golden oak leaves, which Willy had carved round the roof of the carriage, shone brightly as they reflected the sun. The fishermen had found seashells, from which they made mother-of-pearl. Willy used the shell for intricate inlays on the door panels. As the carriage moved, or the doors opened, the mother-of-pearl changed into differing shades of blue, pink, and green, depending upon the light.

The end result was a carriage fit for any king or queen. It would be the envy of all who saw it.

The people were disappointed that Gilda did not wish to wear the crown they had made for her, but they understood her reasons. Besides, they agreed that it was fitting for their Prince Edward to have a crown. However, they still wanted to provide something special for Gilda, and decided to paint her broomstick with the molten gold. Gilda was delighted. Her smile had become crooked, but her eyes showed her delight, and she clapped her hands when she saw her old broom gilded with the metal that was so precious in Briton.

There were no soldiers in Avalon, but swords and other weapons had been taken from the Trajaens. The villagers had captured some of the fine horses which roamed in the valley. The fastest were trained for riding, and the strongest used for pulling carts. Now the best-looking of the strong horses were picked to draw the golden carriage.

The men who would act as guards now had horses and weapons, but no uniforms. Wild sheep which roamed the valley were captured and shorn. Their wool was spun as fine as possible, dyed scarlet, and woven to make long-sleeved, thin vests. The thicker wool was dyed black and made into jerkins.

The village women made both King Arthur and Prince Edward reversible cloaks. One side was dyed black for when they were travelling. The other side, which was dyed red, was to wear when meeting neighbouring royalty. Father and son were delighted with the cloaks.

All the family except Daisy were happy with their outfits. She had accepted Edward's proposal of marriage, and as a future princess, she had been invited to the wedding. However, Daisy was reluctant to "dress up", as she called it. She preferred to wear trousers and a shirt, and to carry a bow and arrow. She also wore a belt with sheath and dagger, which she would not be afraid to use if confronted with danger.

Daisy was a pretty young woman, with long fair hair which she wore loose. Her soft skin was lightly tanned because she enjoyed living an outdoor life. She was slim and agile. However, she saw herself as a warrior and wished to ride with the soldiers, escorting the golden carriage and dressed in the same uniform.

Edward was exasperated. He admired Daisy because she was not vain or pampered. But she would soon be a princess – his princess – and there would be times when he wanted her to behave like one.

"Daisy, you will be a princess soon. You will be expected to attend suitably dressed for the occasion. Will you wear a dress, just once, for me?" he pleaded.

At last, Edward persuaded her to compromise. She would ride dressed in the uniform of an escort throughout the journey, except for the last day. On the day of the wedding, she agreed to wear a red dress trimmed with black, but she insisted that she would carry her dagger in a garter. The only items she did not argue about wearing were a gold necklace and bracelet made from one of the Trajaen armbands; and the ring with an inset pearl, which the prince had placed on the third finger of her left hand.

On the evening before the leaders were to leave for Twydell, the two carpenter boys decided that they would take the golden carriage round the village square to test the wheels. As the vehicle rolled along behind four strong black horses, the whole village stopped what they were doing and came out to watch. The villagers were so delighted with the result of their hard work that they started an evening of music and dancing.

The people of Merlport were glad of a reason to make merry. They had enjoyed the preparations for the wedding. Only a few of them would accompany their leaders from Avalon to Twydell, so they decided they would have a street party to celebrate. It was a dual festivity: it would celebrate both their leaders' invitation to the wedding and Edward's engagement to Daisy.

Edward had always taken pleasure in dancing and was delighted to find that Daisy enjoyed the activity too. He patiently taught her the steps and she was quick to learn and improvise. The prince was disappointed that Daisy still insisted on wearing trousers. But even so, the couple looked a fine pair as they spun round the village square.

The fiddlers played, the singers sang, and the dancers danced. Good food was prepared and eaten. More wine and ale than usual were drunk.

Arthur was worried that the prince and his fiancée would be too tired for their long journey. The next morning, he was relieved to see that the couple were up with the song of the morning lark, and well prepared for the long journey ahead.

181

Chapter 3 – The Journey to Dalton

The party set out five days before the wedding, to allow plenty of time to get to Dalton, the capital of Twydell.

Despite the late night on the eve of departure, it seemed as if the whole of Avalon had turned out to see the party off. Witches and wizards flew alongside the entourage for almost the whole of the first day. Elves travelled along as passengers on many of the broomsticks. Fairies flew along for as far as their wings would allow, and then either waved goodbye or found a space on a broomstick. Other magical people who had not settled in Merlport, preferring instead to live in the meadows or the coppices, lined the route, cheering their kings and queens as they passed by.

In accordance with her agreement, Daisy rode with the men escorting the carriage, her quiver full of arrows slung over her shoulder.

Edward smiled fondly at his fiancée as she rode at his side.

Leo and Sybil trotted along beside Daisy. The lions seemed to be very happy to accompany their mistress on the expedition through the countryside.

Rosalie travelled in the carriage with Maud, Queen of the Fairies, and her husband, King Selogon. Allarond, King of the Elves, and his wife, Queen Farainne, travelled with them. Gilda started off travelling in the carriage too, but sometimes chose to float alongside on her golden broomstick, of which she had become very proud.

Sometimes Esmerelda and Tannus, the young warlock she had brought with her, shared the carriage as well; as did Merlin. Merlin adored Comet, the white stallion which King Frederrick had given him, but the sorcerer was now at an age where he enjoyed the comfort of the padded seating in the carriage.

A wizard called Yzor and his warlock son, Jonathan, had also joined the party. Yzor, who was an herbologist, had married a woman with no magic. She had named their son after her own father. However, Jonathan had turned out to be like his father, a skilled plant magician, who could bring even the weariest of flowers back to life. Yzor and Jonathan could make any garden flourish. Although the herbologists were not invited to the wedding, the party from Avalon intended visiting the Forbidden Forest after the ceremony. The father and son were keen to see the bindweed which surrounded the forest, and to ask the Bramble family to share the spells they used to open and close the entrance to the forest.

"Did you send the Brambles a message to tell them we were going to visit them?" Yzor asked Merlin.

"No need," replied Merlin. "They will know we are on our way. Helen-Joy, the soothsayer, will tell them."

For three nights, the party camped on the roadside in makeshift tents. On the fourth night, they stayed at the Swan Inn, in Belchamps, a village on the outskirts of Dalton. One of the escorts had ridden ahead to make sure that there was room at the inn to accommodate the party. News soon spread about the approaching travellers from Avalon. As a result, crowds were waiting to see the grand procession arrive. The Twydell villagers had heard that the girl who might one day be their princess was in the carriage, and they wanted to see her. They were not disappointed when they saw Rosalie waving to them from the window.

Merlin rode on Comet, and the Twydellers knew who he was instantly. The fame of the old wizard who had saved their country from the dragons' fury had reached every corner of the land. The description of an oddly dressed man, with long grey hair and beard, riding a white horse, made the wizard instantly recognisable.

They pointed at the witch and three wizards soaring high in the sky. All their lives, they had shunned that type of person. That is, until they heard of Merlin's bravery in dealing with the angry dragons who would have destroyed their homes. They had also heard of the defeat of the Trajaens at Merlport. Stories of the battle had spread rapidly. Twydellers knew that Merlport would have fallen to the enemy had it not been for the skill, and sacrifices, of these strange magical people.

The villagers murmured with awe at the golden carriage and the witch floating alongside on a golden broom. Dark blue velvet cushions had been placed on top of the carriage for the fairy and elf royalty. There they sat, for all to see and admire.

The carriage came to a halt outside the inn. The crowd gasped in amazement when the proud elves alighted by simply walking down the straight side of the carriage, as if their feet were coated with some sort of adhesive. They nimbly jumped onto the backs of the two waiting lions, where they stood proudly, one on each of the mighty creatures, as the lions trotted into the inn. The winged fairies breezed above them.

There was no coin in Avalon, so Arthur paid the innkeeper with a piece of a Trajaen's silver arm ring. The innkeeper's eyes almost popped out of his head when he saw it, and he asked if they would like to stay again on their return. Arthur realised that he had overpaid the man. However, the innkeeper used the silver generously and did the party proud. He produced a delicious spread, with plenty of wine and ale, and paid a group of musicians to entertain his guests.

In turn, the guests provided the villagers with entertainment by demonstrating their own special magic. The fairies turned a yellow primrose blue. To the innkeeper's delight, Tannus turned a sour wine, which was going to be thrown away, into a sweet, honey-tasting nectar.

Yzor brought a shrivelling rose bush back to life, with just a few words and a magic wand. He and Jonathan visited some of the villager's gardens, and cast spells to make their produce bigger and better than ever before. Runner beans stretched extra long and tender, cauliflower developed very large heads, and pumpkins grew fatter than ever before. Once their skills were known, the herbologists became very popular with the gardeners in the village.

The elves amused the children by running up the side of a tree without falling off. The children clapped their hands with glee. No one could understand how their tiny feet seemed to cling to the bark.

Edward and Daisy sat at the trellis tables with the men escorting the coach. To Edward's amusement, Daisy demonstrated how she could down a mug of ale as quickly as any man. He looked at Rosalie, his half-sister, and noticed how delicately she sipped the sweet wine from her glass. *They are complete opposites, but I love them both – each in a different way, of course.*

Arthur walked over to the couple. He looked serious. "Don't drink too much, or you'll both suffer headaches in the morning. Tomorrow you must look and act your best."

They knew he was right, and under the king's watchful stare, they bid each other goodnight and made their way to their separate rooms.

The inn was full of hustle and bustle the following morning as the travellers donned their best clothes in preparation for their entrance to Twydell.

Merlin washed his hair and beard, and carefully combed out all the tangles. He put aside his old grey travelling outfit, and put on his velvet gown and multicoloured cloak with matching hat. He admired his reflection in the mirror, wondering if he should wear his best clothes on his next visit to the Forbidden Forest.

Queen Maud and King Selogon wore outfits of the finest fairy silk, spun from spider webs and dyed with an assortment of colours to match their fairy wings. They wore tiny crowns of silver, which shone so brightly that they reflected the bright hues of their wings. Maud held her silver wand in her hand. The star

186

at the end of her wand was inset with sparkling diamonds. Selogon carried a plain silver staff.

King Allarond and Queen Farainne both dressed in dark blue velvet. They wore the elfin crowns of twisted gold set with small sapphires. Neither was more than eighteen inches tall, but both stood straight and proud. Their hair was dark and shone like ebony. Allarond carried an ornate golden staff inlaid with sapphires, and Farainne carried a gold wand with a single large sapphire in the middle of its star.

The witch queen and her warlock friend looked a fine couple. Both were slender, with long black hair, and could easily be mistaken for brother and sister, were it not for their eyes. Whilst Esmerelda's eyes were as green as the richest emeralds, Tannus's eyes were dark brown, almost black. They both dressed in green velvet, but Esmerelda's gown was trimmed with orange-dyed ermine. She wore a hat with a long point, but, instead of stretching into the air, it drooped long against her back to below her waist.

The blue satin gown which had been altered for Rosalie fitted her perfectly. Her pearl and gold earrings made excellent accompaniments to the golden thread and seed pearls sewn into the gown. Daisy brushed Rosalie's long dark hair till it shone. The end result was a young woman who looked as pretty as a picture. Arthur and Gilda looked at their daughter's appearance with pride, and felt sure that their Princess of Avalon would be a fit match for the Prince of Twydell.

Meanwhile, Daisy was not so reluctant to wear her dress as she thought she would be. She saw how everyone else was trying to look their best, and their enthusiasm became infectious, so she decided she would do the same. She allowed Rosalie to use curling tongs on her hair and pin flowers into her silky, fair tresses. Daisy looked at herself in the mirror and laughed. She was enjoying dressing up after all. However, she did not forget to place her dagger in her garter, just in case she might need it.

The walk to the carriage was not an easy one for Daisy. Rosalie had lent her a pair of shoes with heels, which she found it difficult to walk in. Edward suggested that she take the shoes off, but when she did so, the dress was too long.

"Never mind, Daisy. I'll keep my arm round you, and won't let you fall." Edward had never seen his fiancée in a gown before, or with her hair coiffured. He smiled lovingly at her as he gently guided her to the carriage.

As the party came out of the inn, a crowd of village folk clapped, cheered, and called out their best wishes.

Merlin led the procession that departed the village. He looked magnificent on his fine white stallion, his best velvet clothing shimmering in the sun. He carried his staff, and the crystal knob at the end glowed purple.

As they left the village, the Avalonians found that the road to Dalton was lined with people from other Twydell villages who had come to see them. The Avalonians could not fail to feel the warmth and affection greeting them.

Of course, everyone wanted to see Princess Rosalie, and she obliged by leaning out of a carriage window to wave to the crowds. Daisy leaned out of one of the windows on the other side of the coach, waving too.

The fairy and elf kings and queens sat on the blue velvet cushions on the roof of the carriage. They, too, waved to the crowds, who were so pleased to see the charming little beings.

The Twydellers were nervous of the lions, but the animals passed, seemingly disinterested in the humans around them. Nevertheless, parents held their children firmly, lest the big cats felt a sudden hunger.

Esmerelda and the wizards soared above, dipping towards the ground and then rising into the sky again to amuse the onlookers.

The day began happily. The humans hoped that it would continue as well as it had started, but in the background remained the concerns about the missing men from the Forbidden Forest.

Chapter 4 – The Ceremony

The procession was welcomed in Dalton, with even more crowds and more rapturous applause. Merlin was greeted with shouts of hooray. The last time the Daltonians saw the sorcerer was after he had miraculously appeased the angry dragons which were destroying their homes. He was responsible for the peace which they now enjoyed.

Within the city, there were the same gasps of awe as had met the unique procession on its way through the countryside. Never before had such a sight been seen – fairies, elves, wizzwits, and even lions travelling with humans. As for the golden carriage, well, the Daltonians had to admit it surpassed the one owned by the Twydell royalty.

Like the people who had lined the country roads, the townsfolk nodded their approval when they saw Rosalie. Would this be their future princess?

When the Avalonians entered the palace gates, the trumpeters hailed their arrival. There was tumultuous applause as Maud and King Selogon fluttered down from the roof of the carriage. King Allarond and Queen Farainne alighted by simply running down the side of the vehicle, again hopping easily onto the backs of the waiting lions. The crowd gasped in amazement as the elves stood tall and proud on the backs of the golden beasts that trotted into the entrance of the outer hall.

Edward dismounted and made sure he was at the carriage door to help Daisy down. Rosalie stepped down behind her. The prince bowed grandly to his fiancée and half-sister. Placing an arm round Daisy's waist and taking Rosalie by the hand, he walked with them to the outer hall. He held Daisy tightly, making sure that she did not stumble walking in the shoes to which she was not accustomed.

Arthur walked alongside Gilda as she floated side-saddle on her golden broom. All received huge cheers from the crowds who had gathered outside the palace.

Merlin had been steering Comet round the courtyard, speaking to some of the people he recognised in the crowd, including some of the soldiers who had shooed him away on his first visit. Now those same soldiers saluted the wizard. As he dismounted, there was spontaneous applause from the people of Twydell. Cheers of thanks to him for saving them from the wrath of the dragons could be heard all around.

Fingers pointed and mouths gaped at Esmerelda and the three wizards flying high in the sky. There were gasps of amazement as they swept down, landing gracefully in the palace courtyard.

Merlin waited for Esmerelda and Tannus to land before making his way to the outer hall. Two of the escorts took their brooms for safe keeping, and Merlin walked with them to the open doorway. Before entering, the three turned and bowed to the watching crowd.

Yzor and Jonathan, the herbologist wizards, had not been invited to the wedding, so they stayed outside with the townsfolk. Carefully watched by the palace soldiers, the father and son amused the crowd with some of their spells. They turned the red roses, which grew in the courtyard, blue. They also baffled their audience by plucking one of the blue flowers, only for another to grow immediately in its place.

Meanwhile, in the outer hall the party enjoyed light refreshments whilst waiting their turns to be announced into the great hall.

Edward noticed one of King Frederrick's secretaries had come forward to greet Merlin. He spoke quietly, but Edward moved into a position where he could hear what was said. Following his father's instructions to listening and learn was becoming a habit.

"I have some good news, Lord Merlin. The three men from the Forbidden Forest, whom you spoke of when last you were here, have been located. Even as we speak, King Frederrick's men are in Kerner, ready to escort them back to their home in the forest."

"That is indeed good news! Were they held in prison? Are they well?" asked Merlin.

Esmerelda and Tannus heard Merlin's voice, and came to his side. Inquisitive eyes and ears surrounded the king's secretary, a small, timid-looking man. The poor man looked very uncomfortable. The little man looked even more nervous as the witch queen drew near. Nevertheless, he could not help but to gaze into Esmerelda's eyes, which glittered green sparks of anger.

The secretary again looked at Merlin. "I believe that they were imprisoned. King Frederrick negotiated their release as part of his daughter's marriage contract. I cannot tell you any more than that they are on their way home."

"Cannot or will not?" Esmerelda asked sternly as her eyes flashed like emeralds.

"Cannot, my lady. I am sorry that I have no further information." The secretary bowed to the Queen of the Witches.

Turning again to face Merlin, the secretary said, "The king requests that you and King Arthur and his family stay overnight here, in the palace. Tomorrow, he invites you to join a parley with him and King Jeffrey of Kerner. That would be an appropriate time to discuss the men of the Forbidden Forest. I ask that for today you enjoy the festivities and leave other matters till the meeting."

"I notice that I am not invited to the parley or an overnight room." Esmerelda's resentment sounded in her voice, "Is Jeffrey afraid I'll ask too many questions about how our kinsmen have been treated?"

The secretary gave Merlin another worried look as he turned his attention again to the witch. "My apologies, my lady. I should have made it clear that all in your party are invited to stay. We have a room ready for you, which I hope will be to your liking."

Merlin put his arm round Esmerelda in an effort to console her. "My dear, I am as upset about the men from the Forbidden

Forest as you are, but we must respect King Frederrick's hospitality. We must not cause any argument on his daughter's wedding day. You know that I will make our feelings clear to the Kernans."

"Thank you for offering us accommodation," Esmerelda said, trying to keep her tone even. "But we will leave as soon as the wedding is over, to meet our kinfolk in the Forbidden Forest. Rest assured, I will not cause a scene at the wedding, but if I find that our people have suffered harm, I will unleash my fury on the King of Kerner at the earliest opportunity."

The secretary breathed an inward sigh of relief and bowed to the witch queen. "Thank you, Lady Esmerelda. Please, if you would be so kind as to follow me, I will have your arrival announced in the Great Hall, where King Frederrick and King Jeffrey are waiting to greet their guests."

The little man then ushered the party towards the archway leading to the Great Hall.

The master of ceremonies prepared to announce the Avalonians' arrival. He expected King Arthur to enter first, but Arthur stood back and allowed the other members of his party to go in front of him. This was a deliberate action to show that the magical hierarchy were his equals.

The two lions entered first, carrying King Allarond and Queen Farainne on their backs. Having practised their act several times now, both lions and elves felt confident. Nevertheless, Edward and Daisy watched with bated breath, fearing that something might go wrong. The golden beasts trotted down the red carpet which led to their hosts. Magic spells issued from Allarond's staff and Farainne's wand, sending up golden rays towards the high ceiling.

Queen Maud and King Selogon fluttered above the lions. The fairies sent out a host of silver sparks, from wand and staff. As the silver sparks rose up and then fell, they met the golden rays sent up by the elves. The spectacle lit up the dark, austere room like a host of shooting stars.

194

At the end of the red carpet, King Frederrick and King Jeffrey were seated side by side on ornate thrones set upon a dais. Frederrick was as short and plump as Jeffrey was tall and lean. Frederrick was a gentle man who found it easy to laugh, whereas Jeffrey was a very solemn man who found it hard to smile. Their wives sat on lesser thrones on either side of them.

Queen Elise, like her husband, was warm and friendly. She smiled with delight as she saw the strange spectacle approaching.

Queen Shirley-Poppy was a pleasant-looking woman with a big round face. Her mouth had fallen wide open with amazement at the scene in front of her. She was so excited that she could barely stay seated as the tiny people and the lions approached.

King Frederrick laughed and clapped his hands.

For a second, a crack of a smile even appeared on King Jeffrey's face as their extraordinary guests approached the dais.

The lions stopped in front of the thrones. They gracefully stretched their front legs and lowered their heads towards the floor, just as Daisy had taught them. They appeared to be bowing to their hosts.

The elves hopped down effortlessly from the lions' backs. The fairies fluttered down beside them, and all bowed low to acknowledge the royal couples on the dais. The royal families of Twydell and Kerner nodded their greeting.

An official ushered the tiny people towards a small table and chairs which had been set upon one of the main tables. The table prepared for the Avalonians was nearer the royal family, and closer to the red carpet walkway than those prepared for any of the other guests. Places of honour had indeed been given to the guests from Avalon.

The lions trotted back to Daisy, who breathed a sigh of relief that her pets had performed just as she had trained them to. Edward gave her a hug and a kiss on the cheek. It was one of those moments when he was full of pride at his fiancée's accomplishments.

The witch queen, escorted by Merlin and Tannus on either side, made her way down the red carpet. At the end of the carpet, neither Merlin nor Tannus bowed. Esmerelda stood still, making no effort to curtsey.

Despite the lack of formality, Frederrick and Elise welcomed the Queen of the Witches and her companions with genuine amity.

Jeffrey and Shirley-Poppy mouthed their welcome, but their eyes held no warmth. In fact, Queen Shirley-Poppy looked noticeably uncomfortable. Nevertheless, before the trio took their seats, Jeffrey stood up and came forward to shake Merlin's hand. As his frosty grey eyes looked directly into Merlin's twinkling blue ones, he said, "I thank you for the service you have provided to us by quenching the dragons' anger. I shall look forward to talking to you of this and other matters tomorrow." Jeffrey nodded to Esmerelda and Tannus, but his face remained hard and cold.

King Arthur made his way along the Great Hall. He walked as straight as his damaged limbs would allow. Gilda flew side-saddle on her golden broom, at her husband's side. The couple were welcomed by their hosts.

"I apologise that my wife must use her broom." Arthur bowed to the two kings. "She was injured in the battle with the Trajaens and has lost much of her ability to speak and walk."

"We have heard of the great battle that took place," King Frederrick stated, grasping Arthur's hand and shaking it vigorously. "I am sorry to hear that you were so badly injured, Lady Gilda. My men tell me that you brought down several of the raiders before you were struck yourself."

At this point, a look of surprise appeared on King Jeffrey's face. The thought of a king's consort taking part in a fight was something previously unheard of. Queen Shirley-Poppy's mouth opened wide with amazement yet again, and then closed just as quickly. At times, the Queen of Kerner looked like a pouting fish gasping for air.

"My wife fought bravely alongside *all* the witches and wizards who fought in the Battle of Merlport." Arthur spoke loudly and proudly on behalf of his wife and her kind. "I shall look forward to telling you more when we speak tomorrow."

Arthur and Gilda bowed slightly, and then took their places next to the magic people in their party. They looked on with pride as their son and the two girls were announced.

It was time for Prince Edward to walk down the red carpet. On one arm was Daisy, last of the Brewins and his bride-to-be; on the other, his half-sister, Princess Rosalie. Edward walked tall and straight, but slowly, to make sure that Daisy did not fall. *Please don't fall, Daisy – not here, not in front of all the Twydell dignitaries.* His fiancée held his arm so tightly, he was sure it would leave a bruise. On each flank, Leo and Sybil made their way down the carpet for the second time.

Unaware of the problem with Daisy's shoes, Arthur and Gilda looked on proudly at the prince and the two girls. As the trio reached the dais, Arthur noticed that a young man had made his way to stand next to the Queen of Twydell's throne.

"Look! That young man over there, beside Queen Elise, must be Derrick," Arthur whispered to Gilda.

The good-looking young man was dressed in a pale blue outfit trimmed with gold braid. Coincidentally, his outfit was almost identical in colour to the clothing worn by Rosalie. As Rosalie arose gracefully from her low curtsey to her hosts, he gave her a broad smile, and she smiled back.

Fortunately, so many eyes were on Rosalie that the need for Edward to help Daisy rise from her less-elegant curtsey was hardly noticed. *Thank goodness that's over!* Edward breathed a sigh of relief.

Edward and the two girls sat down opposite Tannus and Esmerelda. Edward liked Tannus. He was usually easy to talk to and had a good sense of humour. However, since his father's death, Tannus had become remote and serious. Edward thought that the young warlock resented him for allowing the Trajaen prisoners to sail off on their boats, unharmed. *Now is the time to try to strike up a conversation with him.*

"This is a magnificent palace isn't it?" asked Edward.

Tannus looked Edward straight in the eye. Other than raising his eyebrows, Tannus kept his face expressionless. "Why do humans need to live in such grand surroundings? Why do two people need such a huge house?"

How do I answer this? "Kings and queens need to style themselves in grandeur in order to gain the respect of their subjects." *What a stupid answer!* Edward chided himself as he heard his own words.

Tannus raised his eyebrows further, in mock surprise. "Well, Esmie, dear, you will have to build a big ornate palace to gain the respect of your covens!"

Esmerelda laughed.

To Edward's embarrassment, the young warlock continued. "Esmie is Queen of the Witches because she has their respect. Not because she lives in a grand palace, but because she inherited her mother's talents as a spell weaver, and also because she is intelligent and hard working."

"And willing to sit in boring meetings, and attend the wedding of the son of a person I would like to kill." Esmerelda eyes glittered emerald sparks for a moment. "What about Merlin? He has no big palace, but he has the respect of your kind as well as mine!"

"Merlin is a nomad," Daisy joined in.

Thank you, Daisy; you're not helping. "Yes, you are right," Edward conceded. "It was a silly thing for me to say. You have to admit, though, it is a nice building, and ideal for entertaining."

"Where are you two going to hold your wedding? Have you set a date yet?" Esmerelda smiled at Daisy. The witch queen's eyes had reverted to their friendly moss green.

The fair-haired young woman and the raven-haired young witch queen seemed to get on well.

"King Arthur told us to wait until after Steven and Jeanette's wedding. So, any time after today!" Daisy gave her fiancé a bright smile, which made his heart melt. She was so pretty when she smiled.

"Father is going to speak to King Frederrick tomorrow. We always visualised a wedding in the Merlport town square, followed by a street party. Now we have to consider inviting King Frederrick and his family, and possibly the Kerner royalty."

Esmerelda breathed in noisily, to show her disapproval at the thought of inviting the Kernans to Avalon.

The prince looked at her apologetically but continued. "Merlin thinks that the Twydellers may have some big tents they can bring. He saw them using the tents to shelter the homeless after the dragons destroyed their homes. Apparently, they are rather grand, and we may be able to use them to provide accommodation for visiting royalty. After all, we have nowhere else for them to stay."

Esmerelda gave a *humph*, but said nothing. She knew that this was not the time or the place to argue. Rather than voice her disapproval, she turned and watched the other guests taking their places.

It was a good hour before the last of the guests from Kerner and Twydell were announced and in their seats. Finally, Princess Jeanette and Prince Steven walked down the red carpet. One and all rose to their feet. The ceremony at which the gold rings would be exchanged had begun. To officiate, the mayor of Dalton stood in front of the two thrones. The ring of Kerner was placed on the Princess of Twydell's finger, and the ring of Twydell was placed on the finger of the Prince of Kerner. Thus, the two countries were joined in marriage.

As the ceremony came to a close, flower petals were thrown by the townsfolk in the galleries. The petals fell like a shower of colourful, scented snowflakes, descending gently upon the happy couple.

No sooner had the ceremony ended than the festivities began. Minstrels burst forth into music and song. Servants brought trays of food and wine, and filled the tables with all kinds of culinary delights for the guest to savour. There was something for every taste to relish. The Avalonians tucked in heartily.

Prince Steven and Princess Jeanette were the first to dance, but they were soon joined by others.

Prince Derrick made his way to the Avalonian table and, after bowing to and greeting everyone on the table, turned to Gilda.

"May I have the pleasure of dancing with your beautiful daughter?" he asked, bowing again.

Rosalie gasped, and her cheeks flushed red. She was on her feet, grasping Derrick's outstretched hand, before her parents could finish giving their consent.

Edward laughed at his half-sister's impetuosity. Daisy, Tannus and Esmerelda all joined in. However, Arthur and Gilda simply smiled proudly.

As the couple took their place on the dance floor, many eyes turned from Jeanette and Steven to the other prince and princess. There were sighs and nods of approval from the attending dignitaries and their wives, directed at both of the couples dancing on the floor.

Soon the dance floor was full of couples spinning and swaying in time to the music.

"Why aren't you two dancing?" Esmerelda asked Edward and Daisy. "I expected you to be one of the first couples on the floor."

"I can't dance in these shoes," Daisy confided. "They hurt my feet, and the heels are too high."

"Take them off then," Esmerelda retorted.

"I can't. If I do, my dress will be too long and I'll trip over it."

Edward's foot was tapping in time to the music. *Sometimes I wish Daisy could be just like other girls. Why can't we be out there dancing with the others?*

"Oh, for the moon's sake!" sighed the witch as she listened to Daisy. She got up and moved round to the other side of the table. "Stand up, and take off your shoes," she ordered.

Daisy dutifully kicked off her shoes, and stood. Esmerelda guided Daisy into a space with ample room to manoeuvre.

Drawing her wand and pointing it at Daisy's hem, she walked round the floaty skirt, muttering words which sounded like some sort of foreign language. The length of the skirt shrank instantly as she did so.

"How does that feel?" asked Esmerelda. "It looks all right to me. Is it the right length, or do you want it shorter?"

Daisy walked around to test the reduced length of her dress. The girl was oblivious to the other guests watching the performance. She felt comfortable in her bare feet, and no longer had any fear of tripping over the hem of her dress.

"Oh, Esmie! That's perfect! You are so clever. Thank you." She gave the witch queen a hug and planted a kiss on her cheek.

Esmerelda smiled.

"Come on, Edward." Daisy pulled him up by his arm. "Let's show them how it's done!"

Prince Edward needed no second bidding, and the couple joined the others on the dance floor. *Thank you, Esmie.* He didn't need to say the words aloud; Esmerelda knew him well enough to know what he was thinking. He smiled at the witch, and she gave him a wink. *I'm sure that was a heart-shaped green spark she just sent me from her eye!*

Even Esmerelda and Tannus eventually took a turn on the dance floor.

Maud and Selogon were afraid to dance on the floor, lest they be trodden upon, so the fairies danced on the table. They were soon joined by the elves, Allarond and Farainne.

Rosalie and Derrick seemed tireless, dancing most of the evening. When they eventually decided to take a break from dancing, Derrick asked the King of Avalon if he could join his table. Arthur welcomed the young man.

"I have heard that you travelled from another world. It must have been very exciting. Please tell me about it," Derrick said excitedly.

"I was too ill to notice the journey, I'm afraid," Arthur explained. "I was badly injured in battle, and my people thought that I was dead. Gilda was already here.

"Gilda was one of the first to arrive, with Merlin, to find out if this new world was safe for us. Merlin returned to Briton. Shortly after his return, I was defeated in battle. I was barely alive when he put me in a boat and set it sail for Avalon. When I sailed, I was on the brink of death. Gilda nursed me back to health, although not all my injuries could be healed. Edward-Arthur, my son, joined me some years later. Gilda and I are now married. We were delighted when Rosalie was born – we thought we were too old to have children. We have been blessed to have had a happy marriage and a beautiful daughter. When Edward joined us, we had a complete family – a son and a daughter."

"I remember the journey," Edward reminisced. "I travelled with the witches, fairies and elves, in a tall ship. I wasn't very old. My real mother was dead, so Esmerelda was given the job of looking after me. It was like having an older sister." He grinned. "She was always telling me off."

"It was like having a naughty little brother." Esmerelda winked at Derrick. "He used to annoy me so much; there was many a time I felt tempted to push him over the side of the ship."

Edward laughed. "It was a new beginning for all of us. Until the attack by the Trajaens, we were very happy with our lives in Avalon."

Derrick was keen to find out more about the battle, and so he leaned towards Edward. "I heard your father say that my Lady Gilda was injured in the battle. Our soldiers told me about the terrible combat with the Trajaens. I wish I had been there to fight with you. Please tell me about it."

"Ah," Arthur cut in. "There will be plenty of time to hear about the battle. It was a battle won, but with many sad losses. Let us enjoy ourselves tonight, and we will tell you about the fight with the Trajaens another time."

Thank goodness Father stopped him. The last thing Esmie and Tannus want to talk about tonight is how their parents died. How was Derrick to know that Elvira and Tannitus died in the battle?

"I am sorry," replied Derrick. "I am just so absorbed with everything I have heard about Avalon and the people who live there." He smiled at Rosalie, who smiled back.

Derrick listened intently as the Avalonians told him about their new country and their desires to live in peace and harmony with nature.

Just as much as Edward had been concerned that his half-sister might be persuaded to marry someone she did not like, secretly he had worried that Derrick might reject Rosalie. She was a half-witch, and until recently, such people had been shunned by the Twydellers. He was afraid that Rosalie might be hurt. *He must be aware by now that she is a half-witch, even if she has no magic. Merlin must have made Frederrick aware that if they marry and have children, any future princes and princesses of Twydell might be wizzwits.*

There was no need to worry. Prince Derrick had been left in no doubt whatsoever that Rosalie was a half-witch, but he still seemed besotted with her. He showed no resentment towards magical people, and chatted amiably with Esmerelda and Tannus. The prince made clear his desire to travel to Avalon.

The evening continued happily for everyone, but ended all too soon.

As the festivities came to a close, King Frederrick's secretary made his way to Esmerelda. Edward looked round for Merlin, but the wizard was engrossed in conversation with a Twydeller. Anticipating a difficult conversation, Edward moved to Esmerelda's side.

"Excuse me, my lady." The secretary could barely look the witch queen in the face. "We have just received a message from the guards escorting the men from the Forbidden Forest. We are advised that they will not be crossing the border back into Twydell until early morning."

"Why don't you and Tannus stay the night, Esmie? You can get a fresh start in the morning," Edward suggested tactfully.

"You and your friend are very welcome to a room in the palace this evening," the secretary reminded her.

"The decision is yours," Tannus told her. "I'm not too tired to travel tonight, but we will all be exhausted by the morning if we don't get any rest."

Reluctantly, Esmerelda agreed to accept the Twydellers' hospitality. She wasn't happy about it, though, and her mouth set in a pout as she approached Merlin to let him know her decision.

Merlin was also relieved to look forward to a good night's rest. He was weary, and he also wanted to attend the parley with the three kings the following morning. The old wizard knew that Esmerelda would be anxious for an early start in the morning, but he asked her to delay her plans to allow him to attend the parley.

"I'll only stay for a short while," the old wizard promised. "I want to speak to the King of Kerner personally, to establish whether there are more of our kind held in Kerner prisons. After that, we will travel together to the Forbidden Forest."

After a pause, Merlin continued. "The Bramble family will be overjoyed to see their men again. They will also be delighted to meet new friends. I'm looking forward to introducing you."

Merlin was also looking forward, more than he had anticipated, to seeing Helen-Joy again. However, he failed to mention to the others his strong desire to see the soothsayer.

"Everything you say makes sense," the Queen of the Witches had to agree. "Sleep well, Merlin, my dear friend. I shall look forward to hearing about what was discussed in the parley."

Chapter 5 – The People of the Forbidden Forest

"That was quick." Esmerelda looked surprised to see Merlin leaving the parley after half an hour. Although Merlin had promised to stay for only a short while, she knew that the old wizard usually enjoyed the opportunity to talk.

"Jeffrey knew what I was going to ask, and was prepared. He said that he was unaware that the three wizards were held in a Kerner jail. He says he will have his prisons searched to find out if any others are held, and if any are found, he will ensure that they are released."

"Do you believe him?" Tannus asked.

"No, but I have made it perfectly clear that he must make sure his jailers are honest with him. I left him with no doubts that we have ways of knowing if we are told lies. There are to be no more excuses."

"I have a feeling we are not going to like what we find out today," said Allarond, King of the Elves.

"I have the same niggling feeling," Merlin admitted. "Now let us go. Arthur has offered us the golden carriage, but I have declined his offer in case he wishes to return to Avalon before we are ready to leave the Forbidden Forest. It might be nice to stay for a few days. Is that all right with everyone?"

The other magical beings of Avalon nodded.

"What else were they discussing at the meeting?" Esmerelda asked as they made their way to the courtyard. "I notice Edward and Derrick were both invited to the parley."

"Oh, trade, security, whether I could ask the dragons to burn the Trajaen boats if they attack any of our lands again."

"What did you say?"

"I said I had no time to discuss such matters. My priority is to ensure that the men from the Forbidden Forest have been returned safe and well!"

"Nice answer," Tannus said with a smile.

The elves, who were perched on each of his shoulders, nodded their approval.

The fairies floated above the little group.

The fairy and elf royalty accompanied the witches and wizards on their visit to the forest. They, too, were anxious to find out more about the mysterious woodland. In particular, they wanted to know whether any of their kind might have taken refuge there.

Merlin rode on Comet, his white stallion. The others flew above him. Maud travelled on Esmerelda's broom whilst Farainne travelled with Tannus. Their husbands travelled with the herbologist wizards – Selogon with Yzor, and Allarond with Jonathan.

The timid secretary came out to see them off. He wanted them to wait until King Frederrick could leave the meeting to wish them well on their journey, but they all refused any further delay. The people of Twydell waved their goodbyes. Even some of the soldiers on guard duty waved their farewells.

It was a pleasant morning. The sun shone, but it was not yet too hot; nor was it cold. They travelled along the foot of one of Twydell's three mountains. The landscape was green and fertile and dotted with wild flowers. Merlin was pleased to have a fresh, light wind blowing in his face. It cleared his head after the abundance of ale and wine the night before. He looked up to see if any thunderbirds or dragons were in sight, but he saw none. The only things flying above him were the four broomsticks with their eight passengers. The forest was less than half a day's ride from Dalton, and he looked forward to seeing it again.

Merlin was maintaining a steady canter on Comet when he saw six Twydell soldiers riding towards him. The sergeant leading the half dozen men raised his arm in greeting. Merlin recognised him as one of the soldiers who had escorted him to Avalon and joined him in the Battle of Merlport.

The sergeant was a middle-aged man whose face was weathered by days in the saddle. Pulling up the reins on his horse, he said, "Lord Merlin, you must be travelling to see the men we have just escorted from Kerner."

"I am indeed. How are they? Their family must be delighted to have them home again!" Merlin kept his voice light, but he'd had bad feelings about the men's home coming ever since hearing of their delayed crossing into Twydell.

The wizard knew his suspicions were justified when all the soldiers, including the sergeant, lowered their heads to avoid meeting his gaze.

The rest of Merlin's party dipped down on their broomsticks and hovered round the group of men.

The horses sensed the unease. They whinnied and reared, wheeling as if they wanted their riders to hasten away.

Merlin felt his stomach clench.

"We do not treat our prisoners in Twydell the way the Kernans treat theirs," the sergeant said. He raised his eyes, and Merlin saw within them genuine anguish. "All three are in poor health. I would be surprised if any of the three survive more than a few days. I will make sure King Frederrick knows how concerned we were when we saw them. I am sorry."

"There is no need for you to apologise, Sergeant. You are not to blame. Please tell your king what you have witnessed as soon as you arrive back at Dalton Palace. King Jeffrey of Kerner is still there, and no doubt King Frederrick will want to speak to him about the three wizards of the Forbidden Forest. Our King Arthur is there too, and he will also wish to hear about the state of these men when you brought them home."

Esmerelda's eyes glittered emerald green with anger, but she held her tongue. The rest of the magical folk did as well, all of them knowing that these soldiers were not at fault.

"I will of course do as you bid, Lord Merlin," said the sergeant. "King Frederrick ordered me to speak to him immediately on my return, so your commands are the same."

The sergeant used his strength to hold his reins firmly and try to calm his horse, which was still restless. He then said, "One other thing was strange, Lord Merlin. We told no one of our mission, and we wondered how we would get into the Forbidden Forest – let alone find the family of the three men we escorted. But when we got there, they were all waiting! The bindweed round the forest had opened up like an entrance, but when they took the men inside, it closed over again."

"Oh, they knew you were on your way all right, Sergeant!" said Merlin. "They had no need for anyone outside the forest to tell them. Please make sure you tell that to King Frederrick as well. Tell him we will know if the Kerner prisons hold any more of our kind!"

The sergeant nodded to Merlin and then signalled his soldiers.

All six soldiers gave the magical people a brief salute, and then they urged their horses back on the road to Dalton.

Merlin and his party gathered speed as they continued their journey. The urgency of their task was now confirmed.

❋ ✦ ❋ ✦ ❋ ✦ ❋ ✦ ❋ ✦ ❋

When at last they reached the forest, Merlin saw an old cart, which appeared to have been abandoned outside the point where he had previously entered. As they drew nearer, the bindweed opened, and Lennox appeared on the other side. The unicorn snorted a greeting to Comet and then turned towards Merlin and his companions.

Everyone was pleased to see the unicorn, especially Queen Maud. The fairy queen fluttered down to greet her old friend, perching on his nose before rising up to sit on his forelock. It was the first time any of them, other than Merlin, had seen Lennox since he arrived in Avalon.

"Hello again, my old friend," the unicorn greeted Merlin. "Please tell Maud I rejoice in seeing her again. Nonetheless, I should be grateful if you would make haste with me. The Brambles are all busy tending their three men. They look dreadful, as if they are not really alive. I will show you the way to the Brambles' house, as you have never been there before. Helen-Joy and my wives are at the waterfall. They are looking after the poor pit pony which brought the men here in that old cart. I shall leave you at the Brambles' house, as I am anxious to get back to the pit pony."

The unicorn led the way into the forest.

Maud did not return to Esmerelda's broom; instead, she sat on Lennox's neck, holding on to his mane. That way, although she did not understand the language of the unicorns, she could hear the tone of any conversation which passed between Merlin and Lennox. Besides, she loved Lennox and was happy to feel the warmth of his body again.

It was midday now, and beginning to get hot, so the cool of the woodland was appreciated by all. Once they were all inside, the bindweed closed over again.

Yzor and his son, Jonathan, were both very interested in the way the bindweed closed behind them. They pointed to the woven canopy of leaves and vines overhead, entwining the branches of trees like a hairnet. The herbologists had never seen a plant quite like this one before, and had many questions for the Bramble family about the creeping organism.

Lennox continued to lead the way, with Merlin trotting behind him on Comet. The others followed, hovering along the narrow pathways on their brooms.

At the point where the pathway widened and Merlin's horse could trot alongside the unicorn, Lennox continued his story.

"The men were put in a cart. They were too weak to walk or ride. The pit pony which brought them could hardly put one foot in front of another himself. The poor thing was covered in sores from the whip he has suffered all his life. He told me he is only seven years old, but he has worked all his life in the tin mines.

He is as thin as a rake and looks more than twice his age. The jailers harnessed him to the cart deliberately because they thought his days were numbered. They laughed and said that he would be lucky to make it to the border before he dropped dead. They thought it would be funny. They made jokes about what the Twydell soldiers would do with the men if the pit pony's legs gave out. They wondered what their families would think when the men they once called wizards arrived home looking like dead men. Anyway, the pony got the cart here with the three men, but we may well have four dead bodies in the morning."

"I hope you are wrong, Lennox. Merlin was grave. "Let us see what we can achieve. The people in our party are all skilled magicians. Our combined magic will be powerful."

Wizard and unicorn were silent a moment.

"I will see these men first and then go to the pit pony," Merlin added after the silence. He knew that the pit pony's health was as important to Lennox as the health of the three men was to their kin. The old sorcerer knew he must use his skills fairly.

As the party made its way through the forest, Merlin translated the conversation he'd had with Lennox, relating the news to the others.

The party then travelled on in silence, each absorbed in bitter thoughts. Grim looks had set hard upon their faces, in dire contrast to their happy countenances at the previous night's festivities.

Lennox left the travellers at the Brambles' cottage. He whinnied his goodbye and trotted on towards the waterfall, where Helen-Joy and his wives tended the pit pony.

The cottage was a strange, topsy-turvy structure made of wood, mud, and leaves. On one side of the cottage was a garden full of vegetables, behind which was a grassy area where two goats grazed. In front of the cottage, on a small lawn surrounded by flower beds, Great-Grandmother Bramble sat on a tree stump, stirring a cauldron of rabbit stew over a fire.

She looked up when she saw Merlin approaching, but a worried frown had replaced the familiar smile on her wrinkled face. As Merlin slid from his saddle, she stood up, put her arms round him, and kissed him on the cheek.

"Thank you for finding our men, Merlin, but I fear it is too late. I don't think they even know who they are, let alone where they are."

The matriarch of the Bramble family then greeted the other visitors.

Even though Esmerelda had never met Great-Grandmother Bramble before, she put her arms round the old witch and pulled her into a friendly hug.

Jerry, Garod, and Isaiah, the three freed men, were lying on the beds just inside the cottage, where Great-Grandmother Bramble and her two daughters, Nora and Maura, normally slept. The brothers were still dressed in the plain white suits of Kerner prisoners. Dilly, Dally, and Sally were trying to feed their husbands on the rabbit stew, with the help of their mother, Nora, and their aunt Maura.

Yzor entered the cottage first. After introducing himself to the family, he examined the three men.

"I am an herbologist, not a doctor, but may I suggest that we take the men out into the fresh air? If they have been working in the mines, they may appreciate the air and light of the outdoors. It won't take us long to move these beds outside, and then we can bring them back in again when it grows cooler."

He stepped outside the front door again and looked up at the trees enveloped by the bindweed. "It's a pity the forest is so dense. They could do with a bit of sunlight."

"Good idea. I only closed it over because it was too hot for me in the midday sun. " Great-Grandmother Bramble stood up and, pointing her wand towards the forest canopy, started pacing round in a circle, uttering a spell. Nora and Maura joined her. As the three walked round and round, using their special steps and chanting their spell, the bindweed opened to reveal the afternoon sun.

Yzor stared up in amazement as the forest canopy opened to reveal the sky above.

"Just a bit too much sun now," Maura suggested, and the three paced in the opposite direction, closing the opening slightly to create some shade.

Next, the four visiting wizards used their wands in a combined effort to lift the first of the beds out into the open. Each stood at the corner of the bed, and, together, they lifted their wands. Although they were only light pieces of wood, the wizards strained as they lifted them, as if their wands had suddenly grown much heavier. The bed rose from the floor in the cottage and, under the guidance of the wizards and their straining wands, made its way out of the door into the garden. The wizards followed the bed outside, guiding it and the patient it held, into a suitable position in the diffused sunlight.

In one leap, Allarond jumped onto the bed and stood on the sick man's shoulder. The elf king touched the man's temple with his golden staff, and then he spoke into the man's ear, to no avail. The elf king fell back, exhausted.

"I thought I might be able to lift his soul," said the King of the Avalon Elves. "But it is so far away, I cannot reach it."

"Let me try," Farainne offered, jumping onto the man's other shoulder. She touched her wand to his temple, but with the same result. She sighed and shook her head, as if the task were hopeless.

The second bed was brought into the garden. This time, Maud and Selogon tried to lift the soul of the shell of the man lying within. The fairy queen and king each touched his temples with their instruments of magic. They, too, found it impossible to lift the poor man's soul.

Finally, the third bed, on which Isaiah lay, made its way outside. Sally, his wife, walked in front; Heather, his daughter, walked behind.

"Do you know what?" Sally asked anyone who was listening, her voice full of hope. "Although my Isaiah hasn't seen Heather since she was a baby, I'm sure there was a flicker of recognition when she tried to feed him. I'm sure he knows Heather is his daughter."

"An excellent sign!" shouted Allarond.

He and Farainne jumped down from the first bed and up onto Isaiah's in just two leaps. They both tried to rouse Isaiah's soul from the depths in which it lay. They both fell back onto the pillow, exhausted.

Looking at Sally, the elf king said, "You are right. I think there is a little more response in this one."

"Excuse me," called a small voice from the ground.

They all looked round, and saw an elf standing half in and half out of the Brambles' garden, as if he were just about to turn and run back through the fence and into the forest undergrowth.

"Excuse me," the elf said again. "I think they may have been drugged. The Kernans have used drugs on elves and the fairies before now."

"Hello," Maura Bramble spoke to the little elf. "We see you in the garden sometimes, but you always run away before we have chance to speak. If you can help us find a cure for our men, we would be indebted to you."

The elf said, "My name is Alfred, but my friends call me Alf. The elves and the fairies used to flourish in the meadows, but then men decided that we would look pretty in cages. A captured elf in a cage is worth a lot of money in the markets. A pretty fairy is worth even more."

Everyone gasped with revulsion as they listened to Alf's shocking revelation.

Maud, Queen of the Fairies, turned white with horror.

Alfred continued. "They seem to think it's like having a bird or butterfly in a cage. Something cute to show their friends. Obviously, the poor dears who are captured try to use their magic to escape, but when the men realised what was happening, they forced their captives to drink a mixture which took away some of their senses. Sometimes they were forced to drink too much, and they died. We rescued as many victims as we could before we sought refuge in the forest. A few we managed to bring back to life, but many others were too weak, and they passed away."

"How did you bring them back to life? Please, I beg you, tell us," pleaded Sally, standing at Isaiah's bedside.

"We gave them lots of fresh water to drink, to wash away the effects of the mixture, and we fed them on lots of fresh fruit. Raspberries are very good. Unfortunately, we picked all the fruits in the forest and trod the plants so much that they have dried up."

"Ah, so that's where out raspberries went," said Maura. "I thought it was the birds who had taken them!"

"Me too! I wondered what happened to all my raspberries." Helen-Joy walked through the gate, carrying a basket of fruit from her garden. "I have no raspberries left either, but I do have strawberries, peaches, and plums,"

Helen-Joy put her basket on the ground and picked out a ripe strawberry. "Would you like a strawberry, young man?" she asked, offering the sweet red fruit to little Alf.

"Thank you!" the elf ran forward and took the strawberry from the soothsayer's hand. However, he immediately darted back to the edge of the lawn, putting one leg through the fence.

"Don't be afraid, Alfred. We won't hurt you," Great-Grandmother Bramble spoke kindly to the little elf.

"You may not, but that big black-and-white cat of yours might! She's chased me away more than once."

"What? Old Fluffy?" the old witch laughed. "She might have done once, but even I'm faster than she is these days! I'll go and find her in a minute, and you can make friends with her. She's probably asleep on the kitchen window ledge – that's where she spends most of her days now."

Alf looked a little more relaxed.

Merlin stepped forward, kissed Helen-Joy on the cheek, and introduced her to the Avalonians.

"How is the little pit pony?" he asked.

216

"Resting. He is still very weak," the soothsayer replied. "Great-Grandmother, do you have any soothing ointment I could use to heal the pony's sores, please? I have a good feeling that he will survive, but if he doesn't, then at least he will die in a little more comfort than he is in now."

"Of course, dear. If you have a good feeling the poor creature will live, then I am sure he will." The old witch stood up, moved through the cottage, and came back carrying Fluffy in one arm and a jar of ointment in the other.

She gave the ointment to Helen-Joy then sat down again. She put Fluffy on her lap, and bid Alfred come and sit beside the old cat.

Alfred nervously jumped up onto the arm of the chair, and Great-Grandmother Bramble introduced them to each other. Fluffy eyed the elf with disinterest for a few seconds, curled up into a ball on the old witch's lap, and went to sleep.

Merlin announced that he would not be staying to eat with the Bramble family and his friends from Avalon. "I will accompany Helen-Joy back to her home. Besides, I need to see the little pit pony and help to heal him, in any way I can."

The soothsayer linked arms with the elderly wizard, and the two set off together.

Esmerelda watched the two depart. Observing how close they leant towards each other, she looked at Great-Grandmother Bramble, who had noticed the quizzical expression on her face. A knowing nod from the old witch met the young witch queen's enquiring look.

"Well!" Esmerelda looked at Tannus. He looked back at her, eyebrows raised, and a wry smile on his handsome face.

"Well," murmured Tannus, "they say you're never too old."

Tannus put his arm round Esmerelda and held her close. He planted a kiss on her lips. It had been a strange and somewhat stressful day, but they were finally beginning to unwind.

"With so much love and support round the three brothers, they must surely survive their terrible ordeal," the good-looking warlock told the witch queen. "Even Merlin seems to be taking time out to relax. Perhaps you should do the same."

"This is such a peaceful place," Esmerelda said with a sigh. "But can any of us really breathe easily until our brethren are healed? Even if they do not regain their magical powers, I would like to see their bodies and minds restored to health."

"I believe they will be restored. Our combined magic is very powerful. But, unless we rest, our powers will be weakened." Tannus spoke in a gentle tone. "I feel the tension in your body. Come, my most wonderful lady, sit with me. Let us relax and enjoy the Brambles' hospitality."

The two lovers, and the other visitors from Avalon, settled down to enjoy a meal with the Bramble family. Alf joined them. The Brambles were keen to know more about Avalon, and the Avalonians were equally eager to learn more about the forest, as were the herbologist wizards, Yzor and Jonathan.

Jerry, Garod, and Isaiah lay on their beds. Their faces seemed empty and vacant, but they also looked peaceful. Everyone, Brambles and Avalonians alike, took a turn to sit and speak with the brothers. Every effort was made to try to mend their broken spirits.

As the cool of the night set in, the magical people lifted the sick men's beds back into the house. The Brambles found places for the visitors to sleep. Throughout the night, the Brambles and their visitors took turns sitting with the broken men.

Merlin had a lot to tell Helen-Joy, as they walked towards her cave, and she was eager to hear all. Comet trotted along behind them. Merlin told Helen-Joy all about the dragons' egg and the wedding. Although the soothsayer had seen in her dreams and crystal ball much of what had passed, she still had reams of questions to ask. She was still asking questions when they neared the waterfall, where Lennox's mares were licking and nuzzling the pit pony. The poor animal lay on the grass, enjoying the last of the afternoon sunshine.

"How is the little pony?" Merlin asked the unicorns.

"Lucky. His name is Lucky," replied one of the mares. "He told us that he has never had a name, and kept telling us how lucky he is to be here, so we have called him Lucky."

The little pony raised his head. He had never heard a human speaking in the language of horse before. Merlin spent some time talking to the sad pony, whilst Helen-Joy gently smeared Great-Grandmother Bramble's healing lotion over the creature's sores. She fetched one of her patchwork quilts to cover Lucky's frail body and keep him warm through the night. The soothsayer then went back into her cave to prepare the evening meal.

Merlin came in later to find a plate of bean stew and cup of hot mint tea waiting for him. He devoured his supper with a hearty appetite, answering the soothsayer's endless questions as he ate. Occasionally, he even managed a question or two of his own.

They finished off their supper with a glass of home-made passion fruit wine. They shared a tête-à-tête for a while longer before withdrawing to Helen-Joy's bed of dreams, on the ledge behind the net curtains.

"Is anyone at home?"

Young Heather Bramble's voice awoke Merlin and Helen-Joy.

The girl had politely stood on the ledge between the waterfall and the cave, calling to them. She had then stepped back down to the grass area where the pit pony was standing. The quilt cover had fallen to the ground beside him. She gently stroked the little pony, carefully avoiding his sores.

Helen-Joy came out, dressed in her pink nightgown, completely unabashed. Merlin followed behind, in his vest and underpants, but looked slightly embarrassed.

"Great-Aunt Maura has sent you some of her blackberry crumble for breakfast. It's still warm, and laced with honey."

"Thank you," said Merlin, taking the bowl. He stuck his finger into the bowl, hooked out a portion of its contents, and placed it in his mouth. "I've never had blackberry crumble for breakfast before. It's delicious!"

"Alfred told her how much the elves like blackberries, and next thing, Great Aunt Maura is making a crumble! Yzor and Jonathan went off into the forest with him this morning to look at the raspberry bushes. Alfred thought they had died, but your herbologist wizards managed to revive them. Yzor thinks they will bear fruit again within a few days."

"Ah, good! Yzor's an expert with plants," Merlin said, his mouth full of blackberry crumble. Helen-Joy had brought out some spoons, and they sat beside each other, eating out of the same bowl.

"I'm utterly spoilt here," Merlin said. "How I wish I had found the Forbidden Forest before."

Heather laughed. Her laughter lit up her very plain face. "We wish you had found your way here before too," she said, reddening. She was in awe of Merlin, and still a little shy when she spoke to the mighty wizard.

"How are your father and his brothers this morning?" Helen-Joy asked, changing the subject.

"Do you know? I am sure Mother was right. Daddy knows who I am, even though he hasn't seen me since I was a baby! His eyes definitely looked towards me when I was feeding him this morning." The young witch smiled. "King Allarond was on his shoulder at the time, and he said he had no doubt that Daddy's soul was lifting."

Merlin was sad to learn that Heather had never known her father, but Helen-Joy looked on the bright side.

"What good news!" She raised her spoon, as if to toast the man's recovery. "Lucky looks a lot better today too!"

Heather looked confused, so Helen-Joy explained. "The pit pony. The mares have named him Lucky."

Lucky was now standing by the pool, drinking the cool, clear, water. Two of the mares were frolicking in the pool and trying to encourage the pony to get into the water too. The pony stood nervously at the edge of the pool, as if he wanted to join the mares but was afraid to do so. Comet trotted up behind him and mischievously gave the pony's rump a strong push with his nose. Lucky lost his balance and stumbled into the pool. The mares whinnied, as if they were laughing, and splashed him with water.

Merlin, Helen-Joy, and Heather laughed too.

"That'll do him good! The water will wash his wounds. Anyone for mint tea?" Without waiting for an answer, Helen-Joy made her way up the stone steps behind the waterfall, returning with two mugs of steaming brew for her visitors.

"You two look after Lucky," she ordered. "I'll go and see what is going on elsewhere."

Chapter 6 – Disturbing Stories about Kerner

Helen-Joy took a look in her crystal ball, whilst Merlin and Heather tended Lucky's wounds. The soothsayer saw soldiers heading towards the forest. However, she did not feel any danger, because they carried the flag of Twydell. Nevertheless, it was clear to her that Merlin and his companions would need to go and see what the soldiers wanted before the day was out.

The three left Lucky in the care of Comet and the unicorns, and made their way towards the Brambles' home.

When the funny, topsy-turvy cottage came into sight, they could see everyone sitting outside. The three patients were sitting, propped up by pillows and cushions. They were still pale, although not quite so ghostly as the previous day. Two lay motionless, with the same vacant expressions on their sickly faces, but the third, Isaiah, looked slightly more alert.

The chattering seemed even louder than usual, and as Merlin, Helen-Joy, and Heather drew nearer, they saw a group of about twenty elves helping themselves to a large bowl of blackberry crumble and honey.

Fluffy lay curled up in the sun. The cat was near the elves but showed no interest whatsoever in them.

"I had no idea that there were so many elves in our forest," Maura told the three visitors. "Apparently, they have been leaving their homes in Kerner to get here."

She turned to the elves. "Tell Merlin about the weed-killer."

One of the elves told the story of how the Kernans had bought some weed-killer from sea traders.

"They are the same traders from whom they buy the drug which makes magical people senseless," the elf told Merlin.

The others, who had all heard the story earlier, became silent. It seemed they wanted to hear the story again, to make sure that they could believe their ears.

The little man told how the traders came from somewhere in the north. They sold the Kernans bags of weed-killer. Kerner did not have vast arable land like the Twydellers had, and the traders had told them that the weed-killer would not only destroy weeds but also promote the growth of potatoes, carrots, and other root vegetables. The Kernans thought that, by growing more of their own vegetables, they would be less reliant on the Twydellers for trade. However, the weed-killer seemed to be destroying the land.

The elf spoke with sadness, and tears appeared in his eyes as he described how the weed-killer was making the fairies and elves sick. Most of their kind had died. Those who survived had made their way to the safety of the Forbidden Forest. The other elves nodded to confirm that what their companion said was true, and they, too, shed tears of sorrow.

Merlin shook his head in dismay. "I, too, have a rather nefarious story to relate."

Helen-Joy took the old wizard's arm, as if to give him strength to tell his tale.

"Last night, I spoke to the pit pony. The poor creature was whipped sore in the mines, and in need of nourishment. I'm pleased to say that I believe he is recovering."

A chatter of voices expressed how pleased the magical people were, but the grim look on Merlin's face soon silenced them again.

Merlin continued gravely. "There are children working in the mines. Men bring them to the mines each morning, on leads attached to collars round their necks. The mine managers use the children to work in crevices which are too small for grown men."

They all gasped in horror at the thought of children working in the mines.

"How on earth can their mothers allow such a thing to happen?" asked Esmerelda. Her long dark hair shimmered in the sunlight as she shook her head in sadness. Glimmers of green sparked from her eyes.

"They might be orphans," replied Merlin. "In any case, the more we learn about Kerner, the worse it sounds. Helen-Joy has taken a look in her crystal ball and seen Twydell soldiers heading towards the forest. We must go and see what they want. May I borrow your broom, Great-Grandmother Bramble? I would like to allow Comet to rest today."

"Of course," replied the old witch, without hesitation.

Riding the borrowed broom, Merlin set off to the edge of the forest. With the exception of Maud and Farainne, the other Avalonians followed. Maura and Nora also had old brooms, and travelled with them. Allarond and Selogon, who were anxious to know what was going on, travelled along with Yzor and Jonathan.

When the group reached the edge of the forest, they peered through the bindweed, but there was nothing there except bison and mammoths grazing on the meadow grass. Nora's spell opened an entrance to the forest wall, and the Avalonians walked out into the meadow to watch the mighty beasts.

Maura and Nora held back; they had never stepped outside the forest. They were reluctant to do so now, but they stood, enjoying the sight of the huge animals which rarely came so far west. The Avalonians spotted riders in the distance. All except Merlin sat on the grass and waited for the horsemen to draw near.

The two sisters, Maura and Nora, decided to sit half in and half out of the opening, just as the little elf had stood half in and half out of their garden the day before. They took pleasure in the view, and pointed to parts of the open countryside which were not so easy to see from within the forest.

Merlin stood tall, scanning the landscape. At last, the Twydell standard could be recognised, fluttering behind its bearer. At the head of the group of soldiers, on a fine bay mare, was Prince Derrick. Prince Edward rode beside him on Challenger. Behind the two princes rode six Twydell soldiers.

The magical people stood as the horsemen approached.

"Good morning, Lord Merlin. Or is it afternoon? In any case, I hope you are well." Prince Derrick's smile was wide as he slid easily from his saddle. "Good day, my lords and ladies of Avalon, and other good people."

Derrick bowed towards Esmerelda and Allarond, who both nodded. They had no quarrel with the Prince of Twydell.

Maura and Nora were not sure what to do, but decided that they, too, should nod to the young prince.

"I have just escorted my sister, Jeanette, and the rest of the Kernan party to the border. She is now travelling to her new home with Prince Steven. My father asked me to return via the Forbidden Forest, to see if you would like us to escort you back to Dalton."

"He managed to prise himself away from Rosalie." Edward winked at Merlin and gave Derrick a sideways grin. "Actually, he only joined the escort because his father told him he had to. He would have much preferred to stay with Rosie."

"The question is, did Rosalie want Derrick to be prised away from her?" Merlin concealed his solemn feelings, smiling kindly at the young princes.

"Not really," admitted Edward.

"Please thank your father for thinking of us, Prince Derrick, but I do not believe any of us are likely to be leaving yet." Merlin turned to Allarond and Esmerelda, who nodded their agreement. He noticed that Esmerelda was biting her lip, as if to hold her tongue.

Merlin continued. "For my part, I wish to visit the dragons again and make sure that all is well with them."

"And we wish to stay with our kinfolk in the forest," the witch queen added meaningfully. She wanted to say much more, but she held back.

Tannus stood close to her and clasped her hand.

Allarond was about to agree but decided to keep quiet, as he thought it best that the Twydellers remain ignorant of the existence of elves in the forest.

226

"Did your parley go well?" Merlin asked politely, but before either of the princes could answer, Esmerelda released Tannus's hand and stepped forward.

It was no good. The witch queen could not stay quiet any longer, simply listening to pleasantries. She came straight to the point. "Tell me," she said as she leaned forward to look Prince Derrick directly in the face. "What did your father say to King Jeffrey about the state in which our kinfolk returned to their homes? I take it your sergeant reported the appalling state that they were in when he collected them."

Green sparks flashed in front of the young prince's face, and for a moment, he looked startled, and his hand automatically reached down for his sword.

Edward came forward to stand at Derrick's side. The situation was tense, but Edward stayed calm. It was he who answered Esmerelda.

"King Frederrick was called out of the meeting to speak to the sergeant who escorted the men back to the forest. When he returned, he asked everyone to leave the room because he needed to speak privately with King Jeffrey.

"We all went into the drawing room, but we could hear the shouting. Queen Elise and Queen Shirley-Poppy were sitting in the drawing room, sewing. They just continued chatting about the garden and the weather, as if nothing were going on, but the whole palace must have heard the row. When we were called back, the two kings sat there, drinking mugs of ale, as if nothing had happened."

Edward looked round. The atmosphere had lightened, and Tannus stepped forward to Esmerelda's side. The witch queen leaned against him.

Merlin watched the situation carefully, ready to issue stunning spells if he needed to do so. However, to stun the Queen of the Witches and the Prince of Twydell would be a last resort. Such an action would not be easily forgotten by either.

Derrick spoke. At first, his speech faltered, but as he gained confidence, he spoke like the leader he would one day be.

"Please remember, Kerner and Twydell are neighbours. We are now joined by the wedding rings of Jeanette and Steven. We work together to protect our borders, and our people trade with each other. My father has asked me to inform you that King Jeffrey has told him that he was unaware that wizards were held as prisoners. He will order his prisons to be searched to ensure there are no more magical people being held."

"And will he see whether any of my kind are being held in cages and sold in the markets like pets?" Now it was King Allarond who could no longer hold back his anger. The little elf had used his wand to raise his voice. Now he stood with hands on hips, glowering with rage.

The two princes and the soldiers looked confused.

"I have met an elf from Kerner," Allarond told them. "He described how elves and fairies are captured by Kernans, held in cages, and displayed like ornaments! He told us that the poor people they captured were forced to drink drugs to prevent them using their magic. The drugs killed many of my kind and many fairies. My kind died just so that humans could show off a cute little being in a cage!"

The two princes looked at each other with horrified expressions on their faces. They continued to listen in silence to the elf king's tirade of anger.

"The elf I spoke to believes that the three wizards who have been released are suffering the effects of similar drugs."

"We have also heard that children are used to work in the Kerner mines." The look on Merlin's face was serious as he spoke, but, like Edward, he also felt for the young Prince Derrick. *It should be King Jeffrey facing these angry people and their accusations, not this boy!*

Derrick shook his head in disbelief, but then he looked Merlin straight in the face. "I cannot answer for what happens in Kerner, but I can assure you that this does not happen in Twydell," the young man stated firmly. He turned to his men. "Do you know anything about this? Tell me honestly because if I find out that you are hiding anything from me, you will be punished."

The soldiers looked at each other.

One spoke. "I have heard of this practice but never seen any small people in cages myself. My mother lives in Thorncombe, a town just this side of the border. She told me men from Kerner come, offering rewards for small people. For my part, I swear that I had never seen a fairy or elf before the people of Avalon came to the royal wedding. My mother also told me that the same men offer to take orphans and unwanted urchins off the hands of the town councils. The councils would otherwise have to pay for their keep. The Thorncombe Town Council refused the offer because they did not know what would happen to the children. I do not know whether other towns have given up their orphans to these men."

Derrick crouched down to look directly into the face of the little elf king. "Lord Allarond, I can assure you that neither my father nor his advisers know anything of the practice of imprisoning your kind. I will tell him about this vile practice upon my return. I have no doubt that he will take the necessary steps to make such practice a criminal act in Twydell. However, we Twydellers cannot answer for Kerner. Having said that, I believe that I can say that my father and King Arthur left King Jeffrey of Kerner in no doubt as to their feelings about further harm coming to people of magic."

He remained crouched at Allarond's side but looked up to face the other Avalonians. "The act of making children work in the mines is abhorrent to me, and would be so to other Twydellers as well. We will make our feelings known to the Kernans. My sister is a kind person who loves children. She does not know much about fairies or elves, but I am positive she would do all she could to prevent them being harmed. I will send a personal message to her to make sure she is fully aware of what has transpired in the past. If it is in Jeanette's power, I am sure she will do all she can to help any children forced into labour. I am sure she will do all she can to stop people harming magical beings."

"Thank you," said Merlin. "Your father is indeed a man of wisdom and diplomacy, and I can see that his son has inherited his talents."

Esmerelda continued to hold her tongue, and her glittering eyes began to soften and turn back to the colour of moss. Tannus put his arm round her waist.

"Your offer to escort us back to Dalton is most kind," Merlin said. "However, my colleagues wish to stay and help nurse our kinsmen. They will not be ready to leave for a while. As for myself, I will travel to the dragons' lair tomorrow to see how the little one is. Perhaps when your father raises these matters to the King of Kerner, he might just mention my proposed visit to the dragons."

Prince Derrick nodded his understanding, and a flicker of a smile passed across his face. The reference to the dragons was to be a reminder of Merlin's friendship with the creatures that could bring terror to Kerner.

"Do you know when King Arthur will leave for Avalon?" Merlin asked.

"His party will leave the day after tomorrow. I will go with him and stay in Merlport for a while, to learn more about your country," replied Prince Derrick.

"And to be close to Rosalie," added Edward, with a grin, as he tried to lighten the atmosphere.

Derrick blushed.

Merlin smiled a knowing smile. "I am unlikely to see you before you leave for Avalon, so I bid you and all who travel with you a safe journey. Please tell your father that I will call on him before returning to Merlport."

The princes started to say their goodbyes to each of the Avalonian folk. Derrick nodded towards Esmerelda and Tannus, and they returned the gesture.

Edward approached Esmerelda and gave her a gentle kiss on the cheek. This time, she gave him a little peck too. "Tell Rosalie

I'm glad she's getting on so well with Derrick. He seems a nice enough chappie. I'm sorry I frightened him."

"You frightened everyone. Now everyone will know how scary you are!" Edward winked at her. "We are all horrified to hear how the wizards from the Forbidden Forest were treated by the Kernans, but please don't blame the Twydellers."

"We're not," said Tannus, still standing close Esmerelda. He drew her closer and felt her body taking deep breaths to calm her wrath. "How did you get on with King Jeffrey?"

"He's a cold fish," Edward answered.

"Good description," Tannus said with a smile. "I thought that wife of his looked a bit like a big cod, the way she kept opening and closing her mouth and then pouting."

Edward was relieved to hear Esmerelda let out a giggle. "Shh!" he urged. "I have to go. We'll catch up when we next meet in Merlport."

The other riders were ready to leave. The Prince of Avalon swiftly mounted Challenger, and took his place next to the Prince of Twydell. The two young men and the soldiers saluted the magical folk, and then rode off. The two future kings rode, side by side, at the head of the soldiers.

"Those two boys look truly regal," Merlin said to Esmerelda and Tannus. "I wish Frederrick and Arthur long reigns, but both of those lads will make good leaders when the time comes."

Tannus looked at his witch, with the eyes of love. "Well, let's hope that Prince Steven of Kerner will be a good leader too. I don't think King Jeffrey will last much longer if my good lady here gets too close to him."

Esmerelda almost smiled at her lover but said nothing. Like the other magic people, she waved goodbye to Edward and the Twydellers. Maura and Nora felt rather overwhelmed by the encounter but copied everyone else by waving to the departing humans.

Once everyone was inside, bindweed spread and sealed the entrance, as if it had never been opened. Yzor and Jonathan watched in awe. The father and son herbologist wizards were fascinated as the ageing Bramble sisters uttered their spell.

The forest always sang to the chorus of birds, but as they approached the cottage, they could hear another strange but lovely musical sound.

"What's that?" asked Esmerelda, but none of them had ever heard anything like it before.

The sight which met them was of equal surprise. The Bramble family and Helen-Joy sat in a semicircle, in front of a group of tiny musicians. About fifteen elves had arranged themselves on the lawn. Some played violins; others, cellos made of wood and strung with the plaited strands of cobwebs. Still others had made pipes out of reeds or the stems of plants. Another tapped a strange instrument, made of a long string of snail shells, with a twig. The shells tinkled like bells as they vibrated. Two fairies, who also played violins, sat in the hydrangea bush above the elves.

When the orchestra finished, their audience clapped and asked them to play again. As they finished a second ensemble of ethereal music, Dilly brought out a batch of home-made hazelnut scones. She had lavished them with goat's milk butter, and cut them into small pieces for the elves and fairies. She then returned to the kitchen and fetched more for the other folk.

The smell of hazelnut scones filled the air. Heather did a little dance of glee when she saw her father sniffing the air and turning his head towards the aroma exuding from the kitchen.

Sally placed a piece of buttered scone in her husband's mouth. Isaiah's improvement was noticeable. He munched the scone, swallowed, and opened his mouth for more.

The music has done them a wealth of good," Farainne told the arrivals. "I am an elf, but I have never seen such amazing instruments or heard such wonderful music before. We must teach our people how to play such delightful melodies."

After eating and drinking, and spending some time discussing the day's events, Merlin decided to walk home with Helen-Joy. He wanted to get a good night's sleep and an early start in the morning. He asked to borrow Great-Grandmother Bramble's old broom again, promising to bring it back safely.

The old witch was only too pleased to be of assistance. "I no longer use the broom myself," she told him.

"Good job!" Tannus whispered to Esmerelda. All the Avalonians knew the fate of the last broom, which Merlin had borrowed when he went to visit the dragons.

Chapter 7 – Thunderbirds and Dragons

The next morning Merlin flew high into the mountains where it would have been impossible for Comet to carry him. Yzor travelled with him. However, they did not head towards the dragons' lair. Instead, they made their way towards the cave where Merlin had previously found Storm and Thor with the baby dragon.

Merlin had hoped that they would not be there; that they would have moved far away from the dragons and their wrath, as he had advised. So, it was disappointing to see that a rain cloud hovered above the mountain. The thunderbirds attracted rain and the cloud indicated that the pair still lived in the same place.

As he approached the cave he saw the pair, at the entrance to their home, flapping their wings in welcome to his approach. The wizard was pleased to see that that their wings and tail feathers were gradually growing back. They had been badly burnt by the baby dragon. However, it was worrying to find the giant birds were still living so close to the dragons.

Merlin introduced Yzor to the giant birds, who were delighted to receive visitors. Storm tried to be a good hostess, offering the visitors raw meat. The wizards tactfully refused, saying that it was not long since they had breakfasted.

The thunderbirds told the wizards (or at least they told Merlin, as Yzor did not speak bird) that their new feathers were growing well, but that they had only attempted to fly short distances. Fortunately, there was a lot of wildlife on the side of the mountain where they lived, so there was no shortage of food. They said they did not believe that the dragons had travelled far lately. The birds felt they were safe as long as they flew west, in the opposite direction to the dragons' lair. Nevertheless, now that their feathers were growing back, they would soon seek a new home as far from the dragons as possible.

Merlin was still concerned for the birds' safety. He thought that the dragons probably did not currently travel far because they did not want to leave their baby for very long. Soon, however, the dragons might be teaching the little fellow to fly. He begged the thunderbirds to be careful.

Yzor was fascinated by the birds and wanted to delay their departure, but Merlin hurried him away. The herbologist was very disappointed. He wanted to stay longer and learn the language Merlin shared with the thunderbirds.

The wizards bid the thunderbirds goodbye but promised to come back soon. They said that they would return after they had visited the dragons, to advise the birds how long they might remain safe in their Twydell nest.

It wasn't a long flight to the dragons' lair. Merlin called his greeting from outside, in case surprise visitors were welcomed by a tongue of flame. However, when the family heard his voice, they all came out to greet him and bid the two wizards come inside and enjoy the warmth of their home. The wizards accepted the invitation, but before entering the cave, they carefully placed their brooms on a ledge above the entrance. On his last visit young Drago had set fire to Merlin's borrowed broom and he didn't want the same thing to happen again.

Ajax and Blitzen had named their son Drago. He was a lively little character. His parents were very proud of the fact that he was only a few months old but could throw flames almost four feet in front of himself. They told Drago to demonstrate, but when he did, Merlin and Yzor had to force themselves back against the wall of the cave, for fear of being burnt alive.

"Do you go out very much?" Merlin asked casually.

"Not really," replied Blitzen, the blue female dragon. "We want to spend as much time as possible with little Drago. After all, we will never get these toddler days back again."

"There is plenty of food here on the mountain," continued Ajax, the green male. "And there seems to be a good variety this year. We never did travel far. Dalton is about the farthest we've travelled – except, of course, when we were looking for our egg. Have you seen any more of those thunderbirds?"

"I can't say I have," replied Merlin, which wasn't exactly a lie – he hadn't seen more of them, only the two he'd already met. He then changed the subject by telling the dragons about the men from the Forbidden Forest who had been released from a prison in Kerner. He went on to tell them about the fairies and elves who had been captured and put in cages, and the children who worked in mines. In fact, Merlin talked about anything he could think of – except the thunderbirds.

Yzor, who had no idea what they were talking about, looked on incredulously. He had been entranced by the thunderbirds, but the dragons were even more fascinating. He envied Merlin and his ability to speak to so many different creatures, and resolved to learn those languages too.

Eventually, Merlin drew the visit to an end by saying, "I am glad to see that you are both well and that Drago is growing into such a fine young dragon. We would like to stay longer, but we must leave you now. We wish to get back to the forest before nightfall."

Once again, Merlin had difficulty getting Yzor to leave. Yzor had never met a dragon before and, although he was unable to speak their tongue, he tried to talk with them by using sign language. The dragons found Yzor's attempts to communicate with them amusing.

"I hope your people soon recover," said Blitzen, as she batted her eyelids. Her long eyelashes framed her blue eyes as she added, "If they are as nice as you and Yzor, they are welcome to come and see us. We don't get many visitors."

The dragons waved goodbye to Merlin and Yzor. However, they were disappointed that Merlin did not show off by performing some acrobatics on his broom, as he had done on his last visit.

"Next time I see him, I'll show him a trick or two," said Blitzen. "He's not the only one who can pretend to be an acrobat."

Ajax put his wing round his wife's shoulders, and, together with little Drago, they went back inside their cave.

Chapter 8 – Merlin's Leaving Party

Lennox and his mares were grazing, along with the other beasts, in the meadow outside the forest. Comet was with them, enjoying the fresh meadow grass too. Heather, along with Yzor's son Jonathan, held the entrance open for them. Jonathan was keen to learn as much as he could about the plants of the forest, and Heather was teaching him all she knew.

When the wizards came into view, Comet and the unicorns trotted back into the forest and along the pathway. Merlin and Yzor hovered along behind, riding their brooms. Once they were sure the forest was securely sealed, Heather and Jonathan followed.

"We are all going back to our cottage," Heather informed the arriving wizards. "We are going to have a leaving party for you before you set off tomorrow, Merlin."

"Am I leaving tomorrow?"

"Helen-Joy says you are."

"Then I must be." The old wizard sighed. He seemed resigned to his fate, even though he was not looking forward to another journey so quickly. *Why does Helen-Joy think I should be leaving so soon? What has happened?*

Before they reached the Brambles' cottage, they could hear the strange haunting music of the orchestra again. As they came nearer, they were met by the appetising aromas of home cooking.

Everyone, including the unicorns, was assembled on the lawn outside the cottage. Lucky was grazing with the goats in the field behind the cottage. They all smiled and nodded, but were reluctant to speak because they did not wish to interrupt the music. The orchestra continued to play, and Merlin noticed that its membership had increased, now including a fairy harpist and more strings of snail and freshwater oyster shells. The strings of shells did not really need anyone to play them, as they could just tinkle in the evening breeze. *This is all so beautiful. Why can't I stay here forever? I am an old man, and I am tired.*

"Aren't they lovely?" Helen-Joy whispered to Merlin as she planted a kiss on his cheek. "Alfred calls it therapeutic music. Allarond says that the souls of all three men have lifted over the last few days."

"Look!" shouted Heather.

The music stopped, and everyone looked round to see Heather's father pointing at the orchestra of elves and fairies. They all clapped their hands, partly in applause to the musicians and partly in delight at Isaiah's recognition of what was going on around him.

"I hear I'm leaving tomorrow." Merlin spoke in a low voice to Helen-Joy. *Please tell me it is not true.*

"Yes. While you were out of the way today, I slept on my pillow of dreams. I'll tell you more later, but you are needed elsewhere," she whispered as the orchestra started up again. "I am sorry, my love, but your journey is a necessary one."

Merlin sighed but enjoyed the rest of his evening with the Avalonians and the people of the forest. When the music finished, good food and wine ensued. There was a lot of chatter, and so much to talk about – the magical music; Isaiah's noticeable improvement; the large beasts which were grazing so close to the forest. With much excitement, Yzor recounted his meetings with the thunderbirds and the dragons.

"If I am leaving tomorrow, I'd best not stay too late," Merlin told Helen-Joy. "On our way home, you can tell me what you have seen which must hasten my departure."

Helen-Joy nodded.

The couple were saying their goodbyes when Tannus stopped them. "Wait, Merlin! We have a leaving present for you." And so saying, he picked up a broom from behind a nearby tree and presented it to the old wizard. Daisy and buttercup chains were wound round the gift, as was the custom when magical people gave presents to each other. "We all thought it was about time you had a new one. It should be very powerful because we have all had a hand in making it and cast our own spells to help preserve it."

Merlin was overwhelmed. He felt his heart swell. He accepted the broom with much pleasure. It was not often the old wizard was speechless, but this was one such occasion. Instead of voicing his appreciation, he simply shed tears of gratitude.

Everyone clapped, and even Isaiah seemed to be trying to join in. He tried to bring his hands together, but they did not quite reach. Instead, he gave the appearance of someone imitating a bird flapping its wings. Sally threw her arms round her husband, tears of joy in her eyes, and kissed his forehead.

Before they left, Helen-Joy gave Merlin a sealed piece of parchment, which she told him he must not open until his task was ended. She asked Merlin to swear, in front of all present, that he would not open the parchment until his mission was over.

"Very well," the old wizard said with a sigh. "I swear in front of all my friends, old and new, that I will not open this sealed parchment till my mission is complete." However, he added, "At the moment, I don't know what my mission is. Nevertheless, if the finest soothsayer I have ever met tells me I must leave, then leave I must!"

The couple walked home, arm in arm. On the way, Helen-Joy told Merlin that she dreamed he was needed in a land far away. She said that the ring of Twydell was in danger, but could not understand how or why. She saw the great beasts of the valleys moving to the higher land in the mountains, but did not feel that the signs were all good.

"I am sorry that I cannot tell you more, but I feel distracted. What I do know is that you must leave me again. However, I feel sure you will return, unharmed."

Helen-Joy pulled Merlin a little closer and felt the security of the old wizard's presence.

❀ ✦ ❀ ✦ ❀ ✦ ❀ ✦ ❀ ✦ ❀

The sun was just rising when Merlin set off on his new broom. Heather and Jonathan were waiting for him on the pathway, and hovered along behind him until they reached the spot where the forest bindweed could be opened to allow him to depart.

Heather and Jonathan uttered the spell together. However, instead of going back to the cottage, after Merlin's departure, they sat in the open entrance for a long time. They enjoyed the sight of the wild horses prancing in the dawn sunlight and rabbits frolicking in the meadow. The mighty mammoths just ignored the activity and continued to feed hungrily on the sweet clover which grew in abundance. Meanwhile, the bison headed steadily, in single file, farther up into the mountains.

The pair sat there for so long that Sally came to look for them. She saw her daughter and the young herbologist silhouetted against the morning sun at the wooded entrance. Scolding them for their tardiness, she bid them to hasten closing the entrance to return the forest to safety.

Part 2:
A Secret
Never to Be Told

Chapter 9 – The Journey through Twydell

The new broomstick was far speedier than the one Merlin had borrowed from Willy. The old wizard was making good time, and would be in Dalton by late afternoon.

Blitzen saw him as he travelled past the base of the mountain where the dragons lived. The blue dragon was eager to show him how well she could fly. She remembered Merlin's antics on the broom that her child had damaged by fire, and she wanted to give him a demonstration of her own acrobatic skills.

She flew down to meet him, and Merlin gave her a friendly wave. The next thing he knew, she was flying along beside him, making figures of eight in the air.

At first, Merlin found her antics amusing. He made a few skilful moves himself, even flying upside down for a while. But, as they neared Dalton, he could see people coming out and pointing at them. He knew the people of Dalton would be understandably worried to see the dragon.

The Twydellers were puzzled because the dragon's flying antics seemed nothing like the start of any of the previous vicious assaults. The sight of the wizard, flying just beneath the large creature which had wreaked so much devastation, made them feel less anxious. Nevertheless, archers took their places and made ready to fire.

Merlin called out a warning to Blitzen. The huge beast understood the alarm in the old man's voice. She rose high up into the sky by means of a series of somersaults. She then waved goodbye to Merlin. The wizard breathed a sigh of relief. The last thing he wanted was more trouble between the dragons and the Twydellers.

King Frederrick and Queen Elise were waiting for him in the Dalton Palace courtyard. They had watched the dragon approaching and, like their people, were worried that it might attack. As Blitzen flew off, the archers were ordered to stand down.

"What extraordinary behaviour!" The king sounded relieved.

Queen Elise looked bewildered.

"The dragon was just trying to be friendly." Merlin sighed. "A good sign, I think."

Merlin spent the evening talking to Frederrick. Queen Elise sat with them, murmuring her agreements and making comment from time to time. She fussed over Merlin, making sure his cup was kept filled and plenty of food was available for his plate.

The old king related what he and Arthur had talked about before the Avalonians made their journey home. Frederrick told the wizard that people from Kerner and Twydell were continuing to move to Avalon, where they thought that they would be better protected from the dragons and the Trajaens. He was disappointed that Twydellers thought it safer in Avalon, but had only good wishes for those who had left. He hoped that the migration of Twydellers would bring the two countries closer together. He had advised Arthur to start a new settlement on the other side of the Great Forest, where the giants lived, to secure the northern border.

Frederrick went on to say that he had told Arthur that Twydell had long wanted to annex the Brewins' land, now known as Avalon, but the recurring attacks by the Trajaens had left him without the resources to do so. He was glad that the Avalonians were now able to inhabit the land because a secure Avalon meant better protection from The North for Twydell. The lands known simply as The North were inhabited by unfriendly people who fought among themselves.

As they sipped sweet dessert wine, Frederrick continued to tell Merlin about his concerns regarding the northern border. He thought that trouble in the north could easily spill over the border into Avalon or Twydell.

The old king was aware that the northerners, like the Twydellers, had also tried to annex the Brewin land. There had been some sort of battle with the giants in the Great Forest. He did not know how the problems had arisen; he simply knew that the northerners had withdrawn after a battle.

Next, they spoke about the Forbidden Forest and the people who lived there. The Forbidden Forest was on the other side of Frederrick's kingdom, close to the border with Kerner. The king promised that he would pass a new law to make it a criminal act to capture any fairy or elf, and another law stopping the sale of children. King Jeffrey had left before Derrick had returned to tell him about his encounter with the magical people. He had sent a message to King Jeffrey, telling him of the stories he had heard about the mistreatment of elves and fairies, and the use of children in the tin mines. He was waiting for a reply.

Queen Elise tut-tutted, shaking her head. "Terrible," she muttered. "Terrible."

Nevertheless, Frederrick said he would be surprised if King Jeffrey was aware of such practices, but that he might just prefer to "turn a blind eye", as the king phrased it. He considered Prince Steven to be a genuine, if not misguided, person. He felt sure that the prince loved his daughter, Jeanette, and that they would be happy. The exchange of rings would strengthen the ties between Twydell and Kerner. Jeanette would help her husband to understand points of view different from those of his father.

"Jeanette will be a good influence on Steven," said Queen Elise, listening to every word, but speaking as if to herself.

The king went on to tell Merlin that he was delighted in the way Rosalie and Derrick had taken to each other. After asking her father's permission, Derrick had slipped an engagement ring on Rosalie's finger before the party from Avalon had left for home.

"Another ring – this one to tie Twydell to Avalon!" The king smiled triumphantly, raising his mug of ale in the air.

Merlin raised his own mug and clinked it against Frederrick's. "Congratulations! I hope the union between Avalon and Twydell will be a long and happy one."

"They make such a lovely couple." Queen Elise beamed with pride.

Merlin was very pleased. He liked Frederrick's company and would have liked to stay longer, but it was not possible. He confided to the king that he must leave early the next morning because Helen-Joy, the soothsayer, had told him that his presence was needed urgently in Avalon, although she did not know why. He thought it wise not to mention her prediction about the ring of Twydell. He was sorry to leave so soon, but he trusted the soothsayer's words.

Despite an early start, and a swift broom, it was evening before Merlin reached the small village of Birdsmoorgate. He had taken a slight detour, and, although he had not visited the village before, the inhabitants knew who he was without introduction. The picturesque little village was near the border with Avalon, and only a few miles from the border with The North. It would be the Twydell community nearest the spot which King Frederrick had suggested as an appropriate place to build Avalon's second town.

Merlin ate in a tavern and chatted with the locals. They told the now familiar story that a large number of wild beasts were moving into Twydell and Avalon. The beasts appeared to be leaving The North, but they did not know why. They had also noticed that, for no apparent reason, there were fewer birds than usual for this time of year.

Merlin left Birdsmoorgate the following morning and arrived back in Merlport in the late evening.

King Arthur was surprised to see him so soon, and without any of his travelling companions. Merlin told him that Queen Esmerelda and the other wizards had stayed behind to help nurse the three brothers. However, despite his desire to stay longer in the Forbidden Forest, the soothsayer had told him to return to Merlport, with haste.

Arthur was not aware of any reason which necessitated the wizard's immediate return. Nonetheless, he was pleased to see his friend and keen to learn more about what had happened to the wizards from the Forbidden Forest.

Arthur listened intently to all that Merlin had learnt in the Forbidden Forest and other parts of Twydell. He, too, was concerned about the stories of children, fairies, and elves held as prisoners in Kerner. He was sad to learn that fairies and elves were dying from weed-killer.

In contrast, Arthur had better news to relate to Merlin. He told him that Prince Derrick had gone to Bowers Gifford to see the royal family's villa there. His father had thought that it might be a good place for him and Rosalie to live when they were married. Arthur and Gilda liked this idea, especially as Bowers Gifford was much closer to Merlport than Dalton.

Merlin laughed when Arthur told him that the prince was reluctant to leave Merlport. However, the young man knew better than to disobey his father's instructions.

Good ale and days of travelling had taken their toll on the old wizard, and he bid Arthur goodnight. He was disappointed that he appeared to have journeyed back to Merlport so soon, for no apparent reason. He ate a hearty supper and then took to his bed for a good night's sleep.

Chapter 10 – Seven Magpies

The next morning, Merlin took the opportunity to rest his weary body and lie in bed until late. When he got up, it was already after noon, and he went to look for Rosalie. He wanted to assure himself that she was happy with her intended marriage to Prince Derrick.

The young princess was in the new Garden of Remembrance, which was still being created, not far behind Arthur's house. The blacksmith had made a pair of wrought-iron gates for the garden, called the Alexandrew Gates, after his two sons, Alexander and Andrew, who had died during the battle with the Trajaens. White rose bushes had been planted in memory of each of the Avalonians who had died. Rosalie had been out in the meadow that morning to dig up some wild forget-me-nots. Now she was busy planting them round the border of each of the rose bushes.

"Congratulations!" said Merlin as he sat on the grass beside Rosalie. He started playing with the little white kitten which had followed her to the garden. "So, let me see this wonderful ring I have heard so much about."

"I would not wear my gold and diamond ring when I'm gardening! I am always careful to put it back in its box, on my dressing table, when I'm working."

"So, how do you like the idea of going to live in Bowers Gifford?"

"I've never been there, but as long as I am going to live with Derrick, then I will be happy."

The two chatted amicably for an hour or so whilst Rosalie worked. The kitten had grown tired of playing; it curled up on Merlin's cloak and went to sleep.

Rosalie put her trowel to one side, and stretched. "Oh, my back! I wish there were an easier way of putting these plants in. You don't seem very busy. Would you mind helping me with these last half dozen?"

"Why didn't you ask before?" Merlin smiled. He drew his staff out of the deep pocket in his cloak, trying not to disturb the kitten as he did so. He merely pointed his staff at six points in the flower bed, and the earth moved aside. He then pointed his staff at each of the six plants, in turn. The plants lifted out of the wooden tray in which they had been carried, and placed themselves in the holes.

"A little water, next."

As Merlin pointed his staff again, the watering can lifted itself off the ground, poured water into each of the holes in which the forget-me-nots stood, and then replaced itself on the ground.

Finally, the wizard pointed the staff at each of the holes, in turn, and the earth fell in effortlessly round the plants.

Rosalie watched. Her face was a picture of exasperation. "Oh, Merlin! Why didn't you do that before? You could have saved me hours of work!"

The old man laughed. "I don't like to interfere. Besides, I thought you were enjoying yourself. Tell me, Rosalie, do you have no magic yourself? Have you not inherited any of your mother's skills?"

"If I had, I wouldn't have broken my back digging up flowers in the meadow and re-planting them here!"

"Have you tried?"

"Yes, as a matter of fact, I have tried many times. Unfortunately, I do not take after my mother. If I did, I would turn you into a toad for laughing at me!"

The two sauntered back to Arthur's house. Rosalie was interested in listening to Merlin's stories about his adventures in Twydell. The little white kitten followed behind.

Merlin knew he would be invited to enjoy a mug of beer with his old friend. Sure enough, as soon as Rosalie opened the door, Arthur called his friend in and took two mugs off the shelf. The king filled the mugs from the barrel of dark ale from which they had been drinking the night before.

"I'll go and fetch my ring for you to see." Rosalie ran up the stairs to her room. She was eager to show off the ring of Twydell.

Arthur and Merlin were sipping their ale when they heard a cry from Rosalie. They rose to see her running back down the stairs. She was clearly in distress. "My ring is missing. Someone has stolen my ring!"

"But I've been here all morning," said Arthur. "No one has entered the house since Merlin's visit earlier, and no one could have passed me to go upstairs. Did you leave your window open?"

"Yes," cried Rosalie. "But only since I got back from the meadow. I went upstairs when I got back, to fetch a hat to keep the sun off my head. I opened the window because it was stuffy in my room. The ring was there then. I know because I stood and looked at it for a while, admiring the diamonds glittering in the sunlight."

"Then someone must have got in through the window!" replied Arthur. "I still cannot understand how, because your window is just above the one in this room. I would have seen anyone who tried to put a ladder against the wall."

"If someone had entered by the window, they would have been seen from the Garden of Remembrance," said Merlin. "I was sat on the grass facing the back of your house much of the time, and I saw no one."

Tears started to pour down Rosalie's face.

"Are you sure you did not move the ring?" asked Arthur, starting to get angry. "Have you looked everywhere, to see if you put it somewhere else and then forgot?"

"I have not put it anywhere else! It was in its box, on top of the dressing table, in front of the window!" Rosalie wailed.

"What will King Frederrick think when he learns that you have lost the ring of Twydell after such a short time?" Arthur's anger continued to rise.

"There were some fairies in the garden earlier. Let us find them and ask whether they saw anything suspicious," suggested Merlin.

The three hurried back into the garden, followed by the white kitten. A group of fairies lay in the shade, behind one of the rose bushes. They sat up when they saw Rosalie coming towards them, with her tears falling fast, and the serious looks on the faces of the two men.

Rosalie explained what had happened. "Please tell me if you saw anything suspicious, or if you have any ideas as to what has happened to my ring," she begged.

The fairies talked among themselves for a while, and then one of them, whose name was Hawthorn, spoke. "The magpies like Rosalie, so they always make sure that six of them are close by when she is in the garden. However, this morning, there were seven."

"Six magpies! Seven magpies! What possible difference could that make?" asked Arthur irritably as his pulse throbbed faster and faster.

Merlin repeated the old rhyme: "One for Sorrow, Two for Joy, Three for a Girl and Four for a Boy, Five is for Silver, Six is for Gold, and Seven is for a Secret Never to be Told."

Arthur shook his head with annoyance, but Merlin remained patient.

"Do you speak magpie?" Merlin asked the fairies. "If you do, please, would you ask them whether they saw anyone near Rosalie's bedroom window this morning?"

The fairies chattered again among themselves. This time it was Celandine who spoke. "We do speak magpie, and we heard them asking the seventh where it had come from. We didn't hear its reply. The stranger was a lot thinner than the other magpies, and we noticed him on the roof of Arthur's house. We saw it drop down onto the window ledge, just after you and Rosalie left the garden. We did not see it enter the window, nor did we see it again, but we weren't really looking. We will speak to the magpies for you, and try to find out where the stranger lives."

256

"Thank you," replied Merlin. "Magpies do like collecting bright shiny things. I can't imagine our local birds stealing it if they like Rosalie so much that they try to bring her gold. But it is possible that the strange magpie took it."

The fairies flew off to find the magpies.

Meanwhile, Arthur was becoming more agitated. "I will order every bird's nest in Avalon to be searched," he snapped.

"I should wait." Merlin tried to pacify the king. "Let the fairies find out if the magpies can tell us more."

Arthur didn't calm down, but he did not issue any orders to search birds' nests either.

Rosalie continued to sob. "How can I possibly tell Derrick I've lost his ring? What will King Frederrick and Queen Elise think of me?"

Just like any other young girl in distress, she then ran off to find her mother. The kitten, of course, followed behind.

Merlin sat patiently in the shade of a tall tree, awaiting the fairies' return. He felt as if every muscle in his body still ached from his long journey. It was good to rest.

Arthur had returned home and brought back a chair to sit on. He was afraid that if he sat on the grass, he would not be able to get up again, and he did not want the embarrassment of asking someone to help. He sat in the shade, brooding. He looked alert each time he saw a creature flying nearby, in case it was the fairies coming back with news.

After weeping on her mother's shoulder for an hour, Rosalie had also returned to the garden. She was trying to take her mind off the missing ring by deadheading the white rose bushes.

At last, the fairies returned, bringing with them one of the magpies. "This is Bertie." Hawthorne introduced the bird. "Bertie was here this morning. He tells us that the seventh magpie did not come from around here. He was looking for a new home for his family because there was not enough food where he lived. He had spent a few days in Merlport and had eaten well. He said he would visit Rosalie's garden this morning to see if she had left any breadcrumbs. After that, he was going to make the journey home. He was looking for something nice to take back to his parents to cheer them up."

Merlin had more questions for the magpie. "Please ask Bertie whether the strange magpie told him where he lives, and whether he took Rosalie's ring."

Hawthorn chattered to Bertie. Merlin listened carefully, trying to understand the language. An expert in creature languages, Merlin was able to learn very quickly.

"Bertie says that the strange magpie lived somewhere the other side of the Great Forest. He said that the usual crops of wheat and barley had all died, and there was very little food left. His parents were very sick when he left, as were many other birds. He says that he does not know what happened to Rosalie's ring. Magpies love shiny things, but none of the Merlport magpies would steal from her."

"I am sure they would not!" Merlin replied.

Hawthorne translated Merlin's words, but the comment seemed to annoy the magpie.

"Bertie says if you believe that the Merlport magpies did not steal the ring, why is Rosalie's white kitten searching their nests?"

Merlin was taken aback. "Searching the magpies' nests?"

"And the jackdaw nests," added Hawthorne. "Bertie says the magpies and jackdaws are most upset!"

Rosalie and Arthur looked puzzled.

"I expect the kitten is just being a playful kitten, climbing trees," Merlin replied tactfully. "Please ask Bertie to apologise to the magpies and the jackdaws for us. In fact, let me try myself!"

Merlin spoke to Bertie, and the magpie felt honoured that the famous wizard was trying to learn his language. He accepted the apology and said he would pass it on to the other birds. However, he still thought that the white kitten's actions were somewhat odd.

Merlin, Arthur, and Rosalie thanked the fairies and Bertie for helping them, and told them that Rosalie would look for the white kitten and take it home.

"And I'll leave some breadcrumbs in the garden for you, Bertie!" she called back as she left, hoping the magpie would understand. She thought he did because Bertie flapped his wings before flying off.

"Now I know why Helen-Joy sent me home," Merlin said with a sigh. "To look for a ring! I am disappointed. Nevertheless, I suppose I had better be on my way to the northern border to see if I can find it. I don't think there is a lot of hope, though."

Arthur decided that he would travel with the wizard. "The building of Arthurton is beginning on the other side of the Great Forest, and I need to visit the site. I will go to see how the new settlement is being planned. Migrants from Twydell are moving there, and I should be seen. These people need to know who their new king is. I have to see how they are getting along with our own people. I don't like leaving Merlport while Esmerelda is still in the Forbidden Forest, but I'll leave Edward in charge while I'm away. I fear it will not be long before Edward is king."

"That will not be the case for some time to come," Merlin said with confidence. "I have left Comet in the Forbidden Forest, with the unicorns, so I will fly on my new broom."

"No need," replied Arthur. "We'll take the new golden carriage. It's very comfortable and travels quite fast. There will be plenty of room on the roof to carry your new broom."

Chapter 11 – Arthurton

Arthur and Merlin left at first light the following morning. Two men accompanied the pair, a driver and a scout. They wanted to make sure that there were sufficient men left in Merlport, in case the Trajaens attacked again.

Before departing, Merlin briefed Wormald the Wise. Wormald had not been happy that the leader of the wizards and the king were departing together. He decided to call as many of his brethren together as he could to ensure that Merlport had sufficient protection. Merlin and Arthur thanked the wise wizard.

The carriage travelled at a steady pace. The small party camped overnight and then hurried on the next day. When they reached the site of Arthurton, they were relieved to see that all their people were well and working hard together. There seemed to be more people than expected, and progress on the new settlement was taking place faster than anticipated. Foundations had been put in place to support several of the dwellings still to be built.

The people at the settlement were pleased that their king and the famous wizard Merlin had come to visit. George, whom Arthur had appointed to lead the settlers, stopped work to update the visitors on all the news. He told the visitors that some people, who had lived in the small hamlets on the northern side of the border, had also joined them.

George repeated some strange tales that he had heard from the new settlers. They had told him that the fields in the north no longer bore crops. The big beasts which had provided winter food for them in the past were leaving, heading to the sweeter grasslands in Avalon. Families were worried that they would go hungry if they stayed in The North, and this explained why they had crossed the border to live in the new settlement of Arthurton.

Merlin nodded sagely. The story of animals leaving the north was the same tale he had heard in Birdsmoorgate. If the northern lands were no longer arable, then it followed that there might not be grass either. This would explain why so many beasts were making their way, through Avalon, to the Twydell mountains.

George went on to tell Arthur and Merlin that the northern tribes were now all ruled by one clan. The land was called Barrmin; its people, Barrmen. The people had told him that many years ago, the King of Barrmin had tried to annex this part of Avalon to his own kingdom. The Barrmen traded in timber and had tried to cut down trees from the Great Forest. There had been an argument with the giants, who claimed ownership of the Great Forest. A fight had taken place, which had ended with the Barrmen being driven back to their own country. The giants had warned the Barrmen not to cross the border again.

Next, Arthur spoke to the Barrmen who had joined the Avalonians. He told them that he was happy for them to join his people in Arthurton, providing they respected Avalonian law. The king made it clear that the newcomers should respect the people of magic, and treat them in the same way as they would other people. He told them that they had an agreement with the giants, who lived in the forest, not to cut their trees without permission. Anyone who broke the law would be punished.

The Barrmen said George had already made them swear their loyalty to Avalon, but they would be happy to do so again in front of Arthur. They told Arthur that once their land was full of trees, but their King Rabbart had ordered the trees to be cut. A lot of timber had been sold to the Vanddals, who lived in a country far across the sea. Since the trees were cut, it had been harder to grow crops because in the summer, the sun was hot and there was little rain. The ground had become hard, and only weeds flourished.

They believed that the Vanddals had used some of the timber to build houses and boats because their own land, which was even farther north, did not have many trees. Vanddalasia was a country reputed to be cold, and a large part of it was said to be covered in ice and snow.

The Vanddals had sold the Barrmen large quantities of weed-killer powder, which they had sprinkled on the once arable land, near the border with Avalon. The powder had not only killed the weeds but the crops as well. The Barrmen believed that the powder also contained the seeds of a strange climbing weed which was immune to the weed-killer. The hardy weed had grown fast and furiously in their fields, and they could not get rid of it. People had been forced to leave their homes, as the weed had even managed to creep inside their houses. They hoped that the strange plant would not spread to Avalon, which they now regarded as their home.

The wizard shook his head in dismay. The story that the people from The North were telling him was the same story he had heard before. He remembered how little Alf, the Forbidden Forest elf, had told him about the weed-killer northern traders had sold to the Kernans. The evil powder, which was supposed to kill weeds and promote the growth of root vegetables, had killed the crops it was supposed to promote. The same powder had killed many fairies and elves who lived in the fields.

The wizard took to his broom, and Arthur borrowed a horse, to travel the short distance to the border with George. Some of the men who used to live in Barrmin went with them. As they travelled farther north, they noticed several dead birds and rabbits. As they neared the border, they found that the strange climbing weed had already started to grow within the Avalon border.

George knelt to look at one of the weeds sprawling across the ground. He tried to pull it out of the soil, but it stayed firm, and he only succeeded in breaking off a few leaves as he tugged. The stem was very strong, and George found that even with a sharp knife, it was difficult to cut. In some places, the long vines had criss-crossed each other, forming strands which were as strong as rope.

"I've never seen anything like it!" George exclaimed.

"I have," said Merlin. "This plant is very similar to the bindweed that seals the Forbidden Forest to strangers. How I wish that I had learnt the spells which the Bramble family use to open and close the bindweed that surrounds the forest."

From inside the Avalon border, the men could see the once arable fields of Barrmin. The areas of the fields which were not covered by the sprawling weeds were arid and brown.

The men took their horses across the border and examined the ground beneath them. It was dry and powdery. Along with the bodies of small animals, fairies and elves could be seen lying lifeless under the bindweed.

"The weed-killer did that! Don't let your horses eat any of the grass – not that they would want to!" said one of the Barrmen. "This was once my field. The soil was rich and moist. I grew potatoes here. I made my living off the land. Look at it now. It is not fit for anything! Even the large beasts, which once provided us with meat, have left Barrmin and travelled to Avalon.

The man looked worried. "If this weed continues to grow at the rate it is growing now, we will soon have to move out of our new home in Arthurton and farther into Avalon.

"It is has certainly covered more ground since I was here last. It is growing much faster than anyone could have imagined."

"How long would it take to deliver a message to the King of Barrmin?" Merlin asked the man.

"It used to take two days on horseback to reach the Rock Palace. Now, with this weed, a rider would have to be careful that his horse's hooves did not get tangled. So, I would say, at least three days."

"I need two volunteers from the men who used to live in Barrmin to ride to King Rabbart and tell him that I know someone who might be able to get rid of this bindweed. I need them to tell him I will meet him here at midday in ten days' time. If we can stop the bindweed penetrating Avalon, then we may be able to rid it from these Barrmin fields too."

The men who once lived on the now devastated land spoke among themselves. Two men came forward as volunteers.

"We hope that you will be able to find a way to rid Barrmin of this terrible weed which is spreading like a disease. But, even if you do destroy the weed, the ground beneath it will still be poisoned."

"I think we might be able to help with that too," said Merlin. "But I make no promises."

Having satisfied the wizard that they understood the message perfectly, the two men went back to Arthurton, to prepare for their journey.

Merlin turned to Arthur. "I must return to the Bramble Family. They know how to control the bindweed which forms a defence against unwelcome visitors to the Forbidden Forest. The Brambles are reluctant to leave the Forbidden Forest, but they have been teaching Yzor and Jonathan their spells. If the Brambles are unwilling to help, our herbologists may be able to do so."

Arthur turned to the wizard. "Go with haste, my old friend. I am sorry that it seems you are to have no rest since bringing us to this new world. I will meet you here in ten days' time. I hope that King Rabbart will join us, for I would like to meet him. I wish to ask him if he has sold timber which has been used to make Trajaen boats. He and I have a lot to talk about!"

"Yes, and I have a few questions I would like to ask him too!" added Merlin.

The wizard mounted his broomstick and flew high in the sky, looking down on the ravaged ground beneath him. Just as he was crossing the border back into Avalon, he noticed something beneath him glittering in the sunlight. He dipped his broom and saw that the sparkles came from a bird's nest in a dead fir tree. It was a gold band, with a large diamond surrounded by several smaller ones. It's Rosalie's ring! He looked round for the culprit and saw three dead magpies on the ground beneath him. *That must be the thief and his parents.*

He flew back to Arthur and gave him the ring. "If Rosalie had not lost her ring, we would have not have visited the northern border so soon. Nor would we have been aware of this plant which is spreading into Avalon. Everything happens for a reason. Please tell Rosalie that she is not to blame for losing the ring."

Arthur barely had time to thank the wizard before he set off in the direction of Twydell's Forbidden Forest.

Merlin flew long hours and rested little. However, he made one important detour on route. He stopped off at the home of the thunderbirds. They were thrilled to see him again especially when he told them that he might be able to arrange a new home for them, in another country. It was a land in need of plenty of water, so their presence would be welcome because of their ability to create rain. He explained to the thunderbirds that an abundance of rain was needed to dilute poison in the soil. He hoped that continued showers would eventually wash the poison down, so far into the earth, that it would no longer be harmful.

However, the wizard also made the huge birds promise that they would do nothing to hurt the people who lived in the new land. They must do nothing to harm the farm stock. In return, the people would feed the giant birds until it was safe for them to hunt in the wild without fear of being poisoned.

The thunderbirds knew that they must find a new home as far away from the dragons as possible. Their feathers had almost fully grown back, and they felt that they were strong enough to make the journey. They were happy to know that someone, somewhere, might actually want their help. They knew that they were not normally liked by people. The couple promised that they would hurt no one. However, they were worried about travelling east, in case they were seen by the dragons.

Merlin explained that in one week's time they should travel north and then east. They would see a settlement being built near the forest where the giants lived. He would watch out for them, and, when he saw them in the air, he would signal to them. The wizard bid the huge birds goodbye, and flew on to the Forbidden Forest.

Chapter 12 – The Old Lady Comes to the Rescue

Heather and Helen-Joy met Merlin at the woodland entrance. Helen-Joy was riding Comet. The white stallion followed the two broomsticks, and their riders, as they hovered along the pathway to the Brambles' cottage.

The family sat in the garden, with the Avalonians and some of the forest fairies and elves. Merlin was pleased to see that Isaiah was up and walking, although he appeared to still be in some sort of trance. Garod and Jerry were looking much better: some colour had risen to their cheeks, but they were still sitting with vacant expressions on their sad faces.

The group greeted Merlin. As he delved into welcome refreshments, he told them about the problems in Barrmin which were spreading into Avalon.

"Not just Avalon," one of the forest elves informed him. "Don't forget there are problems in Kerner too. Some of our kinfolk have died, and others have made their way to the forest, to get away from the poisonous ground. I have not heard of any bindweed taking over the land, though."

Merlin sighed. "It seems as if the poison is in the weed-killer, along with bindweed seeds. If the weed-killer has only recently been spread in Kerner, then the seeds may not yet have formed into plants."

Merlin said that Yzor and Jonathan should travel with him to see the plants. He asked the Bramble family if any of them would be willing to travel to the Barrmin border. Maura, Nora, and Nora's three daughters were all reluctant to do so, but old Great-Grandmother Bramble surprised everyone by stating very firmly that she would go. Her daughters and granddaughters were horrified, and tried to dissuade her.

269

"I shall go." The old witch was adamant. "I came to the forest as a child and have never since crossed its boundary. My family can manage well without me now. It would be good to be of some use to the outside world before I die."

"But how will you get there?" Maura tried to talk sense into the old witch.

"Well, for a while now, I've been thinking about taking one of the rugs you made for me and fastening either end to two of the new broomsticks which Tannus made for us. That way, I may not travel very fast, but I can sit in comfort. I will be able look at the land beneath me, which I have heard so much about, but have no memory of ever seeing."

"I would like to go too," Heather stated. "I am good with plant spells, and I can help look after Great-Grandmother."

"It's too dangerous!" Sally snapped at her daughter.

"Yzor and Jonathan will be there to help protect us," Heather argued. "I really do need to get out of the forest and see the world for myself. I am sorry, Mother. I love the forest, but I need some freedom."

"Please let her go," pleaded Jonathan. "I promise I will look after her and bring her home safely."

Sally looked beaten. "If I told her not to go, she would go anyway. That morning, when I saw the two of you together at the opening to the forest, I knew this day would come. I could see the look of longing on your face, Heather. I can't say that you are going with my blessing, but I wish you well. Your great-grandmother will need the company of one of our family, so it is probably for the best. I just ask that you both come home as soon as the task at hand is over."

"We will be racing back to tell you all about it!" Heather gave her mother a hug.

"I'm not sure I'll be up to racing!" Great-Grandmother Bramble cackled.

Merlin thanked Heather and her great-grandmother. It was getting late, and he and Helen-Joy bid their friends goodbye. The couple travelled back to the cave behind the waterfall. The soothsayer rode on Comet, of whom she had become very fond, and Merlin hovered along behind her on his broom.

Once inside the cave, Merlin asked, "Can I open the parchment now?" He smiled at Helen-Joy as he sipped a nightcap cup of buttercup wine.

"Not yet," she said. "You can open it at the end of your mission. I fear you still have much to do."

As they lay in bed, Helen-Joy told Merlin what she had seen in her dreams, and confirmed in her crystal ball. She said that the northerners were selling weed-killer to the Kernans. She also told him that she had seen the Vanddals selling King Rabbart's timber to the Trajaens. She feared that the Trajaens were building new boats and would return to Avalon to seek their revenge.

"Is it possible that the Vanddals are working with the Trajaens?" asked Merlin.

"Possibly," replied Helen-Joy. "I am sorry that I cannot tell you more."

"And I still can't open the parchment?"

"No. Not yet. Now get some sleep. You have a long journey ahead of you and a lot of work to do when you reach your destination."

"Yes, my dear. I'll turn out the lamp."

❀ ✦ ❀ ✦ ❀ ✦ ❀ ✦ ❀ ✦ ❀

It was sunrise as the visitors left the forest. The three sisters – Dilly, Dally, and Sally – had come to the edge of the forest to wave them off.

Selogon and Farainne stayed behind to help with the sick men and to learn more from the forest fairies and elves.

However, Esmerelda and Tannus decided to travel home to Merlport, carrying Maud and Allarond with them. The witch queen, fairy queen, and elf king felt the need to return to Merlport because, with Arthur at the Barrmin border, the only leader in the village was young Prince Edward. They still lived in fear of another Trajaen attack.

Maud and Esmerelda had been given some of the musical strings of shells as leaving presents. They called them wind chimes because the instruments played their own tune, in the breeze, without the need of a musician. The wind chimes tinkled as the travellers rose up in the air, ready for their long flight home. They waved goodbye to Merlin's party and the people of the Forbidden Forest, and then flew at high speed towards Merlport.

Next, the party leaving for Barrmin said their goodbyes. Merlin led the group. Behind him sat Great-Grandmother Bramble, flying on her strange contraption. She sat on the rug, which was fastened between two broomsticks. There was enough room on the rug to carry a bag of "useful things she might need" behind her. The old witch had wrapped up in her warmest clothes, and sat, not gracefully, but definitely alert and interested in all that was going on round her. Heather and Jonathan flew either side of the old lady, whilst Yzor brought up the rear.

The Dalton guards alerted King Frederrick and Queen Elise as soon as the strange group of travellers were sighted in the sky. The king and queen were already in the courtyard waiting for them when they landed.

The party was offered overnight hospitality by the Twydellers. During dinner, Merlin updated the king and queen as to the problems that had befallen Barrmin and were now becoming apparent in Kerner.

King Frederrick and Queen Elise were alarmed by what they learnt, worried that the problems might spread to Twydell. The king did not hesitate in sending a messenger to King Jeffrey, telling him the news. The message included a warning that the King of Kerner should stop his people using the weed-killer.

Heather and Great-Grandmother Bramble were fascinated by the size and the elegance of the palace. They were very tired from their journey, but when Queen Elise offered to show them round, they eagerly accepted.

"I wish I could stay here forever," said Heather with sigh, as she admired the beauty of the great hall, with its windows of coloured glass. She touched the intricate carving on the stone pillars and spent some time gazing at paintings.

For once in her life, Great-Grandmother Bramble was awestruck and silent.

The party set off again at sunrise.

The next night was spent in less comfort at the small tavern in Birdsmoorgate. The villagers had come to know Merlin, and welcomed his companions. They were anxious to hear the news the travellers carried with them. The wizards spent some time talking to the villagers, enjoying the tavern ale, before retiring for the night.

They arrived at Arthurton the following afternoon. Great-Grandmother Bramble was very tired, but when Arthur offered to share his golden carriage with her, she agreed to go to the border that evening rather than wait till the morning. Heather and Merlin travelled with her. Yzor and Jonathan flew beside the carriage on their brooms, and several of the settlers followed on horseback.

Great-Grandmother Bramble and Heather looked at the bindweed. "It's a bit different to ours," the old witch said to her great-granddaughter. "Never mind; let's give it a try, and see what happens!"

The two witches withdrew their wands from their cloaks, and danced anticlockwise round one of the plants, uttering their spells. Yzor and Jonathan watched carefully. The bindweed started to shrivel and die. The long stem could be seen shrivelling along its length, almost as far as the eye could see.

The men from Barrmin, who had settled in Arthurton, stared in amazement. They shook their heads in disbelief, scratching their chins thoughtfully.

Yzor and Jonathan took a turn next, but the bindweed stayed green and healthy.

"You're not holding your wand right," Heather told Jonathan, grabbing his wand and pointing it a few degrees lower. "And you need to say 'sharrer', not 'sherrer'."

Heather walked around with the two wizards, correcting their footsteps and words when needed. Eventually, the plant weakened and shrivelled. They looked on, with satisfaction, as the long vine diminished back towards the direction of its root.

"You work with me," Great-Grandmother ordered Yzor. Turning towards Jonathan, she added, "You, young man, work with Heather. It's the best way to learn."

The two pairs each found a different plant, and then repeated their performance. Two more weeds withered away.

Merlin clapped his hands, and the rest of the party copied his example. The applause was loud. The former Barrmen cheered. One of them threw his hat in the air.

Heather and her great-grandmother beamed with pride. Great-Grandmother Bramble even did a little curtsey for her audience before setting to work again.

The two pairs killed a few more plants before Merlin stopped them, bidding them to travel back to Arthurton to rest.

Over the next few days, the Brambles and the herbologists cast their spells, experimenting with changes to their chants, words, and movements. Eventually, they found improved ways to work their magic. As soon as one long vine perished, it seemed to take the spell back to its root, and others around it wasted away too.

Merlin watched carefully, and Great-Grandmother Bramble encouraged him to join in. "You're never too old to learn," she told him.

Chapter 13 – The Arrival of the King of Barrmin

By the time the King of Barrmin was due to arrive, all the creeping plants on the Avalon side of the border had been destroyed.

On the appointed day, a large number of people had gathered at the border, along with Arthur and Merlin. There were the two herbologists and the two Brambles, of course, plus most of the Arthurton settlers, who were simply interested in seeing what would evolve from the historic meeting.

Since seeing the various flags and standards at the Twydell wedding, the Avalonians had created an emblem of their own. In Briton, Arthur's standard had been a bear on a white background. Now a black bear had been embroidered on to a piece of red cloth.

The Avalonians proudly placed the red-and-black banner in the ground to mark their territory.

Arthur intended to entertain the Barrmen. A tent was being erected. Fires were lit outside the tent, and pots of stew were hung to cook over the fires. The baker was busy kneading dough to make bread and dumplings. Several barrels of ale had been brought from Merlport, and Gilda and her women had sent some home-made cakes.

The King of Avalon was busy giving instructions on the preparations for the visit when a cloud of dry, brown, dust was seen in the distance.

The yellow banner of Barrmin soon came into view. At the front of about forty horsemen, a tall man rode on a large black charger. However, he stopped quite a long distance from the border, sending forward a messenger.

The messenger rode forward, stopping short of the Avalonians. "King Rabbart lll of Barrmin is here, at your request. He is willing to parley, but he and his advisor will speak to two Avalonians only. He will meet you on our land, an equal distance between your people and ours. The two who come must be unarmed and on horseback. King Rabbart does not wish to speak to any person riding on the handle of a brush."

Arthur agreed, on the condition that Rabbart and his advisor also came unarmed. The messenger went back to his king, and then rode forward again to confirm agreement on the terms of the meeting.

Arthur took his sword out of its scabbard and lifted it high, so that it glinted in the sun and Rabbart could see that he was disarming. However, he hid his knife beneath his vest. "I'll bet Rabbart and his advisor will have knives and small swords hidden somewhere on their persons. I don't trust them," he said in a low voice.

"Neither do I," Merlin said. The old wizard muttered a few words, running his hand over his staff with the crystal ball at the end. The staff instantly turned into a crooked stick which looked as if it had just been cut from a tree.

Arthur mounted his horse, ready to meet the Barrmen. Merlin had left Comet in the Forbidden Forest, but was able to borrow a good looking grey mare. King and wizard rode side by side over the border into Barrmin. As they drew nearer they could see that a double sided axe, with blood dripping from it, was depicted on the yellow standard of Barrmin.

Rabbart trotted towards them, with an equally tall warrior, also dressed in black, at his side. The other man was younger than his king. They were both strong, muscular men who wore the scars of battle. Their dark hair was partly shaven at the sides but grew long from the centre of their heads, falling onto their backs. Both had neatly trimmed beards.

"He doesn't look much like an advisor," Merlin whispered to Arthur, "He looks more like a bodyguard."

"They both look like Trajaens to me." Arthur spoke softly so the approaching men could not hear. "Same dark skin and black hair. And, look at their standard – didn't the Trajaen standard have axes on it, too?"

"Greetings, King Arthur," growled Rabbart. "I would like to say, 'welcome to Barrmin', but our land is not very welcoming at the moment." He looked at the ground beneath him, with the bodies of small animals lying dead at his horse's feet.

Rabbart then added, "This is Jaeggar, my adviser." The Barrmin king's companion nodded.

"Greetings," said Arthur loudly, in his regal voice. "This is Merlin, who is my adviser."

The two Barrmen glared at Merlin, who simply bowed his head and smiled pleasantly.

Arthur continued. "I am sorry to learn that your land has been poisoned and your crops replaced by this terrible plant which grows so quickly. It had started to spread into Avalon, but we have people of magic with us." He gestured towards the sorcerer. "They have used their spells to kill this creeping plant. In fact, the plants which had spread into Avalon are all dead. Merlin here believes that he can destroy the weeds that have taken over your land. He also has a plan to make your soil rich and moist once more, but it will take a long time.

"If you cross our border into Avalon, we will show you what magic our herbologists have done. If you do not wish to come any closer, then I will ask our herbologists to come forward. They can then give you a demonstration of what they can do."

"Ask them to come forward so I can see for myself." Rabbart's words sounded like a command rather than a request.

Merlin turned his back on the Barrmen and, putting his stick to his throat, uttered a short spell. When he spoke, his voice boomed five times louder than normal. "Yzor, Jonathon, will you come forward, *please?*" He emphasised the word *please* purposely, intending it for the King of Barrmin's ears. "King Rabbart would like to see you kill the bindweed. If the girls are willing to come with you, that will be fine – the more dead bindweed, the better – but if they prefer to stay where they are, they should do so."

Merlin only expected Yzor and Jonathan to fly forward, but Heather rode between them. They stopped a few yards behind Arthur and Merlin, but still close enough for the Barrmen to see what they were doing. They put their broomsticks down and drew their wands.

As the wands were drawn, Arthur noticed Rabbart and Jaeggar each put a hand to their saddles. *So that is where they have hidden their daggers,* he thought, *beneath their saddles.*

Heather and the two herbologist wizards paced round a patch of bindweed, using very deliberate steps whilst muttering their spell. Soon the whole patch visibly yellowed, and then withered back in the direction of its roots. They were so intense on watching the patch of bindweed shrivel that no one noticed Great-Grandmother Bramble fly up on her vehicle of a rug harnessed to two broomsticks.

"I'm not missing all the fun," she laughed. She clambered down from her conveyance, which awaited her return, sitting motionless in the air. The rug looked very odd strung between the two broomsticks, with no support from the ground. Great-Grandmother Bramble's bag remained perched on the rug.

The old witch raised her wand, and almost danced round a fresh patch of bindweed, which soon wasted away. She laughed at her own success.

Heather and the wizards laughed with her. "My great-grandmother really is the bindweed expert," she said proudly, and then she, too, started to dance round the bindweed, singing her spell, making the plant wilt and shrink back into the ground.

Rabbart and Jaeggar seemed stunned by the odd spectacle before them.

"King Rabbart," Arthur said, commanding the King of Barrmin's attention. "If you wish us to rid your land of this plant, then I must ask you some favours in return."

"Speak." Rabbart looked suspicious.

"First, tell me whether you have sold this weed-killer, which kills all except the bindweed, to the Kernans."

"We sold it before we knew it was harmful," Rabbart replied abruptly.

Arthur guessed the other king was lying and had sold the weed-killer to the Kernans deliberately to undermine their strength.

"Did you sell timber to the Trajaens?"

"No," replied Rabbart.

"Are you sure?"

Rabbart looked suspicious that Arthur already knew the answer. Nevertheless, his gaze did not waver as he looked the King of Avalon in the face. "We do a lot of trade with the Vanddals. If the Vanddals traded some of the timber we sold them to the Trajaens, we were not to know."

"If you wish our people of magic to rid your land of the bindweed, I ask that you give me your oath firstly. I ask you to swear that you will not harm any of the people, magic or otherwise, who live in Avalon."

"Does that include the giants?" Rabbart asked gruffly.

"It includes all the people of Avalon. Witches, wizards, fairies, elves, people like me who have no magic, and giants."

"Add thunderbirds to the list, please," Merlin said.

Rabbart and Jaeggar looked puzzled.

"No harm to thunderbirds either," added Arthur.

"I have no wish to harm any of the people or creatures of Avalon, so long as they do not harm any people of Barrmin," Rabbart stated firmly.

"Good. I can assure you that we wish no harm to the people of Barrmin. Secondly, would you be willing to offer a home to two thunderbirds in your country, where they will not be harmed? They need to be fed daily and they like living in caves. The thunderbirds bring rain. We believe that over time the rain will dilute the poison, and eventually it will wash deep into the earth where it will no longer be of harm. If you wish the thunderbirds to leave Barrmin at any time, you must consult us first. You must not harm them whilst they live in your country."

Rabbart laughed. He considered Arthur's terms to be very easy. "We have caves in our granite hills over there." He pointed to a distant mountain. "Would that be a suitable abode for the birds which bring rain when needed?"

"That would be perfect!" agreed Merlin.

"Then I will order my people not to harm the birds. We will make sure they are well fed."

Arthur continued. "Finally, I wish you to promise that you will no longer supply the Vanddals or the Trajaens with timber."

Rabbart did not like this condition but considered that he would rather lose the trade of one product than risk his crops and the loss of large beasts from his land. He reluctantly agreed, saying, "We have not sold wood to the Trajaens. We cannot afford to lose our trade with the Vanddals, who are also my relatives by marriage. However, Avalon is now our neighbour. If you are prepared to enter into trade negotiations with us, I will add a term in any future contract with the Vanddals to ensure that they do not sell our timber to the Trajaens."

Arthur considered Rabbart to be a good politician. He did not concede, even though he had no choice, without a condition of his own.

"We will be more than happy to look at what trade you can offer us." Arthur smiled. "Would you like to join us for lunch? The soil here is poisonous, but if you wish to cross the border into Avalon, our cook has made a tasty stew and fresh bread. We have also brought a few barrels of ale from Merlport."

The Barrmen accepted the hospitality offered, moved forward, and entered Avalon. They were cautious, though, and kept their horses close by in case they were being led into a trap.

The meal was progressing well when two large birds were seen on the horizon. Merlin ran forward, waving his wooden stick in the air. He ran his hand over the stick and it turned back into the staff with the crystal knob at the end. This time, the crystal glowed green as a signal to the thunderbirds.

Merlin tapped his throat with the staff to increase the volume of his voice. "Do not harm these birds. They are here to help!"

Storm and Thor, the thunderbirds, landed some distance away from the large group of people. Despite Merlin's assurances, they were still concerned that arrows or spears might be aimed at them. As they landed, the weather changed, and it started to rain.

"That's just what we need," said one of the Barrmen as he stepped under the cover of a sack canopy which had been erected.

"Oh dear," said Merlin with a sigh. "We didn't want the rain quite yet. It might put out the fires on which we are cooking our meal."

He welcomed the thunderbirds and asked if they could fly round the dry patches where the bindweed had died. He told them it would help wash the poison from the soil and that, eventually, with enough rain, the poison would dilute and wash away.

"Show this lot what you can do!" he whispered to Storm and Thor. "And then I'll get you some food. Whatever you do, don't eat the small creatures on the land. They have died of poison."

Patches of rain started to pour over all the areas where the giant birds spread their wings. The onlookers were astonished. No one, except Merlin and Yzor, had ever seen birds as big as these let alone birds which brought rain.

The bystanders were a little surprised to see Merlin give the birds a large joint of meat each. But, by this time, they had stopped questioning the wizard's actions.

The birds were now very happy because they had never been welcomed anywhere before.

The plan of action was now clear. The Brambles, Yzor, and Jonathan would take responsibility for clearing the bindweed – a task which Heather and her great-grandmother seemed to relish. As a patch of ground was cleared, the thunderbirds would create rain to wash away the poison.

The problem was that, at the moment, the large creatures were creating too much rain. Merlin pointed the birds in the direction of the mountains indicated by Rabbart, and suggested that they find a suitable cave and take some much-needed rest. He told the birds to return in the morning, when more bindweed had been cleared. The humans would provide meals for them until they were able to find food for themselves.

The birds were excited to find a new home where they did not have to hide in fear of the dragons. They took as much food as they could carry in their talons, and set off towards the caves.

Rabbart and the Barrmen soldiers left in good spirits, if not a little wet. The Brambles continued their work, with the help of the two herbologist wizards.

That evening, as they sheltered in a tent, Merlin asked Great-Grandmother Bramble if she would teach others their spells. He wanted more witches and wizards to help with the work so that the weed could be cleared as quickly as possible.

"I am sorry," the old witch replied. "We taught Yzor and Jonathan our secret spells because Helen-Joy had already told us you would bring a young warlock with you. Even before you first arrived, she said that the young warlock who would one day come to the forest with you would be a husband for Heather. When Jonathan and Heather exchange rings, then it is logical that his father will want to come and visit them in the forest. But, if we reveal our secrets to too many people, our forest will be open to trespass by anyone, at any time."

She smiled a wide toothless smile to placate Merlin, but he was not unhappy. He was considering Helen-Joy's safety, as well as that of the Bramble family. He knew that there was good and bad in all races of people.

"Do Heather and Jonathan know they will be exchanging rings yet?" the old wizard asked.

"They haven't said anything so far." The old witch gave Merlin a sly smile. "But I think it's fairly obvious, don't you?"

"I didn't mind teaching you our spells either," she added. "Helen-Joy's not said anything, but I've got a feeling we will be seeing quite a lot of you too."

It was several weeks before substantial areas of land were clear of the poisonous bindweed. The two Brambles and the two wizards worked ceaselessly. Sometimes Merlin joined them, and they found that when the five of them danced round the bindweed, his tremendous power enabled them to clear much-larger patches.

"I never knew you could dance!" Arthur teased the old wizard when he saw him helping to weave the bindweed killing spells.

Regular messengers were sent back and forth to the Forbidden Forest, keeping the folk there up to date on the progress of killing the creeping weed. Messages came back to tell them that the three men were improving, and Isaiah was even beginning to put words together. Heather was anxious to get back to her father.

Arthur offered the witches the use of his golden carriage and an escort. He considered that the two women should have only the best. The offer was gratefully accepted. However, Heather was sad to leave. She said she would return if the work was still unfinished after the time she felt she needed to spend with her family.

Merlin decided to travel with them. He said he wanted to see what damage the weed-killer had done to Kerner. Besides, the use of the golden carriage, for an elderly wizard with aching limbs, was an offer too good to miss.

Just before they left, Thor flew across the border into Avalon, bringing with him the usual rain, but also a piece of good news. The thunderbird told Merlin and Yzor that he and his wife had found some eagle's eggs which had been left in a nest. The parents had died from pecking seeds from the poisoned grass, but the eggs were still healthy.

"Storm has taken them back to our cave and will keep them warm," Thor told Merlin. "I can manage to make enough rain to wash the soil on my own."

Merlin was delighted. "Please tell Storm that I am thrilled to hear your news. I am very glad that the young eagles will have a happy home when they hatch out."

"I would very much like to visit Storm, if that is all right." Yzor had learnt the thunderbird language whilst working with them to clear the creeping weed.

Thor was delighted to think that anyone would like to visit his cave. He said that he and Storm would be very pleased to receive visitors. Bidding the two wizards goodbye, he spread his massive wings, and flew off in search of suitable bedding for the nest.

Jonathan's disappointment that Heather was leaving was obvious to all who saw him. His long face looked even longer than usual, and his customary smile was missing. He vowed to work long hours and to make his way to the Forbidden Forest if the work was completed before Heather was ready to return. Anyway, if Merlin was right, Jonathan suspected he would shortly be wanted to do a job in Kerner, and the Forbidden Forest was close to the Kernan border!

Chapter 14 – The King of Kerner Seeks Help

On the way back to the Forbidden Forest, whilst travelling through Twydell, the party met a messenger from Kerner.

He was escorted by a mixture of Kernan and Twydell soldiers. The messenger had come from King Jeffrey, to ask for Merlin's help in clearing their land of a strange creeping plant which had started to form a footing in the soil. He said the invasive plant seemed to have poisoned the land, and was spreading rapidly.

The magical people in the carriage looked at each other knowingly. The message and plea for help, from Kerner, was hardly unexpected.

The Brambles smiled as Merlin stated his terms clearly to the messenger. "Tell King Jeffrey that we will clear your land, but he must first ensure that all people of magic are released from Kerner prisons. This includes all fairies and elves held in cages. No more children are to work in your mines, and those children working in them now are to be released into my care. I shall know if anyone tries to conceal any prisoners or children from me. King Jeffrey is to meet me at the Kerner border in one week from today. I will expect your prisoners and the children to be handed over at that time. Your king must provide three months' worth of food to feed the people you hand over. I should also like three barrels of the best ale King Jeffrey can find."

The messenger repeated the terms which the sorcerer had set. He and the escorting soldiers turned their horses, preparing to ride back from whence they had come. However, Merlin stopped them. He asked that one of the Twydell men travel to Merlport instead. He was to tell Esmerelda, Queen of the Witches, of the message and the demands Merlin had sent to King Jeffrey. One of the Twydell soldiers left the group and did as Merlin bid.

When they reached the Forbidden Forest, Maura and Nora were waiting at the entrance. Helen-Joy was with them. Comet and Lucky were there as well. The Bramble sisters were thrilled to see their mother seated in the golden carriage. Great-Grandmother Bramble cackled as she stepped down from the splendid vehicle, with the assistance of one of the escorts. "Well, this is a day I bet you never imagined you'd see!"

As Heather stepped down, Nora rushed forward to embrace her granddaughter. "I have missed you so much," she said, and tears of joy fell from her eyes.

Maura and Nora had brought some refreshments for the escort. The men were grateful for the gesture. They would rest in the meadow outside the forest for a while before returning, with the golden carriage, to Merlport. The Brambles were now getting more used to meeting people from outside their forest home but were still nervous of contact with humans. Nevertheless, they considered it polite to offer hospitality to the Avalonians, and they felt safe with Merlin present.

Leaving the escort in the meadow, they made their way along the woodland paths. Helen-Joy rode on Comet, with Lucky trotting along behind, followed by a parade of broomsticks and their riders, all flying apace. The soothsayer and Merlin did not stop at the Brambles' cottage, but made their way straight back to the cave behind the waterfall.

Merlin was relieved to rest his aching body in the comfort of Helen-Joy's bed.

"Ah," said Merlin. "A few days off, then back to work again. Can I open the parchment now?"

"Yes," replied Helen-Joy.

Merlin read aloud.

1. You will require the help of the thunderbirds, and you will find them a new home.

2. You will meet a new king, but you must be wary of him. Quite rightly, you will not believe all that he tells you.

3. You will rescue children who need your help.

However, when he got to the fourth point, he stopped. His mouth dropped wide open in astonishment. He did not read aloud, but took Helen-Joy in his arms.

The fourth prediction read:

I will cradle twins within nine months.

At the appointed time, Merlin met Jeffrey at the Kerner border. Standing beside Merlin were Esmerelda, Queen of the Witches; Maud, Queen of the Fairies; and Allarond, King of the Elves. Crowds from both Avalon and Twydell had gathered to wait for the arrival of Jeffrey, the prisoners, and the children who had worked in the mines. Lucky the pony was also there, waiting to see if any of his friends from the mines would pull the carts.

Merlin had ordered all wizards and witches to keep their wands inside their cloaks so that the Kernans did not feel threatened. Esmerelda and Tannus had argued with him but reluctantly agreed to do as he bid.

Jeffrey arrived by carriage. Five wagons followed. One contained seven sick-looking men whose hands were bound. Two others contained children wearing collars, with leashes attached. The leashes were tied to the carts. Three of the children had their hands tightly bound. The other two carts carried boxes, which Merlin assumed held the food supplies he had demanded.

The King of Kerner came forward. His face was unsmiling and full of humiliation. "I am sorry," he said. "I did not know that these people were being held in the prisons. Neither was I aware that the guards were using drugs to weaken those with magic powers. The guards are being punished."

The cart containing the seven men came forward. "Why are their hands tied?" Esmerelda said with a snarl. Her green eyes glinted dangerously, reflecting the fury she felt.

"I am told that if they were not tied throughout the journey, they might have cast their magic on the drivers. The drivers are innocent of harming them," Jeffrey replied.

Esmerelda raised her hand and pointed it at the men in the carriage. She was so powerful a witch that she did not need a wand. The ropes binding their hands fell undone, and witches and wizards rushed forward to take the sick men into their care.

Next, the two carts containing the children came forward. The children looked around anxiously, full of fear. They were dressed in rags, stained by dirt from the mines. Their pale faces made their eyes, staring wide from the surrounding dark circles, look enormous.

"The mine managers told me that they had to leash the children to the cart to stop them running away. The children whose hands are bound are those whose parents disowned them because they showed magical powers."

Jeffrey wanted to look away from Merlin's angry face. However, as a king, he knew that no matter how ashamed he felt, he had to look the wizard straight in the eye.

A burly man, who had driven one of the wagons containing the children, climbed into the back. He unhitched the leashes which were attached to the wagon. He ordered the man who had driven the other wagon to do the same. The children climbed down from the carts, but the men still held the leashes attached to the collars round their scrawny necks.

Tannus walked steadily towards the men. They offered him the leashes.

"We don't want the kids any longer anyway," taunted one of the men. "We've found stronger creatures to work in our mines. Creatures who do what they're told, without argument, and who don't need the whip. They're happy to work for us and don't try to run off!"

The warlock did not take the leashes, but raised his hand and snarled a spell. The collars fell away from the children's necks. The men were left looking foolish, holding the dangling leashes.

Tannus's dark eyes did not hide the rage he felt. He uttered a second spell, and the ropes binding the wrists of the three magical children fell to the ground.

One of the children was frightened, and ran towards the forest. However, he stopped and turned, and then, raising his hand, sent a ball of fire rolling through the air towards the men holding the dangling leashes.

Tannus pointed his hand at the fireball and sent it spinning into the air, where it turned into a small cloud. He pointed at the cloud and guided it till it reached a point just above where the men were standing.

The men looked up, dumbstruck. Their mouths gaped open.

Next, Tannus gave a quick flick of his wrist. Rain fell from the cloud, onto the heads of the two men.

The children and the crowd watched with amazement. They all started to laugh.

"Very good," muttered Merlin to himself. "I was wondering how we would deal with washing the poison from the soil, without the help of the thunderbirds. Now I have an answer."

The men tried to run away – one in one direction, and one in the other. As they ran, their legs became tangled, and they tripped and fell. They tried to rise, but the same thing happened again, and they fell against each other. Their heads bumped, one against the other, with a loud bang.

Merlin looked round, to see who had cast the spell, and spotted an old man and woman in a rickety old cart. He just caught sight of the man hiding his wand beneath his coat.

One of the witches walked over to the boy who had created the ball of fire, and offered him her hand. The boy took her hand, and they walked away from the cart, towards a welcoming group of wizzwits. Others followed the witch's example, including Maura and Nora, who took the hands of the other two children of magic.

All the children, except those of magic, were taken to Merlport, where homes would be found for them.

The blacksmith and his wife, whose two sons had died in the battle with the Trajaens, wanted to adopt two boys. The couple promised to take good care of the boys and love them like their own.

The children of magic, who had been drugged to try to deaden their powers, would be nursed back to health in the Forbidden Forest. The seven men of magic, who had just been released, were also taken to the forest.

Jeffrey urged the fourth cart forward. In the cart, along with boxes of food, were what looked like bird cages containing limp fairies and elves.

The forest fairies and elves, who had found viewing points in the branches of trees, sprang forward onto the cart. Using their own magical powers to open the cages, they carried off their sick kinfolk. The elves shook their fists furiously at the Kernans but resisted using their magic to seek revenge. These poor creatures would also go to the Forbidden Forest, where every effort would be made to try to nurse them back to health.

Finally, the fifth cart came forward. This was filled with more boxes of food and the three barrels of ale.

Lucky whinnied, and the sad-looking ponies who had pulled the carts answered.

"These pit ponies don't look in very good condition," remarked Merlin to Jeffrey. "Do you really want to take them back to Kerner? They look as if they are on their last legs!"

Jeffrey did not argue. "Keep them."

"We will keep our side of the agreement," Merlin told Jeffrey. "I can see the creeping weed from here. We will start at this point, and work our way into Kerner. So saying, he walked across the border with Heather and Great-Grandmother Bramble. The onlookers watched the trio dancing anticlockwise round a large patch of creeping weed. They saw the terrible plant shrivel up and die before their very eyes.

Chapter 15 – Secrets Start to Unfold

That evening, Merlin and Helen-Joy celebrated with their friends at the Brambles' cottage.

The sick magical people were being nursed by the Bramble family and other witches and wizards from Avalon. Tents had been set up in the Brambles' garden to accommodate everyone.

Fruit bushes flourished under the spells the herbologists had cast. Fresh food was in constant preparation. Musicians from the forest orchestra took turns playing soothing music.

Despite all the work going on in the Forbidden Forest, the witches and wizards promised to keep their side of the bargain, to prove their honesty. They would destroy the creeping weed, and by doing so, they would not just help the Kernans but also save many small creatures.

The three brothers were looking much better. Merlin noticed that the elderly man and woman he had seen in the rickety old cart were sitting with them. The old woman appeared to be reading them a story.

"Who are they?" asked Merlin, indicating the couple. "I saw that man perform a spell today."

"That's the parents of Isaiah, Jerry, and Garod." Great-Grandmother Bramble smiled.

"As you know, we hadn't seen them for years. Apparently, they stopped coming to the forest because they thought they were being followed by bounty hunters. They were afraid that they would put us and their sons at risk if the bounty hunters found out that we lived in the forest.

"They didn't think that the boys would go looking for them. They feel dreadful to think that the boys were captured on their way to see them."

The old witch continued. "It is so good to see the boys' parents again. They had never seen Heather, their own grandchild, before. They were so proud when they saw her destroying the creeping weed."

Much to everyone's delight, the whole orchestra assembled to play therapeutic music.

When the orchestra finished, rapturous applause arose from one and all.

Merlin and Helen-Joy stood up, taking the opportunity to ask for the attention of everyone present.

Merlin started by thanking the orchestra and all the helpers who were working to heal the sick. He then asked Helen-Joy to tell the gathering their good news.

It was unusual for Helen-Joy to be shy. At first, she hesitated, but then, lifting her head high, she proudly announced that she was expecting twins.

The news took the whole assembly by utter surprise. Everyone wanted to rush forward to offer congratulations.

However, before anyone could do so, the famous wizard raised his arm to stop them. Taking the soothsayer's hand in his, he knelt on one knee in front of her. "My good lady, will you do me the honour of exchanging rings with me?" he asked.

Helen-Joy blushed but did not hesitate in accepting. It was then that everyone came forward to offer their best wishes to the happy couple.

At last, after speaking to almost everyone, the couple sat beside Great-Grandmother Bramble. They wanted to relax for a while before walking home.

"I can't believe I'm going to be a father at the age of 130!"

"I can't believe that I'm going to be a mother at the age of 107! I'm beginning to feel very tired already. I am sure it is affecting my ability to foresee, but I don't care. I have always wanted children."

"Ah, I was tired when I carried Nora and Maura," Great-Grandmother Bramble said wisely. "You will need to spend more time resting, my dear."

"Are Maura and Nora twins?" asked Merlin.

The old witch nodded with a smile.

"And, Dilly, Dally, and Sally … ?"

"Triplets." She chuckled, knowing what he was going to ask.

"How old was your husband when he died?"

"Barley was about 150. He was a lot older than I when we met."

"It must be the water." Helen-Joy laughed.

"Which is one of the reasons we don't want to tell too many people how to get in and out of the forest," Great-Grandmother Bramble said knowingly. "If our secret is known outside, people will destroy our home, trying to find fertility and long life. If too many people came here, the forest would lose its purity and its power."

Merlin understood. He also understood the rhyme about the magpies. He told the two women about the magpies, and how they always tried to make sure that six were in the Garden of Remembrance when Rosalie was working there, but on the day she lost her ring, there had been seven of them.

"Well, she has her gold, all right," said Helen-Joy with a smile. "A rich prince, who has given her a gold ring and who will probably shower her with gifts."

"And now you know the secret of the Forbidden Forest," added Great-Grandmother Bramble. "A secret never to be told!"

"How true," agreed Merlin. "A secret it must remain."

Merlin and Helen-Joy stayed awhile longer, to listen to the orchestra strike up once more. However, the sorcerer seemed lost in thought.

"What is wrong, my sweet?" asked Helen-Joy.

"I am worried by what was said by the man who brought the children to us. About the strong creatures which have replaced the children who worked in the mines. Is this a story yet to unfold?" asked Merlin.

"Well, we will worry about that another day." Helen-Joy took her husband-to-be by the hand. "Now it is time to walk home and get some well-deserved sleep."

Characters

List of main characters, in alphabetical order.

Ajax: green dragon; husband of Blitzen

Alexander: the blacksmith's son (usually referred to as Alex); brother of Andrew; friend of Edward.

Alfred: an elf.

Allarond: King of the Elves

Andrew: the blacksmith's son; brother of Alexander; friend of Edward.

Arthur: King of Avalon (once King of Briton); husband of Gilda the witch; father of Edward-Arthur and Rosalie.

Azgoose: a witch who can create clouds of goo

Bizzbuzz: a wizard who specialises in making honey

Blitzen: blue Dragon; wife of Ajax

Bramble Family:

Comet: Merlin's white stallion

Connie: the baker's daughter

Daisy: the last of the Brewins

Derrick: Prince of Twydell; son of King Frederrick and Queen Elise

Edward-Arthur: illegitimate son of King Arthur (usually referred to simply as Edward)

Elise: wife/consort of King Frederrick of Twydell (given the title of queen at the time of marriage)

Elvira: Queen of the Witches in Briton and in Avalon; many of her witches migrated to Avalon

Esmerelda: Queen of the Witches (after Elvira); daughter of Elvira

Farainne: wife/consort of Allarond, King of the Elves (given the title of queen at the time of marriage)

Frederrick: King of Twydell

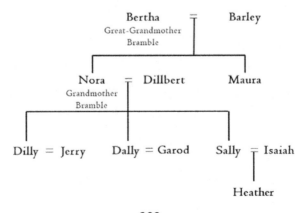

Gilda: one of the first witches to migrate to Avalon; she later married King Arthur; mother of Rosalie

Greatog: former leader of the giants; killed in an earlier battle with the Trajaens; father of Zog

Helen-Joy: a soothsayer

Jeanette: Princess of Twydell; daughter of King Frederrick and Queen Elise

Jeffrey: King of Kerner

Jonathan: a young warlock who specialises in plants (herbologist); son of the wizard Yzor and a half-witch

Lennox: last of the unicorns of Briton

Maud: Queen of the Fairies; married to Selogon

Merlin: powerful wizard who organised the migration to Avalon; advisor to King Arthur

Rabbart lll: King of Barrmin

Rosalie: daughter of King Arthur and Gilda the witch

Selogon: husband/consort of Maud, Queen of the Fairies

Shirley-Poppy: wife/consort of Jeffrey, King of Kerner (given the title of queen at the time of marriage)

Steven: Prince of Kerner; son of King Jeffrey and Queen Shirley-Poppy

Tannitus: powerful wizard; father of Tannus

Tannus: powerful young warlock; son of Tannitus

Willy the Wood Wizard: wizard who can talk to trees

Wormald the Wise: wise old wizard

Yzor: a wizard who specialises in plants (herbologist); father of Jonathan

Zog: leader of the giants; son of Greatog

About the Author

Daisy Bourne was born in England in 1917. Nothing much is known about her real parents except that their lives were changed dramatically by the First World War. At the age of six, Daisy was unofficially adopted by a farmer and his wife. They changed her name and took her to Canada.

There are several similarities between the real Daisy Bourne and her namesake in this book. To a small child, Canada, with its heavy snowfalls, huge forests and grizzly bears must indeed have

seemed like some kind of new world. Although Daisy loved Canada and the farm on which she lived, she was not happy and ran away. She returned to England at the age of 16. In later life, she took up farming again. She also enjoyed her garden and preserving much of its produce. This is where the similarities between the real Daisy and the character in the "*Tales of Avalon*" series end.

I am proud to use my mother's birth name as a pseudonym when writing the *Tales of Avalon* series. My ambition is to one day write the story of the real Daisy Bourne. In the meantime, I will continue to complete the *Tales of Avalon* series.

DAISY BOURNE

A note from the Author

I love hearing from my readers. If you would like to contact me, please use the link on my website: TalesOfAvalon.co.uk or message me on my Facebook page: Tales of Avalon Series

If you enjoyed reading this book, why not recommend the Tales of Avalon series to your friends. But please suggest that they start on Book 1, right at the beginning of the tale, so that they do not miss out on any of the adventures.

More from the Tales of Avalon series

Lennox's Story is the fifth book in the *Tales of Avalon* series and is to be published early in 2018.

It tells the story of Lennox, the last unicorn in Briton, and how and why he made the decision to travel to Avalon. In *The New Land,* Lennox left his fellow travellers on the beach and headed straight towards the scent of other unicorns drifting from the Great Forest. We do not see him again until he greets Merlin at the entrance to the Forbidden Forest in *The Land of Twydell and the Dragon Egg.* How and why did Lennox travel through Twydell? What secrets has Lennox yet to tell about his journey to the Forbidden Forest and how is it connected to the zanite locket that Tannus has given to Merlin? Who are the strong creatures who work in Kernan mines? All is revealed when Lennox's magical story is revealed.

Edward's Story, the sixth book in the *Tales of Avalon* series, is also planned for publication in 2018.

Is Princess Rosalie safe from King Rabbart's scheming? Will he murder the young princess before her marriage to Prince Derrick? You will have to read *Edward's Story* to find out.